Deceived

THE DEVIL'S SYNDICATE
BOOK ONE

SARAH BAILEY

Cover Art by Sarah Bailey

Published by Twisted Tree Publications
www.twistedtreepublications.com
info@twistedtreepublications.com

Paperback ISBN: 978-1-913217-11-2

To all those left out in the dark
One day, you'll find your way home

CHAPTER ONE

Ash

I could pinpoint the moment in my life when everything fell apart to the day the love of my life walked out. At least I thought he was the love of my life. Nate Tucker was the epitome of perfection. From his signature ice-blue eyes to his always neatly styled blonde quiff and blue suits which clung to his muscular body. A body I knew intimately. For instance, I knew he liked to work out every morning before he took a shower and that his health was very important to him. Meals had consisted of grilled chicken, salads and these disgusting green smoothies he'd whizz up every morning. He never put anything in his body that wasn't good for him. Junk food was banned from our house, although I managed to sneak it in every so often when he wasn't at home.

I should've known it was too good to be true, but I was blindsided by his handsome features, southern American charm and the attention he paid me. I thought we were going to get married, have babies and grow old together. That was the plan. I guess sometimes plans got derailed because here I was left with the broken shards of my heart in a mess on the floor. Two years of my life wasted on a man who clearly cared very little about me.

How did I know he didn't care?

Well, the fact he was cooing over this leggy blonde with fake tits and a nasally laugh which grated on my ears across the room from me might cue you in. Trust me, the daughter of a man who led a prominent crime family in London to fall for the first man her father approved of. He practically shoved Nate in my face. It was all "Nate is my new American associate, Ashleigh, you should show him the town" and "Nate is a nice guy, he'll treat you right". Pity Papa didn't tell me Nate was only using me to get in his good graces.

How did I know that?

The second Nate received an invitation into Papa's inner circle, he dropped me like I was an annoying fly buzzing around his head.

The worst part of all?

Papa wasn't even mad. It's like he knew Nate was using me. I hated them for it. Hated they'd used me so cruelly. I'd loved Nate. Took care of him. Moulded myself to fit in his life. And it was all for nothing. All I had left was our flat, which Papa bought for me and the memories of the life I'd shared with Nate haunting every inch of it.

Nate knew I was staring at him, but he refused to even glance at me. Fully engrossed in Ursula fucking Gregory. I hated that bitch. Not because she was flirting with Nate. No, she'd sneered and belittled me from the first day I'd arrived at

Hawkshead Prep School until the day I left. Now she'd wormed her way into one of Papa's inner circle parties like the sneaky bitch with no shame that she was. Ursula had no idea what she'd got herself into. She didn't know about the criminal empire my father ran. His investment company was a front for his drugs and illicit dealings.

"Ashleigh, darling, it's rude to stare," my mother hissed in my ear.

Isabella Russo, née Davenport. A force to be reckoned with. Coming from money and marrying into a family like my father's was seen as a power move. There was no love lost between my parents these days. She attended his parties to keep up appearances. That's all they cared about. Making sure their image in polite society wasn't tarnished.

"Yes, Mother," I mumbled, dragging my gaze away from Nate and Ursula.

"That boy never deserved you."

I looked over at her. Mother was always impeccably dressed in the latest designer brands. Nothing but the best for Isabella. Today she was sporting a deep red cocktail dress which pushed her breasts up and complimented her hourglass figure. Her blonde hair was up and her smoky eyeshadow perfectly highlighted her blue eyes. I'd inherited her looks rather than my father's dark hair, olive skin and dark eyes. It's why I hated the fact that Nate had gone after Ursula. He clearly had a type. Blondes. Not for the first time, I wished I didn't look like a younger, much shorter version of Isabella Russo.

"He deserves to have his dick cut off."

"That could be arranged."

3

I couldn't bring myself to smile at that. In my world, if you messed with our family, you'd likely turn up in hospital with broken legs or in a body bag in the morgue.

"Papa would never allow it."

He'd likely be looking around at his men as we speak, deciding which one to marry me off to. The Russos kept things within the family. I was expected to marry for strategic purposes rather than love. Papa never shielded me from the harsh realities of his world. I'd witnessed things which might make a lesser girl's stomach turn.

"Your father wants what's best for you. That boy will never be it."

I wisely kept my mouth shut. No point arguing with Isabella. She'd only tell me I was being naïve. Instead, I scanned the room again until my eyes fell on a group of men in the corner. Normally I wouldn't give a shit who Papa had invited to these things. This group I hadn't seen before. Four of them. All equally striking in their own right. One had dirty blonde hair with a scar running across his right eyebrow. Another had chestnut hair with dark eyes the colour of an evergreen forest. The third slouched against a bookcase with a whisky tumbler in his hand, his auburn hair glinting under the lights and his blue eyes piercing. It was the last man who caught my attention. He had dark hair and eyes as black as night. He looked like he'd walked right out of hell, wearing all black with a single red handkerchief in his suit pocket. The look in those dark eyes as he scanned the room with a sneer on his face sent a chill down my spine.

If I was the superstitious type, I'd say these men were a bad omen. Something about them made me want to shrink into the background so they couldn't see me. Especially the dark-haired one. He could gut a woman with a single glance. I decided then and there, I never wanted to make their acquaintance.

"Who are they?"

"I advise you not to ask that question, Ashleigh."

I turned to her, my eyes wide.

"Why not?"

"Forget you saw them. They're not men you want to know."

My mother's eyes were narrowed. She gripped her glass of champagne tighter. Her reaction only confirmed my suspicions. They were not good men. Why were they at my father's party? How had they gained entry?

"Mother..."

"Don't. Stay far away from them. Promise me you won't go looking for trouble."

As if. I knew what type of men graced this world. Growing up with hardened criminals changes a person's perception. You'd think Papa might have shielded his own daughter from the horrific nature of his business. No such luck there.

"I won't."

She eyed me for a moment longer before nodding and sauntering off towards the games room where my father was gambling. I decided I'd seen enough. Papa expected me to make an appearance tonight, and that was it. I'd done his bidding, now it was my time to escape.

Glancing around one last time, my eyes lingered on the man from hell. His eyes were fixed on the open doors of the gaming room where my father could be seen laughing. The rage and hatred in his eyes were unmistakable. Whatever problem he had with Papa, it was no concern of mine.

I slipped from the room into the hallway and walked towards the stairs. That's the last thing I remember of that night. My foot landing on the first stair before a hand slammed over my mouth and the sharp sting of a needle slicing through my flesh. I never got a chance to scream. Darkness overtook me, dragging me down as my body slumped against a solid chest and all my senses faded to black.

CHAPTER TWO

Ash

rip. Drip. Drip.
    The sound rang in my ears.
    Drip. Drip. Drip.
Why was it so loud?

Drip. Drip. Drip.

Sleep tugged at my senses, but that sound was maddening. I tried to move and found my body unresponsive. My fingers wouldn't even twitch. Willing my eyes to open, I heard the low murmur of male voices.

"We should move her."

"Is she awake?"

A shuffling of feet brought the voices closer.

"No, but she can't be comfortable there."

"I don't give a shit about her comfort."

Who are these men? What happened to me? Why can't I move?

"I don't hurt women."

"It's his daughter. Why the fuck would you care about her?"

Had these men taken me because I was Frank Russo's daughter?

"There's just no need to keep her like this."

"Oh, because you're such a paragon of virtue and morality."

"Fuck you, Knox."

The footsteps came closer. I could feel the heat of another body. It made me aware of how cold I felt and how I seemed to be trembling despite my inability to move.

"She's freezing," the one who'd sworn at this Knox said.

"Do I look like I care?" Knox said, although he sounded further away.

"Might I remind you we need her alive."

"Fine. Warm her up but don't give her any fucking creature comforts, you hear me?"

"Whatever, Knox."

The sound of retreating footsteps echoed in my ears.

Drip. Drip. Drip.

"Fucking prick," muttered the man who'd come closer to me.

Drip. Drip. Drip.

I felt his hands tuck under my legs and back. A low whimper escaped my lips as I realised they'd stripped me bare. What else had they done?

"Shh, it's okay, angel, I've got you," he murmured close to my ear as his warm breath fluttered across my face.

I still couldn't move. He tucked me up in his arms and I felt the sensation of being carried. The sound of his heart beating in his chest where my head was resting lulled me back into oblivion.

When I next regained my senses, the dripping sound was gone. My body ached all over like I'd been sleeping on a hard concrete floor all night. I attempted to move my fingers, finding them twitching with the effort. I cracked open my eyes. The light was almost blinding. My head pounded immediately. I squeezed them shut again, groaning at the pain.

"So you are still with us," came a male voice, one I recognised vaguely from before.

"Wh… what?" I croaked.

My mouth felt like it was full of cotton wool. My lips were dry and cracked as I ran my tongue over them.

"You're awake."

I opened my eyes again, wincing at the light. I couldn't move my head yet, but above me was a white ceiling and a single bulb shining down on me. My eyes flicked down and I found a man sitting in a chair at the end of the bed I seemed to be laid out on. He had auburn hair cropped close to his scalp. His heavily tattooed arms rippled with muscle as he turned to me. His piercing blue eyes were like beacons in a storm, drawing me in.

"Wh… who are you?"

"No one important, angel."

"What happened?"

I couldn't remember anything. The last solid memory I had was of talking with my mother at one of Papa's parties.

"Not really meant to tell you anything."

My eyes flicked down to my own body covered by a thin blanket. Underneath said blanket, there wasn't a stitch of clothing on me. I let out a choked gasp, my eyes finding those blue ones again.

"Where are my clothes?" I rasped, realising I should've been asking for water.

He raised an eyebrow.

"Don't worry, angel, no one has taken advantage of you."

The gleam in his eye told me he'd thought about it. My stomach churned at the implications.

What the fuck?

It wasn't as though this man who called me angel was unattractive, but clearly he was complicit in taking me. Somebody had kidnapped me. So regardless of whether he was hot or not, there was no way in hell I was letting him or anyone else touch me.

He looked away from me and fiddled with his phone for a moment. Then he stood, stretching as his joints popped. He came around the bed, picked something up from near my head before sitting down next to me. He reached over, tucking a hand behind my head and lifting it. I almost protested, but then I realised he had a glass of water in his other hand. I gratefully sipped at it with his help.

He placed it back on the bedside table as the door to the room slammed back on its hinges. Both of us looked over at it. Blue eyes huffed and muttered, "Here we go," under his breath.

"I told you no fucking creature comforts, Xav," growled the black-haired demon who'd appeared in the doorway.

The memory of last night came flooding back in full force. I looked between blue eyes and the demon from hell as two other men appeared behind him. It all clicked into place.

10

The four men from last night.

They were all here.

They had taken me.

The question which formed on my lips was, "Why?"

All four men fixed their eyes on me, making me realise I'd spoken out loud.

"Why what, angel?" blue eyes asked.

"Why am I here?"

He looked over at the other three men as if to ask what he should say in response. No one spoke for a long moment. Then the demon advanced into the room, ripped the blanket from my body and practically dragged me off the bed.

"Hey, Knox, be careful with her."

"Back off, Xav," the demon hissed, his dark eyes wild.

I stumbled, unable to hold myself up as the drugs still coursed through my system. Falling against him as my knees buckled, he gripped my arms to steady me. Next, I found myself hoisted up in his arms and pressed against his solid chest. He didn't look down at me, but I took a moment to study him as he carried me from the room. He had one of those devastatingly attractive faces if you didn't count the fact that he had a scowl etched deeply on it. High cheekbones and a beautiful jawline most women would swoon over with incredibly long eyelashes fluttering across his cheeks when he blinked.

"Knox, you don't have to do this," called blue eyes.

"I said, back the fuck off."

His jaw ticked after he clenched his mouth shut with his retort. Perhaps his stern look should've scared me, and in many ways it did.

"Xav's right, we don't have to keep her chained up," another voice sounded down the hallway followed by footsteps.

"You can fuck off too, E."

The footsteps stopped. I continued to stare up at my kidnapper, wondering what I should say.

"Who are you?" I croaked out.

"Quiet," he snarled, not even deigning to look down at me.

If he thought because I wasn't able to struggle against his grasp due to the effects of the drugs they'd given me that I'd do what he said, he had another thing coming.

"Who are you?" I repeated, my voice a little louder this time.

"I told you to be fucking quiet."

My hand twitched where it was resting against his chest. I should've probably been embarrassed about being in his arms when I was completely starkers, but they'd all seen me now, so what did it matter. Blue eyes, or Xav, said none of them had taken advantage of me. I doubted this Knox wanted to either judging by the rage radiating off him, but who knew what was going on behind those piercing eyes.

"No. Why did you take me from my father's house? Surely he knows it was you. He'll have everyone looking for me."

His dark eyes flicked down to mine. The hatred in them made me flinch.

"You want to know why we took you?"

"Yes."

"Because fuck Frank Russo, that's why."

His eyes snapped forward again. Papa had enemies by the dozen. The way he'd practically spat my father's name told me this happened to be personal for him.

"So you hate my father. How original."

"Listen here, little girl, you have no idea how much fucking shit you're in right now so I suggest you shut that little sarcastic trap of yours and keep your childish thoughts to yourself."

I rolled my eyes. Typical really. Thinking he could just tell me to be quiet and expecting me to listen.

"I'm not a child. I'm twenty-one."

His eyes met mine again. The deadly gleam in them had me regretting my words.

"I'm well aware you're a grown woman." His eyes roamed across my body in his arms. "But if you think you can use that to your advantage, you'd be mistaken."

He clearly didn't realise how hungry his eyes had turned when he looked at my naked flesh.

"Trust me, I'd rather die than sleep with any of you."

His expression darkened.

"That can be arranged, sweetheart."

I scowled. He had no right to call me that. I hadn't much minded Xav calling me angel, but he seemed to want to take care of me.

"Going to kill me then? Might as well get on with it. No point wasting time."

I didn't have a death wish, but I understood my situation happened to be precarious.

"If I wanted you dead, I wouldn't have gone to the trouble of taking you from right under your Daddy's nose."

I stowed away that piece of information for safekeeping. Perhaps I should be more freaked out than I was. I'd stared into the faces of monsters before. The things I'd seen left scars on my soul. So being kidnapped wasn't top of the list of most fucked up events in my life.

Knox walked into a room and set me down on the floor by the back wall. I slumped against it, only just getting the feeling back in my limbs. He grabbed my wrist roughly and attached a steel cuff to it.

"Why won't you tell me who you are? I've seen all your faces, not like you're being very secretive."

He didn't look at me as he picked up something else from the floor and gathered up my hair with one hand. He snapped a steel collar around my neck with a chain attached to it. If I thought it was worth it, I'd have complained about him chaining me to the wall. His general attitude towards me told me it would fall on deaf ears. He dropped my hair and stood up. His dark eyes raked over me, hunger burning inside them.

"You're far too curious for your own good."

"I'm not what you expected, am I?"

He cocked his head to the side. He was wearing all black again. Whilst Xav had been all bulging muscles, the demon from hell was more athletic in build. He'd carried me with ease, which meant he had upper body strength in spades. He flexed his hands at his sides.

"I'm sure you heard what they called me."

Ignoring my question, I see.

"Knox."

He let out a low hum of agreement.

"That's not your first name."

His eyes narrowed and he took a step towards me, his feet nudging against my bare thigh. I flinched back away from him.

"And how would you know that, little girl?"

I almost spat at him for calling me that again.

"I'm not stupid that's how."

"Clearly not. Stupid little girls would be screaming and begging for their lives right now."

I shrugged. No point in begging a demon for mercy. Monsters didn't deal in mercy and kindness. They dealt in death and destruction.

"I'm under no illusions about my father and the kind of company he keeps. You don't scare me."

"I'm not in business with your father," he spat, venom seeping from his words.

"No, I'm sure it's all just some convoluted revenge plot you've cooked up because you think he's wronged you. You're not the first man to want Papa dead. You won't be the last."

I could tell Knox wasn't happy with my response. His eyes narrowed to slits and his fists clenched by his sides.

"You think you know everything, Ashleigh Vittoria Russo."

He squatted down on his haunches, his eyes hardening. Reaching out, he gripped my face and forced me to look at him.

"You have no idea what kind of man I am or what I'm capable of." He leant closer until his nose was almost brushing against mine. "Unless you wish to wake the beast, I suggest you keep your smart remarks and questions to yourself. I'll take pleasure in punishing you if you keep pushing me." His eyes lowered to my mouth. "I can think of many ways to punish that smart mouth of yours. Many, many ways, sweetheart. Don't think I won't follow through. I don't care who your father is nor am I scared of what he'll do when he finds out I have his little princess."

My bottom lip trembled. For the first time since I'd woken up, my confidence wavered. Isabella said they weren't men I wanted to know. Knox's words confirmed that for me. The conviction in his voice had my heart racing in my chest. What kind of man wasn't afraid of Frank Russo? A man who possessed more darkness than the head of the Russo family himself.

"Do you know what your family call me?" he whispered, his breath fluttering across my face.

I shook my head.

"*Il Diavolo*."

I'd been right. Knox had walked out of hell itself. And he was known by two words.

The Devil.

"But you, Ashleigh, may call me Quinn."

"It's Ash," I whispered.

I had no idea why I told him that. My mother and father insisted on calling me Ashleigh, but everyone else referred to me as the boss' daughter or just Ash.

His eyes flickered with heat for a moment before it was gone. Then he stood, turned and walked away. I stared at his back, realising just how much I didn't understand about what was happening to me. He hadn't explained anything. Not really.

He paused in the doorway, turning back to me slightly.

"If you think you can cry to the others, you'd be mistaken. You belong to me now, Ash."

Before I had a chance to formulate a response, he walked out of the room and the door slammed shut behind him.

Quinn Knox is the devil incarnate, was the first thought I had. The second was I happened to be screwed. Well and truly screwed.

I shifted, testing my limbs, which moved with some complaint. At least the drug they'd administered to knock me out had all but worn off. The room he'd put me in was another matter entirely. There was a small metal-framed bed with a thin mattress to my right and a metal toilet to my left. That was it unless you counted the window above me with metal bars across it and the single bulb hanging from the ceiling.

I shifted up on my hands and knees with some effort and dragged myself over to the bed. The chains tethering me to the wall gave me enough slack to lay down on it. I fingered the cold steel collar around my neck. The rational part of my brain told me there was no way out of this. Trapped as a prisoner at the mercy of a man who was beginning to terrify me to my very core.

Hot, salty tears erupted from the corners of my eyes as I shivered. I had no blanket. Nothing to cover myself with. He'd left me naked and alone, chained to the wall with no hope left in my heart. So instead of being brave like I ought to have been, I cried silent tears of regret and shame, wondering what the hell would happen when Papa found out who had me. I'd heard the words *Il Diavolo* whispered before. If Quinn really was The Devil, then my situation was dire.

"Papa," I whispered. "Please come for me. Please don't leave me here alone."

I curled myself up into a ball, my tears soaking the thin mattress below me until I drifted off, allowing exhaustion to consume me.

CHAPTER THREE

Quinn

I had no interest in dealing with Xavier, Rory, and Eric's concerns about the Russo girl. They'd all agreed to this course of action. They didn't get to question me now. Not when we had her in our clutches. Admittedly, I shouldn't have asked them to strip her bare. Having the image of her naked skin branded on my retinas did nothing to quell my dark mood. The stupid girl had talked back to me. Made my fingers itch to punish her for her insolence. I'd teach Ash how to show me the respect I deserved if she insisted on testing me.

My three partners in crime barged into my office within minutes of me entering and sitting down after placing the Russo girl where she belonged. Chained up and unable to escape.

Ashleigh Vittoria Russo is mine.

"You really are a piece of shit," Xav snarled, slamming his hand down on my desk after he'd advanced towards me.

"Don't tell me you're having second thoughts now," I replied, looking down at my nails.

"You know what, I think you take that fucking title they gave you far too seriously. What the fuck happened to treating a woman with decency, huh?"

I looked up at him, noting the burning rage in his blue eyes. That was Xavier's problem. He'd always been a hothead. Barging in all guns blazing without a second thought for the consequences of his actions. He had a hero complex and clearly, he thought Ash needed saving. Little girls who did their father's bidding didn't need saving at all. They needed to learn their fucking place. My hand curled into a fist under the table. I couldn't allow that girl to get under my skin.

"We all agreed, Xav," Rory said quietly, saving me from answering.

Did I care they'd given me the nickname *Il Diavolo*? Not particularly. It served my agenda. Having them fear me. Xav thought it had gone to my head. He couldn't see beyond his own fucking need to save lost souls. Everything I did had a bigger picture. Every move I made brought us closer to our ultimate goals.

Xavier paced away, glowering at Rory. He'd fall in line. His bark was far worse than his bite. Xav might look like a jacked-up bodybuilder, but he had a soft heart underneath that façade. Besides, they all deferred to me one way or another. I'd kept them alive this long. I'd fought their battles since we were kids.

"That was before you decided to chain her up naked."

No one spoke for a long moment. The elephant in the room had reared its ugly head. I doubt any of us could say we hadn't looked at Ash and wondered what it'd be like to slide inside her lithe little body. And it wasn't as though we hadn't fucked the same woman before. Never at the same time, but sharing women had never been a big deal. Not when you lived in the way we did with all the shit we'd done over the years.

Eric had been the one to remove her clothes. Rory kept his distance, which wasn't unusual for him. He didn't much like human contact unless it was on his terms. Xav didn't want any part of it. He hadn't minded picking her up and carrying her into one of the spare rooms. Hypocrite.

"Did you forget who she belongs to?" I asked, my voice barely above a murmur.

"As if I could fucking forget. You and your sick fucking games, Quinn. When will it end?"

I flinched. He rarely called me Quinn. I'd been known as Knox by the world for longer than I cared to remember.

"What do you want me to do? Act like she's an innocent? That girl is not innocent and you know it. I suggest you get off your high fucking horse, pipe down and let me deal with Ashleigh Russo."

Xav clenched his fists, staring at me with unconcealed disgust.

"You'll regret treating her like this." He stabbed a finger in my direction "Mark my fucking words."

He stormed out of the room, barging past Rory.

"Xavier," Eric called, hurrying after him. "Come on, man, you know Quinn's doing what he thinks is best."

I rolled my eyes as Rory shut the door behind them. He leant up against the wall and levelled his gaze on me.

"What?"

21

He didn't speak, just continued to watch me with those discerning hazel eyes of his. Like he could strip the world bare and make it his bitch. In all honesty, he probably could.

"Those two fuckheads can go deal with their hardons for each other." Rory raised a single blonde eyebrow. "You think I don't know?"

"I didn't say anything," he replied smoothly.

I glanced over at the monitors on my desk, noting Ash had curled up on the bed and was fast asleep. She looked like a little blonde angel, just like Xav had called her. Except I knew that girl was no angel.

"Those two have been obsessed with each other since forever."

"You really are a prick, Quinn."

I shrugged. Xavier was bisexual and Eric had always said he loved people, not genders. I didn't give a shit who they stuck their dicks in. As long as they did their jobs and didn't let whatever went on between them effect that, I wouldn't interfere.

"If they're happy then what do I care? Say… I wonder who fucks who."

Rory gave me a look as if to say 'what the fuck, man?'. I put my hands up.

"Okay, you're right, it's none of my business."

He shook his head. Rory was used to dealing with me.

"You need to get your shit straight," he murmured. "You can't let this girl blind you."

"What makes you think she has?"

He gave me one of his signature looks. Rory. Ever the silent stoic type. Only speaking when he had something

22

important to say. Everything else was conveyed with a single look.

"Spit it out already. I'm tired of having to work out what you're trying to say without words."

He shoved off the wall and walked over to my desk, taking a seat in front of it. He tapped his fingers on his thigh.

"Xav and Eric don't know you like I do."

My eyes flicked back to the monitors again. Rory knew exactly what I'd do to little Ash Russo if I had half the chance. We met Xavier and Eric in school, but Rory and I had grown up next door to each other. We knew what it was like to rise from the ashes of the shitty lot we'd been given in life. We kept each other's dark and depraved secrets.

"So?"

His stare told me exactly what I needed to know.

"I'm not going to touch her."

His eyes flicked towards the monitors and back to me. I knew Rory's type. Little angelic girls who liked a man to do depraved shit to them. Ash fit the bill in some of those respects. Quite honestly, I think she fit the bill for all four of us even if Xav and Eric were preoccupied with each other.

"You don't believe me."

He shrugged, continuing to tap his fingers on his thigh.

"Talking to you is like pulling teeth, you know that, right?"

"Says the man who doesn't know when to shut up."

Touché old friend.

I flashed him a grin.

"Are you going to stop me if I do?"

I wasn't sure I trusted myself not to if she chose to provoke me further. What I needed was to stay away. The boys could take care of her.

"You're going to do what you want regardless of my intervention."

I shrugged and ran a hand through my hair.

"Don't touch her, Quinn. You know it will only lead to trouble."

Rory had a point. We had her here for a reason and that had nothing to do with my innate urge to have my way with her. The things I'd do to that lithe body.

Stop thinking about her like that.

"I won't."

His eyes roamed over my face.

"You will."

I didn't answer. He stood up, nodded at me and walked towards the door.

"For the record, nothing has happened between Eric and Xavier. If it had, I would know."

"They need to get on with it then. I'm tired of those longing looks E gives Xav."

"You should worry more about yourself and the girl."

Fuck Rory. Fuck him knowing everything about me.

I sat back and stared at the monitors. A part of me wanted to reach out and touch the screen as if I could stroke her hair back from her face. She looked very much like her mother but so much younger and infinitely more angelic. Deceptive which made her dangerous. Too fucking dangerous.

Deceived

I had to reign in any urges I had towards her. Regardless of her sins, those were not part of the plan. We had her for a reason and jeopardising that could cost us everything.

CHAPTER FOUR

Ash

I was cold. Too cold. My body shivered as I curled in on myself on the narrow bed. Why had they taken my clothes? Why were they doing any of this to me? Yes, I was Frank Russo's daughter but that didn't mean shit. If they wanted information, then they'd be sorely disappointed. Papa would hurt me if I told them anything.

I had the distinct impression eyes were on me. Peeking out from my knees, I found the dirty blonde-haired man with the scar on his eyebrow leaning against the doorframe watching me intently.

Unnerving. Totally unnerving.

Didn't make him any less attractive than the others. Honestly, it was like four bloody gods had a hold of me, although I hadn't particularly studied the last man with the green eyes.

"What do you want?"

He didn't speak. Just stared at me.

"You're one of those quiet types."

Nothing. Not even a hint of an acknowledgement. I shifted, uncurling my legs and sitting up against the wall. I crossed my arms over my breasts. I didn't think he had any interest in me but being naked for their perusal was starting to make me uncomfortable.

"Quinn said none of you will help me."

His lip twitched.

"Is he just going to leave me here to starve and freeze to death?"

"No."

That single word conveyed so much. His voice was deep, rich and calming. I cocked my head to the side.

"Then can I get some water… please?"

My throat was dry and scratchy. I had no idea how long I'd been asleep.

He didn't say anything else, just turned and walked away. Who knew if he was going to get me something or not. Perhaps he'd got bored of me speaking to him.

Why had these four men taken me? Why would they be complicit in something like this? Keeping a naked girl chained up against her will. Xav made it clear he didn't like what Quinn was doing but I had no idea about the other two men.

I looked around the room again. Nothing had changed but reality started to set in. Would I see the outside of these four walls again? What if the blonde-haired man was lying and Quinn really would let me freeze and starve to death?

I trembled, trying not to allow myself to cry again as tears pricked at the corners of my eyes.

"You belong to me now, Ash."

28

Screw that shit. I wasn't Quinn Knox's possession. I didn't even know anything about him other than he hated my father. But who didn't hate Frank Russo outside of his inner circle? He was ruthless and took no prisoners. He'd shown me that on more than one occasion.

Images of the last man he'd brutalised in front of me flittered across my retinas. I shut my eyes, trying to flush those out of my brain.

The blood. So much blood. It ran down his chest in rivulets and dripped from the chair onto the bare concrete floor.

I dug my palms into my eyes. Those reminders weren't welcome.

Drip. Drip. Drip.

I shivered again, a slight whimper escaping my lips. The things my father and his men had done haunted my dreams. Except Nate. I'd never seen him hurt another living soul. Unless you counted him breaking my heart. Desolation began to sink into my soul. That prick probably didn't care I was missing.

I felt something being settled over me. I dropped my hands and stared up into the hazel eyes of the blonde-haired man. He'd draped a thick blanket over me. Unable to form words to thank him for his simple kindness, I pulled it up to my chin.

He sat on the bed before handing me a glass of water. I took it and sipped at it.

"Will he take this away from me?" I indicated the blanket with my head.

"Probably."

"Then why give it to me?"

He stared at me. His eyes were far too discerning like he could rip me open and learn everything about me with one glance.

"I'm not Quinn."

I almost scoffed. Well, that was obvious, but it didn't mean he had to be nice to me.

"Well, not Quinn, thank you."

His lip twitched.

"Rory."

I gave him a half-smile. Whilst he still unnerved me, it didn't seem like he would hurt me. At least I hoped not.

"Does he know you're here?"

He inclined his head once before his eyes flicked around the room. I followed his gaze, noting there were cameras. Why didn't that surprise me? Had he been watching me sleep? Why would I assume Quinn had been watching me? Perhaps it was the way he'd looked at me with such hunger in his eyes. Like I was a meal he wanted to feast on. A shiver ran up my spine at the thought of it. There was no way in hell I would allow him to touch me up in any way shape or form. Quinn might be devastatingly handsome, but he was dangerous, sinful and downright terrifying. I knew men like him and I had no interest in playing his games.

"You can tell him he's a creep for spying on me."

Rory's lip twitched again. I drained the glass and handed it back to him. He stood before turning and walking away to the door.

"A word of advice if you want to survive this. Don't provoke Quinn."

Deceived

He left, not shutting the door behind him. I trembled at his parting words. They sounded ominous. Like if I pushed Quinn's buttons I wouldn't like the outcome at all.

I lay down on the small bed again, hugging the thick blanket around me to keep warm. And vowed to myself I'd survive whatever Quinn Knox and the others had in store for me. I had no idea what these men wanted with me. I had to find a way to stay strong and resolute.

No more crying.

No more wishing my father would come and get me.

If I knew anything about Frank Russo, it was that he protected his own, but not at the cost of his own interests.

Would his own daughter be worth the effort for him?

Only time would tell.

CHAPTER FIVE

Eric

avier paced the room like a caged wild animal. I sighed, rubbing my face. This situation weighed heavily on all of us. Quinn had never steered us wrong yet, but kidnapping Frank Russo's daughter was a whole new low even for us. We all knew what was at stake. What we had to achieve. Fractures in our friendships wouldn't do. The four of us had to stick to the plan and see this through.

"I don't know why he has to treat her like she's a dog," he growled.

"I don't agree with it any more than you do."

He turned on me, his blue eyes blazing.

"You fucking undressed her so don't tell me you're not in agreement with him."

I put my hands up. Undressing her had been a bad idea. Ashleigh Russo's subtle curves and pretty tits were hard not to stare at. I think all four of us had sucked in a breath after I'd unzipped her dress, unbuckled her shoes and removed her little lacy set of black underwear. Underneath her innocent exterior lay a girl whose body was sinful. Taunting us with thoughts of what it'd be like to sink into her every which way we could.

"I didn't want a fight."

He rolled his eyes and started pacing again. It was the truth. Fighting with Quinn only led to trouble and none of us needed that right now.

"Always the goddamn pacifist. Keeping the peace doesn't always work, Eric. Sometimes you have to stick up for your fucking principals."

I sighed. When Xav got in a mood like this, it was hard to get him to see sense. Not that any of this was rational in the first place. I questioned myself and the guys almost daily, wondering whether this was really necessary. Yes, we had our reasons. Didn't mean I had to like it. Didn't mean any of it sat well with me. I still had a moral compass and this went against it.

"You used to trust Quinn."

"I still fucking trust him, I just don't like this. He could at least make her comfortable, but no, he has to be a dick and treat her like she's less than human."

"You know what she did."

He growled in response, slamming his hand against the wall and bowing his head to his chest.

"I wish I didn't."

I approached him. Spooking Xav would be a mistake. We'd known each other since we were kids. All four of us had met at school. So I knew how to handle him, it's just I wanted to do more to help. My fingers itched to reach out and touch him. Soothe him. Take away the ache in his chest. Xav lived with so many demons and I wanted to calm his soul. But I couldn't. Risking our friendship would disrupt the fine balance between the four of us. So I kept my hands to myself.

"Xavi, I know it's hard, but we have to stay the course."

He tensed at my address. I hardly ever called him that. It was usually Xav.

"Stay the fucking course? The cost... what if it's too high? What if this destroys everyone? Destroys her? Will he feel fucking vindicated then? And don't fucking tell me she's not innocent. I know that, but it doesn't make it feel any less... wrong."

Xav had a thing about not hurting women after what happened to his family. I understood why this riled him up and made him want to punch Quinn's lights out.

"It's not about vindication. And we'll make sure he doesn't destroy her, okay?"

How we'd stop Quinn, I had no idea. The thought of there being nothing left but a vacant shell when we were through with Ashleigh Russo left a bad taste in my mouth. Her light blue eyes were so full of intelligence and life. When she'd looked up at Xav like he was her saviour, it caused a stabbing pain in my chest. Feelings I refused to acknowledge surfaced inside me. Whilst Xav might be attracted to men and women, he certainly had a thing for broken birds who needed saving. Ashleigh Russo would end up being one of those broken birds by the time Quinn was done with her. And Xav would want to rescue her in the end.

Bile rose up in the back of my throat at the thought of it. He had no idea the torment he caused inside me. No idea of the longing and shame I felt whenever I looked at him. The burning sensation in my chest grew and grew. I took another step towards him, unable to help myself.

"How?"

"Give her comfort when we can and make sure she knows she isn't alone."

"As if fucking Knox would let us."

The urge grew too strong. Gently, I placed a hand on his shoulder. Xav's tense muscles loosened after a few moments, filling me with relief.

"What's he going to do? He needs us. And she will too."

Xav looked at me, his blue eyes glinting and a rueful smile gracing his lips.

"He doesn't need anyone."

"He might like the world to think he's a lone wolf, but you, Rory and I know that's not the truth."

He rolled his eyes, straightening and my hand dropped. My fingers tingled from the loss of contact.

"Oh no, he's just a fucking prick."

I smiled. Quinn was many things, including a prick, but he'd also got us through the darkest of times. All four of us were loyal to a fault despite the tensions between us over the situation with Ashleigh Russo. And after I'd undressed her, there was a lot more fucking tension in the room. None of us could deny wanting her. Even our silent, stoic Rory who barely said a word to anyone. I'd seen the dark glint in his hazel eyes. The one which told me he'd do depraved shit to her if he had half the chance. Rory might like to think he was a locked vault, but we all knew each other too well for that to be the case.

"He's still the only one who has the balls to go up against the worst of the worst."

Xav shrugged and rolled his shoulders.

"They need to be put down like the animals they are."

I wouldn't dispute that. We weren't any better in all honesty, but we had our own reasons for the depraved shit we'd gotten into. All of us did.

"Just remember who we're doing this for."

He sighed before reaching out and touching my arm. I knew it meant nothing, but my skin heated at his fingers brushing over my bare skin.

"I don't know what I'd do without you, Eric. You're the only one who keeps me fucking sane."

I gave him a tense smile. One which didn't betray my inner turmoil. I hoped.

"I'll always be here for you."

In more ways than you'll ever know.

CHAPTER SIX

Quinn

eeing Rory give her a blanket made me wonder what the fuck he was playing at. Was he messing with me on purpose or had the girl affected him? Rory never allowed anything to get to him, so who knew? If she had, then she had a heck of a lot more to answer for.

The steady rise and fall of the blanket told me she was asleep, then again, so was everyone else at this hour. No one had fed her, which was an oversight on my part. I couldn't starve her. I wouldn't call myself a nice person. I had chained her to the wall naked which weren't the actions of someone who had a kind bone in their body. But I also wasn't a complete monster.

I turned off the cameras, knowing Rory would notice when the recording went blank but not caring in the slightest what he thought. He could spend fucking eternity wondering what I did with Ash tonight. All of them could. They didn't get to dictate what I did with her.

Sighing, I rose from my office chair and walked down the hallway to the kitchen. Eric had left a plate in the fridge for me, but I wasn't hungry. I took it out, sticking it in the microwave for a couple of minutes. Setting everything up on a tray, I took it down to her room and shut the door behind me. I set the tray down on the floor and stood over Ash's sleeping form.

The urge to see her uncovered lashed against me. Rory was right to be concerned, but I wouldn't tell him that. Crouching down next to the bed, I reached out and slowly pulled the blanket off her, exposing her body to me inch by inch. The cool air made goosebumps rise all over her skin. Luminescent skin which taunted me. You'd be a fool not to notice how beautiful she was. How angelic her features appeared to be. I brushed her blonde hair out of her face. It was long and flowed down her back. She was lying with her head resting on her hands. Perfectly still other than the soft rise and fall of her chest.

"Ash."

If I touched her right now, I wouldn't stop and I really wouldn't care if she screamed. Would certainly teach her a lesson about who she belonged to now.

"Ashleigh."

She let out a soft moan which had me clenching my fists. She blinked, staring up at me for a moment. Then she screeched and reared back.

"What the fuck?"

I cocked my head to the side. She scowled at me, looking down to find herself bare all over again.

"Don't even think about covering yourself up."

I should probably let her given this wasn't helping quiet the need coursing inside me, but I was clearly a fucking sucker for punishment. She ignored me, putting her hands over her breasts and shutting her legs tight.

"What do you want?"

"You haven't eaten."

That is why I was here. Not to touch her in the ways I wanted, but to feed her.

"And why would you care about that?"

I smirked. Ash had no idea. I swivelled slightly and picked up the tray before popping it on the bed for her. She looked down at it, eyes narrowed. She needn't be suspicious, I wasn't trying to poison her.

"Eat, Ash."

She sat up against the wall and put the tray on her lap. I sat down on the end of the bed and watched her. The chain rattled as she ate, the noise ringing through the room. Seeing her restrained was like a drug, intoxicating me. Even if she ran, she couldn't escape.

"Why are you staring at me?"

My eyes roamed down her chest, noting how her dusky pink nipples were hard little nubs against her ample breasts.

"You belong to me."

Her face contorted with irritation.

"I'm not a piece of property."

My tongue flicked over my bottom lip, imagining how sweet those nipples would look clamped. Would she pant because of the pain when I tugged on the chain I'd attach in between them? Would she beg?

"That's where you're mistaken."

She put her fork down and crossed her arms over her chest, hiding her breasts from my gaze. My eyes flicked back up to hers, finding those iridescent blue eyes dark with anger.

"You can't own another person. It doesn't work like that, and stop staring at me."

"Why? Does it bother you?"

"Yes."

I reached out and trailed my fingers along the top of her foot which was next to me. She let out a little gasp, her eyes falling on my hand.

"Too bad. I don't take orders from little girls."

The scowl etched on her face deepened.

"I'm not a fucking little girl."

She was little compared to me. So small and lithe. My fingers trailed higher, tracing lines across her ankle. She trembled and I knew she was affected by this simple touch.

"No? Aren't you daddy's little pampered princess?"

"If you think my father has ever pampered me, then you really have no idea."

I looked down at her plate. She'd mostly finished everything including the glass of water I'd brought her. Leaning forward, I plucked the tray from her lap and set it on the floor. Ash's eyes widened when I gripped her arms and tugged her down so she was flat on her back. I crawled over her naked form, settling my legs in between hers to make sure she couldn't do anything like knee me in the balls. My hands rested on either side of her head.

"Do you think your father is coming for you?"

She stared up at me, anger seeping out of her pores.

"He loves me."

42

I smiled, leaning closer until I was inches away from her face.

"Your father loves no one but himself and his own interests."

She clamped her mouth shut as her pupils dilated, telling me she wasn't unaware of what seemed to pulse between us.

"You're my little girl now, Ash. I will use you as I see fit. If you fight me, you'll regret it."

I rose a little and lifted one of my hands from the bed. My fingers landed on her chest, right above her breasts. Her skin was so soft against the pads of my fingertips. So delicate and fragile. Pity I'd break her down piece by piece.

"Rory told me not to provoke you."

"You should listen to him."

My fingers trailed down her chest, in between her breasts and lower. I splayed my hand out across her stomach and I heard her breath catch in her throat.

"What are you doing?"

"Taking what's mine."

Not that I should be. Too damn tempting. That's what Ash was. Her skin against mine felt like fire and I couldn't get enough. Lifting my fingers from her stomach, I brushed my knuckles over the small thatch of curls above her sweet, delectable little pussy.

"Don't," she whimpered.

She could say no all she wanted. I needed to know what she felt like. Despite her words, she didn't move an inch, like she was frozen, waiting for me to do what she'd just told me not to.

"No? Tell me, Ash, did that little fuck you used to call a boyfriend ever really satisfy you? Did he make you scream when he fucked you? Because I'll make you scream if you're good for me."

She sucked in a breath, her eyes widening. Oh yes, I knew all about Nate fucking Tucker and his relationship with her. What Ash didn't realise is just how much I knew about the inner workings of the Russo family.

"What?"

"See my theory is you catered to his every need. He only cared about what he wanted. You need a real man to show you exactly what you've been missing."

The air around us was thick with tension. She could choose to fight me if she wanted.

"And that's you?"

I smirked as both of us looked down at where my knuckles rested, brushing back and forth against her curls. Just itching to trail lower.

"It could be."

"I don't want you."

"I think you don't want me to know how wet you are at my touch."

She let out a sharp little huff of indignation, but we both knew the truth.

"Should I prove myself right, Ash?"

"No."

"Then tell me the truth."

She shook her head, her fists clenching at her sides.

"Too bad I'm going to find out anyway."

Deceived

The hold I had on myself snapped. Straightening my fingers, I dipped them lower and stroked my forefinger across her slit, finding her exactly as I'd hoped. Soaking wet. Delving between those lips, I sought out her little bud and stroked her. She let out a pant followed by a whimper.

"Spread your legs wider. Let me make you feel good."

If I wasn't hard as a fucking stone before, I certainly was now.

"No, stop it."

"You want me to stop, Ash? Fight me off. Show me that backbone."

Her pupils were fully dilated now and her fists were still clenched at her sides. I continued stroking and teasing her little bud. Her chest became flushed and her hips bucked of their own accord. She closed her eyes, biting down on her lip.

For fuck's sake, Rory was right and I hated him for it. Where the hell was my self-control right now? Flown out the damn window.

"Please stop, Quinn," she whispered.

The pleading note in her voice fed me, but the way she said my name made me freeze. Her eyes flew open as I tensed above her.

"You said if I fight you, it'll be worse for me. If that means I have to let you do this, then fine, but I don't want it. I don't want you."

She'd thrown my contradictory words back in my face. I wanted to see her blue eyes flash with anger as she struggled. No one ever said I wasn't a sick, fucked up bastard. They called me the fucking devil after all.

45

"Are you quite sure about that? Your mouth is saying no but your body is clearly saying yes."

CHAPTER SEVEN

Ash

I stared up at Quinn, wondering how exactly I answered that question. What I said was true, I really wanted him to stop, but not because I didn't want him. No, beyond all reason, my body wanted the man above me. Now he'd touched me, I couldn't help the way I reacted to him. I could keep saying no. That was an option. But I didn't know if he would stop.

And you don't really want him to.

Damn it to hell. Why did he have to be so sinful and yet devastating to look at?

I wasn't going to let him have power over me. He didn't get to take control. Not when he'd already taken enough by kidnapping me in the first place.

I moved my uncuffed hand and circled his wrist. The sly smile which appeared on his face unnerved me. So I did the only thing I could, tore his hand away and held it in between us.

"You should listen to the words coming out of my mouth."

He cocked his head to the side, his dark eyes assessing me. I almost hated my own body for betraying me and making me wet for him. It really didn't help that all four of these men were far too handsome for their own good.

"I don't want any of you. You've chained me up naked and I don't even know why. What makes you think I want to be subjected to your hands on me as well."

You're a liar. Such a liar.

Better to lie about my real feelings than give in. I'd been here twenty-four hours so they could all fuck off if they thought they could break me so easily.

Quinn's eyebrow quirked up and surprise flickered across his face.

"Any of us?"

Why the hell did I word it like that?

"None, so you can tell them to keep their hands to themselves too."

For a moment, he didn't react at all, then he sat up, ripping his hand away from me and barked with laughter as if what I said was funny. When he calmed down, he levelled me with a smirk.

"So you admit you've thought about all of us, have you? Isn't that a little greedy?" He leant closer. "Do you wonder what it would be like to be fucked by two men at once or maybe you're interested in getting fucked by four, is that it?"

I felt my face heat up at his words as flames licked down my skin.

"You're sick if you think I'd ever want that."

He shook his head, still smirking.

"I think you're really a very dirty little girl deep down, Ashleigh. Pity for you I don't share my toys."

I wanted to spit in his face. Whilst there was nothing wrong with having sexual kinks, I'd never considered myself into anything other than plain vanilla. I certainly didn't want to fuck four men at once.

"I'm not your fucking toy."

He ran a finger down my sternum, which only pissed me off further.

"Get off me, Quinn. I'm done with this conversation."

His smirk fell and his eyes darkened until they were almost soulless pits of black. He grabbed both my hands and pinned them either side of my head.

"You'll only be done when I say we're done. Do you understand, little girl?"

I struggled against his grip.

"Go fuck yourself."

"Now, now, that's not very nice."

I almost outright screamed at him to leave, but something in the way he was looking at me held me back. It made my back stiffen and my body twitch. If I pushed Quinn any further, I didn't think I'd like the consequences.

"I think you need to learn some manners and I'm more than happy to teach you."

He slowly moved off me and sat down on the bed next to me. I blinked, wondering what the hell that even meant.

"Come here."

His tone brokered absolutely no objections.

"Why?"

"Do not try my patience. It will only be worse for you."

I sat up and moved towards him. He grabbed me the moment I was close and within seconds had me bend over his knees with an arm across my back to keep me in place. His other hand ran across my behind and I had some idea of what he intended to do.

"Now, are you going to be good for me or do I have to punish you?"

I twisted my head up to look at him. His eyes were still black as night and his whole demeanour scared the shit out of me. Either way I looked at this, I was pretty sure he was about to hurt me and I really had no idea how I felt about it.

"What happens if I'm good?"

"I'll go easy on you."

I trembled. Quinn was about to spank me like I was some kind of naughty school girl. That could be the only reason he'd put me in this position. I dropped my head back down and rested my hands on the cold floor to steady myself.

"I'll be good," I whispered.

"For each one you're going to say thank you, sir."

"What? I'm not calling you sir."

Without warning, his hand came down hard on my left cheek. It took a second to register what he'd done and then the pain started. It radiated outwards from where his hand had connected with my skin. I whimpered, unable to keep the sound back.

Christ, that hurt.

"What do you say?"

"If you think I'm going—"

Smack.

I almost screamed because he'd slapped me in the exact same place as before and now it stung like a bitch.

"What the fuck?"

Smack. Smack.

Having never been spanked before, this felt exactly like a punishment should. And I equal parts hated and loved every second of it. Hated how Quinn decided I needed to be taught a lesson. Hated him for the pain, but the strange part about it all is it sent my nerve endings crazy. It's like the pain shot right to my core and turned me on further.

What the hell is wrong with me?

How could I enjoy any of this?

"That fucking hurts."

Smack. Smack.

Tears formed behind my eyes. I sucked in a breath. I could struggle and try to escape him, but what would be the point? He was going to do this whether I liked it or not.

"Quinn!"

Smack. Smack. Smack. Smack.

My cheeks were on fire now and all I could do was keep the tears back. My head dropped and I didn't have it in me to rage against him any further.

"Thank you… sir," I choked out.

The next slap didn't come. His fingers brushed over me and I winced.

"Good little girl," he said softly.

He didn't strike me again. Merely stroked a soothing hand over my raw behind.

"Next time you disobey me, it'll be worse. You can go back to sleep now."

It took me a minute to lift myself from his lap when he released me. I crawled back under the blanket, scowling at him. If he noticed, he didn't comment on it. Picking up the tray he brought with him, he stood up and left the room without a word.

"What the hell was all that about?" I muttered, lamenting over my smarting arse.

Whatever Quinn's game was, I didn't like it. He'd left me with a sore behind and a wet pussy. The man was a fucking menace.

I burrowed under the thick blanket further, wanting to disappear. It took me a good long while to fall asleep again because every time I moved, it exacerbated the pain from his spanking.

Damn you, Quinn Knox. Damn you to hell.

CHAPTER EIGHT

Xavier

I didn't give a shit what Quinn said, I wanted to make sure Ashleigh was okay. He could throw all the hissy fits he wanted, that girl still deserved some common decency.

I had no idea if he'd actually taken the time to feed her or not, so I made her some breakfast and went down to her room. I'd tucked a t-shirt into my back pocket along with the keys to her chains. Ashleigh was huddled under a blanket when I stepped in, her blue eyes wide.

"Morning angel."

She sat up, pulling the blanket high on her chest and wincing at the same time.

"Oh, it's you."

I cocked my head to the side as I approached her.

"You okay there?"

"No, but you have your *friend* to thank for that."

The sarcasm in her voice didn't escape my notice. Clearly, Quinn had done something to her and she wasn't best pleased about it. I set the tea and toast I'd made next to her small bed and reached for her. She flinched back away from me.

"What are you doing?"

"Taking this shit off."

I indicated her collar with my hand.

"Oh."

She seemed stumped by that. I reached out again and this time she sat still whilst I unlocked the collar and the cuff on her hand. Pulling out the t-shirt, which was likely miles too big for her, I gave her a smile.

"I thought you might want to cover up a little."

She took it hesitantly with a curious expression on her face.

"Quinn won't like this."

"Well, *Quinn* isn't here to fucking well complain about it."

I got a slight smile out of her for that comment. She tugged on the t-shirt.

"Thank you...?"

"It's Xavier but you can call me Xav if you'd like."

She nodded. I didn't move to lock her up again, figuring she'd appreciate some freedom. I gave her the tea and toast I'd made next. She practically guzzled it down, leading me to think that fucker hadn't bothered to give her anything.

"What did Knox do to upset you?" I asked as I sat down next to her.

"What didn't he do," she muttered.

"You can tell me, angel. I can't promise to stop him from doing it again, but if you need someone to talk to, I'm here."

Even if I wanted to stop Quinn, I couldn't. He was the one who called the shots for a reason. Whilst I trusted the shit out of him, I didn't always like or agree with his methods.

"He…" her voice faltered. "He spanked me."

My stomach dropped. I knew all about Quinn's proclivities. I just didn't think he'd be so fucking brazen as to start on Ashleigh straight away.

"Did he say why?" I asked, trying to keep my voice level and even.

"Said I needed to learn some manners, but I wasn't the one who came in here and started up on about how I'd never been properly satisfied by a man and accusing me of wanting the four of you to have sex with me at the same time."

My mouth dropped open. Did this girl have a filter or was she that pissed off about what Quinn did and said, she didn't care about what she was admitting to me?

And why does the thought of us sharing her make my cock twitch?

"He said that?"

"Yeah, I told him I wasn't interested in any of you… No offence but you're all complicit in kidnapping me. I don't think it'd be normal to want to sleep with your captors. Not that you guys are unattractive or anything."

She waved a hand at me and went back to eating the second slice of her toast. I had absolutely no idea what to say to that. It wasn't often another person rendered me speechless.

"Should I not have said that?"

Her eyes turned curious.

"You can say what you like to me, angel. I won't hurt you."

Eric and I agreed we'd be there for her no matter what she'd done. Besides, I didn't lay hands on women. Not like that anyway. I wouldn't ask her to do anything she wasn't comfortable with even if she'd just called me and the others attractive.

"But I can't. Rory indicated there are cameras in here."

"Rory came to see you?"

Now there was a turn up for the books. Rory rarely spoke to anyone but us. He didn't like human contact either. I couldn't exactly blame him for the way he was.

"Yeah, he gave me the blanket."

I looked down at the thick blanket covering her legs.

"Well I'll be damned," I muttered.

"Does he not do stuff like that normally?"

"Rory? No."

I shouldn't reveal too much about the four of us. I might want to keep her safe, but Quinn would have me strung up if I accidentally told her something I shouldn't.

"Oh. He did seem like one of those quiet types."

I grinned.

"He is."

"What about the other one? I haven't met him properly yet."

"You will, angel."

Eric could introduce himself. Wasn't my place.

"Finished?" I indicated her plate with my hand.

She took a long gulp of her tea then handed me both the mug and the plate.

"Thank you again."

"You're welcome."

I set them down and reached over, picking up her chains and feeling shit about it.

"I'm sorry, I have to put these on again."

"It's okay."

It wasn't, but neither of us were going to say so. I chained her back up, regretting the damn collar sitting around her neck. It made me feel sick. I stood with her breakfast things and made my way to the door, pausing on the threshold.

"See you later, angel."

"Yeah, okay."

I smiled, shaking my head as I walked out and found Rory leaning up against the wall outside. Shutting her door, I turned to him.

"I heard you've been giving our little prisoner things, going soft in your old age, man?"

Rory was actually the youngest at twenty-seven. Eric and I were twenty-nine and our piece of shit esteemed leader, thirty.

Rory didn't reply but I hadn't expected him to.

"You know she told me Knox went to see her last night."

That made his eyes darken. Rory was just as concerned about Quinn's interest in Ashleigh as Eric and I were.

"He pinked up her little behind, not that she showed me. I don't think that's the whole of it."

"He turned the cameras off."

"That fucker… if he took her against her will, I'll fucking kill him. I don't care what she did. Doesn't give him the right to…"

Rory gave me a sharp shake of his head.

"You don't think he did?"

"Even he has boundaries, Xav."

I shook my head. I wish his fucking boundaries didn't include hurting her for speaking back to him.

"Some fucking boundaries."

When he said nothing else, I walked away towards the kitchen.

"Just do me a favour and have a word with him," I threw over my shoulder.

If anyone could get through to Quinn, it was Rory. The two of them had an understanding. Both of them were into BDSM shit in the bedroom so they'd bonded over that. It went deeper though. They'd been close as kids. We'd all had shitty families, but Rory's? They were the worst. Quinn saved us. That's all any of us needed to walk through fire for the man.

CHAPTER NINE

Quinn

y phone kept ringing like it was going out of fucking business. I stared at the screen, wishing the person on the other end would leave me the fuck alone. I'd done what they wanted. Got myself involved in this mess with no real way out. We all had. Going back on this plan would ruin everything. Besides, all of this would eventually work in our favour. Staying the course was never more imperative than in the here and now.

I put it on silent and shoved it away as the door to my office opened. None of them ever fucking knocked. When I didn't get an immediate earful, I looked up to find Rory leaning against the bookcase with his arms crossed.

Why am I not surprised?

"What now?"

"You touched her."

His tone was matter of fact rather than accusatory.

"I didn't fuck her if that's what you're getting at."

He stared at me for a long moment, his gaze piercing through everything as always.

"She needs discipline," I continued when he didn't respond.

Rory cocked his head to the side. No doubt he would enjoy disciplining Ash if he allowed himself to get remotely close to her. Rory hated humanity on the whole. Hated being around anyone except us and never partook in the women we brought around. It wasn't as if he didn't have needs, he just rarely catered to them and if he did, it was done discreetly.

"What do you want me to say, Rory?"

I splayed out my hands, wondering why my best friend felt it his duty to leash me. Rory had always been my conscience even if he was more fucked up than me, Xav and Eric put together.

"I want you to think before you act."

I rolled my eyes. All I did was think about the potential outcomes to any move I made on behalf of the four of us.

"I always do."

"There will be consequences even you can't hide from if you continue in this, Quinn."

A cold shiver licked down my spine.

"Are you telling me to leave her alone?"

He shook his head.

"Then what the fuck do you mean?"

He shoved off the bookcase and took a step towards the door.

"Just be careful."

I almost threw something at his retreating head. Always talking in damn fucking riddles and never giving you a straight answer. That was our Rory.

He ducked his head back in.

"And Xav has fed our guest."

Ash was hardly our guest, more like a prisoner.

Rory disappeared again before I had a chance to say anything else. I rubbed my forehead as my phone vibrated on the desk again.

"For fuck's sake," I muttered, picking it up and answering it. "What do you want?"

"Is that any way to say hello?" came the voice on the other end.

"What do you want?" I repeated, not in the mood for niceties.

"I want to talk to her."

I stood up and kicked my chair back.

"Not happening. So I suggest you stay in your fucking lane and stop calling me."

I hung up.

"Fucking cunt," I growled as I stalked out of my office and down the hallway towards the kitchen.

It wasn't the first time I wished I'd never gone down this road. Whilst it had been necessary, things never went to plan. Our guest, as Rory had put it, had only been with us for a day and a half and yet she'd caused more trouble than she was worth. Trouble I hadn't been looking for. I couldn't have her winding the boys around her little finger. Xav was treating her like she was his to save and Rory, well I didn't know what the fuck was going on with him. He rarely showed any sort of kindness. I didn't want to think about what she'd done to me. The only one who seemed unaffected was Eric, but he hadn't yet interacted with her.

When I reached the kitchen, I found Xav and Eric at the breakfast bar with mugs and breakfast in front of them.

"All right, fucker?" Xav said, his expression darkening when he spied me.

"What have I done to earn your ire this time?"

"What haven't you done," he muttered, turning back to his plate.

I decided it wasn't worth getting into another argument with him. Xav and I had been at odds ever since the subject of taking Ash had first come up. I took a seat next to Eric who nudged a plate towards me. He tended to make our meals since he enjoyed cooking, unlike the rest of us.

"Can I trust you to make sure Ash gets her meals?"

Eric gave me a sidelong look.

"You're entrusting me with her care?"

"Don't be fucking smart."

He grinned and nudged my shoulder.

"I suppose I have to say hello to her at some point, so whatever. She'll get fed."

I nodded and dished myself up some eggs, bacon and toast.

We hadn't exactly discussed what would happen when Ash got here other than she'd be mine to deal with. I couldn't see to her at all times so the boys would have to help out. It was never my intention to let the girl starve or go without basic necessities.

"We need to talk about our next steps now we have her."

Deceived

The first step in my grand plan to bring everything crashing down around us, destroy those who needed taking out and kick the status quo to the curb. No one would come out unscathed. Especially not Ash's cunt of a father, Frank Russo. The man thought he was untouchable, but I'd proved him wrong.

I had his daughter and there was no fucking way I'd be letting her go.

Ever.

CHAPTER TEN

Ash

I t was much too quiet in my cell. At least I had something to wear even if it was an oversized t-shirt which swamped me. I wondered briefly what they'd done with the clothes I'd been wearing the night of the party. What did it even matter? Wasn't like I was getting out of here any time soon. Quinn made it very clear I was his property even though I'd strongly objected to anyone's ownership.

Why had they taken me? If he wanted to get back at my father, I probably wasn't the best way of going about it. Yes, my father would take it as a slight on his name, but did he really care about my well-being? I used to think he did until the whole situation with Nate. If Papa really cared then he wouldn't have allowed someone who worked for him to treat me that way.

As much as I wanted him to come after me, I wasn't exactly sure if Papa would. Perhaps he'd make the effort due to my mother's pressure. Whilst their marriage was just for show these days, she was still his queen. Me being kidnapped would make him look weak.

My thoughts were drowning me. I stared at the wall, wishing for something to distract me. Wishing I could be torn out of my own head for five minutes. I didn't want to think about Papa or my mother. I wanted out of here. Out of this place where four men had taken me and one of them had touched me in ways I was pretty sure I shouldn't like. But I had. And I hated it. Hated Quinn for his maddening touch. For the way he'd spanked me and made my pussy so wet for him.

I covered my eyes with my hand, groaning as my insides clenched at the thought. This had turned into an intolerable situation. Wanting him was unacceptable. I needed to be more resolute. To fight against him harder. I wasn't going to let him get away with this shit.

The door to my cell swung open and I dropped my hand, tensing as I expected it to be Quinn coming back to taunt me all over again. Except it wasn't.

Stood in the doorway with a plate in one hand and a glass of water in the other was the only man who hadn't yet introduced himself to me. The one with green eyes and chestnut hair. His smile lit up his features and made my heart thump against my chest.

What the hell? Stop it!

Why was I having weird reactions to all these men? I didn't understand it and nor did I want to.

"Hungry?" he asked as he strolled towards me.

I lifted a shoulder, unsure of what to say. His eyes drifted over me, a predatory glint appearing in them momentarily before they cleared. I shivered, wondering what the hell that meant.

He handed me the plate containing a sandwich when he reached me before placing the glass of water on the floor by my bed. I stared down at the food before looking up at him. His head cocked to the side then he turned around and started to walk towards the door.

"Wait!"

He paused, his body tensing. I didn't know why I'd called out to him, only that I hadn't had any company apart from Xav today. He could be my distraction.

"What's your name?"

He turned his head slightly towards me.

"Eric."

I blinked. Now I knew all of them by name at least. He started towards the door again. My heart lurched painfully. I didn't want to be alone, but I had no idea what to do to make him stay. Why did I even want that? I knew nothing about these men.

I kicked myself when he walked out, leaving the door ajar and almost threw the sandwich across the room out of sheer frustration. Placing the plate down on the narrow cot, I got up and paced the room, hating the way the chains clanked as I walked. My hands fisted in the bottom of the t-shirt Xav had given me. Everything inside me was a complete and utter mess.

I dropped the t-shirt and raked my hands through my hair. My head turned sharply towards the door. No one was there, but I was fucking done. I couldn't take this. Isolation had always been an issue for me. I'd felt it my whole life because of who my parents were. I'd never really had a normal childhood.

Walking towards the door with determination, I found myself jerked back by the collar around my neck when I was within a few feet of it. That was it. I stamped my foot, threw my head back and screamed, not caring if any of them heard me. Not caring if they came and stopped me. What was the point? None of them would tell me why they'd taken me or what the hell they were playing at.

My hands fisted at my sides. My throat started to burn, but all I could think of was the cathartic release I felt at letting out my frustrations. Letting everything rip because this situation was too much for me. I'd been through so much shit in my life due to my father. These four men didn't get to destroy me further. They didn't get to just kidnap me and turn me into their property like I meant nothing. I'd had enough of men and their dark natures. The ugliness of the world had seeped into my body and turned it against me. Xav kept calling me angel, but I was no angel. I was just a girl with a damaged and bruised soul crying out for someone to take care of her. For someone to take this pain away.

Through my screams, I heard footsteps outside. The door slammed back on its hinges and there stood the devil himself. Quinn's eyes were black and his expression grim.

"Jesus Christ, what the fuck is wrong with you?"

I didn't say anything, just screamed again. He advanced on me, grabbing me by the hair and shoving a hand across my mouth.

"Shut the fuck up, Ash, before I fucking well make you. What the hell are you playing at screaming my fucking house down?"

I winced at the pain in my scalp. He wasn't being gentle and quite frankly, I didn't expect anything else. My eyes met his. All I could see was irritation burning inside those dark depths. He let go of my mouth, keeping his hand hovering over my lips in case I screamed again.

"Fuck you," I spat.

"Well, nice to see you're in a good mood today."

I raised my hands and shoved at his chest, but he didn't budge.

"Get off me."

He only held my hair tighter, pulling my head back.

"Not until you tell me why you're making such a fucking racket."

"Why? Why, Quinn? Isn't it fucking obvious? I'm chained up like a fucking animal." I let out a choked sound of pain as everything about my situation came crashing down on me. My lungs burnt and my chest caved in. "It's making me crazy. All of this. You're making me fucking crazy." I shoved at him helplessly again. "Why are you doing this to me? Why did you take me? I don't understand. What did I ever do to you?"

His eyes flashed with emotions I didn't recognise.

"I don't answer to you." His voice was low and gravelly, making my blood temperature spike. "You're here because it's where you need to be."

"That's not a fucking explanation."

"It's the only one you're getting."

I sucked in a breath and let it rip again. His hand slammed across my mouth and he backed me away towards the wall. Releasing my hair, he pinned me to it with an arm across my chest.

"Stop fucking screaming. Do you want me to punish you again?"

My face felt like it was on fire at the thought of him bending me over his knee again. Of his hand hitting my bare skin. The way each strike had made my pussy clench with anticipation. How empty I'd felt when he left me afterwards.

I shook my head. He didn't need to know how much it turned me on or how every second he was in my presence made me crave him in ways I wasn't ready for. What the hell was wrong with me? I didn't even like Quinn. He was an arsehole who hadn't been remotely nice to me in the time I'd been with him.

He let go of my mouth again, his eyes intent on mine as his fingers caressed the collar around my neck.

"I like seeing you with this," he said in a low voice. "Collared for me. You're mine, little girl, so don't forget it."

What the hell?

"I'm not yours."

He smirked, his full lips quirking up at the sides and making me wonder what they'd feel like against my skin.

"This defiant nature of yours doesn't do you any favours. It only makes me want to punish you for your insolence. Is that what you want, Ash? To push me?"

"No!"

His hand moved lower until he brushed his fingertips over my t-shirt clad breasts. Trailing a finger over my nipple, his

70

smirk deepened whilst I stiffened and let out a little gasp. My body betrayed me entirely as my hips shifted off the wall towards him. The moment he'd entered the room, all I could think about was him. All I could focus on was Quinn and how his touch burnt me. The devil towered over me and I was pretty sure if he kept this up, I would bend to his will.

"You're going to obey me."

I shook my head even though I knew the moment he gave me a command, I wouldn't hesitate to follow through.

"Put your hands on the wall and keep them there."

My fight left me. I put my hands on the wall as instructed, laying my palms flat. If it pleased him, he didn't comment on it.

"Stay."

He pulled back and looked me over, his dark eyes blazed with lust and I couldn't help wondering what he intended to do next. The only sounds in the air were my chest heaving and his slightly laboured breath. The pulsating desire in the atmosphere almost suffocated me. I didn't want to question why I felt this pull towards a man I barely knew. A man who'd kidnapped me, chained me up like an animal and told me I was his.

I watched him as he lowered himself to his knees in front of me. He reached out and tugged up the t-shirt until he exposed me to his gaze. Breathing in, he inhaled me. I let out a ragged breath.

"Your body doesn't lie, Ash. It tells me everything you don't want to voice out loud."

I'd never had a man get so up close and personal with my pussy before. Nate hadn't been interested. He just liked to stick his dick in me, which happened to be very different to what Quinn was doing now. His pupils were fully dilated and he was staring at my most intimate parts like they mesmerised him. Nate never looked at me as if he wanted to feast upon me, but Quinn did. He made my body burn up from the inside out.

"Spread your legs wider."

I shifted my feet, giving him what he asked for.

"So beautiful," he whispered and I felt the truth of his words.

His eyes met mine, the lust swirling in them making my heart pound harder. Leaning towards me, he ran his nose up my inner thigh.

"Quinn," I whimpered, his name falling out of my mouth without my say so.

"Do you want me, little girl? I told you I'd make you scream."

His mouth was mere inches away from where I desperately wanted him. His breath dusted across my exposed pussy and I couldn't take it.

"Please."

His rumble of approval vibrated through me.

"Please what?"

I almost let out a frustrated huff. Quinn wanted me to give him proper respect. That's the only way I would get what I wanted from him.

"Please, sir."

His warmth was gone the next instant. I blinked rapidly before my eyes came to rest on him. He'd risen to his feet and was standing a few feet away from me.

"You think you're going to get rewarded after you made such a racket, Ash? You're mistaken."

And with those words, he left the room, slamming the door shut behind him. I stood there, pinned to the wall with my mouth opening and closing.

What the fuck just happened?

CHAPTER ELEVEN

Ash

I sat down heavily on the cot and picked up the plate with the sandwich Eric had made me. My body ached with desire, but there was no way in hell I was going to touch myself when I knew very well there were cameras in this room. As if I'd give that piece of shit a show after what he'd done to me.

Screw Quinn and screw the rest of them. They hadn't stopped him. They wouldn't. So as far as I was concerned, they were all as bad as each other.

You know that's not true though, Ash.

I stuffed one half of the sandwich in my mouth, taking a bite and chewing to stop myself thinking those thoughts. Hating how they'd all confused me so much with their behaviour towards me. Why had Rory and Xav been nice and yet allowed Quinn to just do what the hell he wanted? What made them so loyal? I hadn't had enough interaction with Eric to know what his deal was. I did know he made a mean chicken salad sandwich though. It really did taste like heaven. I groaned as I ate the rest, downing the glass of water he'd brought me too. I left it and the plate as close to the door as I could get before pacing the room again.

Quinn had only distracted me for a limited period of time. Now all my thoughts were consumed by my predicament again. My new reality. I wanted to rip the t-shirt from my body and scream again, but I knew it wouldn't do me any favours. Quinn would just come back and then I'd be punished for sure.

"God damn it," I huffed. "Fuck my life."

I shook my head. Getting angry at things wouldn't help me. I didn't think anything would at this rate. The chains clinked across the floor, the noise grating on my ears but I couldn't stop pacing. Dragging my hands through my hair and wanting out of this fucking room. I felt unclean. Sullied by that fucking man and his hands on me. My skin itched. I scratched my arms. This was absolute hell.

Why did I have to be born Ashleigh Vittoria Russo? Why couldn't I have come from a normal family? I hated Papa's ties to the criminal underworld. Hated knowing all the unspeakable things he did to those who crossed him. Even more so to those who had only been a mere inconvenience to Frank Russo and his illegally obtained wealth.

"Fuck him," I hissed under my breath. "Fuck everything about him."

As much as I wanted Papa to save me, I wasn't sure going back to that life would be worth it either. Being married off to one of his lackeys didn't appeal to me in the slightest. Or perhaps he'd use me to join our family to one of his allies or, I dreaded to think, one of his rivals.

I threw my hands up in frustration, wanting this all to end. That's when I felt it. *His* presence. I stopped abruptly, my eyes falling on the door and Rory leaning against the wall next to it. How did the man manage to move so silently? I swear I hadn't heard him come in, then again I'd been rather preoccupied with my own inner turmoil.

"Jesus, do you always sneak up on people like that?"

He blinked but said nothing. I took a step towards him, wary as I knew next to nothing about the man.

"Did you want something?"

Still no response. I let out a sigh and looked down at the floor.

"You don't like to talk, do you?"

I glanced up at him under my lashes. His hazel eyes pierced inside my soul. At least it felt that way when he looked at me.

"Will you listen then?"

I don't know why I asked that. Just that my racing mind was driving me up the wall and I couldn't take it any longer.

I took another step towards him. His body tensed. It would've been barely noticeable if I hadn't been paying attention.

"You seem agitated," he said, his deep voice low.

That was an understatement.

"More like frustrated and confused."

Why was I even talking to him? He was Quinn's friend and therefore not on my side. No matter what any of them said, they didn't have my best interests at heart.

I turned away and clenched my fists. No point trying to explain how I felt to anyone. Why would they even care? Though this morning Xav had seemed genuinely concerned about what Quinn had done to upset me.

Doesn't matter. I can't allow myself to let my guard down with any of them.

"Ashleigh…"

Why did my name on his lips feel like a caress against my skin?

"It's Ash," I mumbled.

"You don't like it in here."

I didn't bother agreeing. I hated every part of this. Especially being chained up. I looked at the cuff on my wrist and wished it would melt off so I never had to see it again.

"I'm all alone," I whispered, not caring if he heard me or not.

Even though I couldn't see him, I could feel him. The heat of his body searing into mine. When the hell did he move closer?

"Do you want to get clean?"

I nodded. Maybe I would feel better then. More human instead of this chained up animal Quinn had made me into.

"Here."

I turned, finding him standing right next to me holding a set of keys between his fingers.

"Quinn won't like this. He's already mad at me for screaming the place down."

His lip twitched. So he'd heard me too.

"He isn't here."

Did he go out? Why did I care? Rory was going to let me wash and that was far more than any of them had done for me so far.

I held out my wrist for him. It didn't escape my notice he avoided touching my skin as he unlocked the cuff. It clanked on the floor after it dropped. I moved my hair out of the way and let him unlock the collar. His breath dusted across my neck, making me tremble and my skin prickle with goosebumps. He stepped back abruptly, throwing the collar on the floor.

"Come with me."

I followed him from the room, knowing better than to attempt to flee. Didn't have it in me anyway. Running seemed like a stupid idea. They would only hunt me down and throw me back in the cell. I didn't want to think about what Quinn would do to me then. I wasn't stupid enough to think escaping would be a viable option.

I didn't pay much attention to where we were going, staring at Rory's back. He wasn't overly muscly, but athletic like Quinn. No doubt he could quite easily overpower me if it came down to it. He wore a navy t-shirt and black jeans with black trainers. I wondered if he was the youngest of the group. He had more of a baby face even though he also had that scar on his eyebrow as if he'd been through the wars.

We stopped outside a room. Rory pushed the door open and looked at me.

"You're trusting me alone in there?"

He shook his head.

I sighed and walked in with him following me. The bathroom was huge with a big Victorian toe-clawed tub set by the window. Rory walked over to it, put in the plug and turned on the taps. He poured something into the water and watched it fill up. I leant against the sink counter, wondering if I should break the silence or not.

"Come here, Ash."

Something about the deep notes of his voice had me obeying immediately. I shuffled over to the bath and stood next to him.

"Is this too hot for you?"

I realised he was talking about the water. Leaning down, I tested it with my hand.

"No, that's okay."

He looked at me, his eyes roaming over the t-shirt I had on. His gaze didn't make me uncomfortable. If anything it made my skin tingle. Rory hadn't looked at me like he was interested when I'd been naked before. I doubted it would be different this time.

"Is anyone else here?"

"No."

Did I feel safe being alone with him? Not particularly but mostly because I didn't trust any of them. Rory hadn't actually done anything to make me feel like he was about to take advantage of me.

He turned off the taps and stepped back. My hands went to the bottom of the t-shirt Xav had given me. His eyes fixed on them. I could hardly breathe as I pulled it off, leaving me bare before him. I swallowed as I met his eyes. There wasn't a hint of emotion in them. I had no idea why that disappointed me so much.

Deceived

His lip twitched, the only discernible reaction to me being naked. Did Rory like what he saw? Why did I even care?

I stepped over the lip of the bath and climbed in. As I lowered myself into the water, I couldn't help the moan of appreciation leaving my lips. When I looked up at Rory, his eyes were dark and his muscles tense.

"Are you going to watch me?"

I almost slapped myself for asking that until his tongue darted out, wetting his bottom lip.

"Not unless you want me to."

My eyebrows shot up.

What the hell does that mean?

"I... uh..."

I looked away, unable to stand the sudden tension between us.

"I'm kidding. You don't have to be scared of me. I'm not Quinn."

Fucking Quinn.

I didn't want to think about him.

"Why are you all letting him do this to me?"

There was no point me asking since I knew it wouldn't be answered. I hugged my legs to my chest, feeling vulnerable and exposed.

"I'm scared of all of you," I whispered. "I don't want any of this."

I shivered despite the heat of the water melting away the tension in my body.

Rory sat on the edge of the bath. His closeness affected me no matter how hard I tried to deny it to myself.

"Being touched scares me."

I looked up at him. So that's why he'd been careful not to touch me when he was taking the chains off me. Why would he fear touch?

"What, why?"

"We all have fears we can't control, Ash. I can't promise no one will hurt you but you have nothing to fear from me."

"I don't?"

He shook his head once.

"I won't touch you like he does. Neither will Eric nor Xav."

His words made a pit of despair open up inside me and I had no idea why. I should be pleased to hear him say that, but I wasn't. Analysing why wouldn't do me any favours.

"Okay," I whispered, unsure of what else to say.

"Close your eyes and relax. You're safe for now. I promise."

The weird thing was I felt safer right then than I had done since I'd been taken. I uncoiled my body, settling down in the bath properly. My head lolled against the lip. I closed my eyes, allowing the heat of the water to seep into my bones. And for half an hour, Rory afforded me a sliver of peace and quiet from my raging thoughts with his calming presence.

When this ended and I had to go back to my cell, at least I might be better prepared for my next encounter with Quinn. I could hope, couldn't I?

CHAPTER TWELVE

Eric

"Russo knows she's missing, right?" Xav said from the back seat whilst I drove.

"He'd be a pretty fucking shitty leader if he didn't know his own daughter is missing," Quinn retorted next to me.

I rolled my eyes. These two would be the death of me soon.

"Well, excuse me for wanting to make sure, not like I monitor threats or anything."

Xav did exactly that. Yes, he was a bit of a gym bunny and all that shit, but he was smart with computers. He'd set up all the cameras in the house as well as Ashleigh's cell. I didn't like to think of it like that. If I had my way, she wouldn't be in there at all, but going against Quinn when it came to her would be like playing with fire and I'd be the one getting burnt. Keeping my mouth shut would be better all round.

"He'll know soon enough *Il Diavolo* has his daughter and he isn't giving her back."

"You know you sound like an absolute twat every time you talk about yourself in the third person."

Quinn practically ground his teeth.

"Fuck off, Xav."

"Why don't you fuck off? You're the one who's acting like this is some kind of joke. Russo is dangerous as shit. You, of all fucking people, should know that."

Quinn turned his head and glared at Xav.

"Do *not* fucking bring that up."

"Would you two kindly stop bickering like children?" I interjected before one of them threw himself at the other in the car and made me lose my concentration.

I watched Xav cross his arms over his chest and stare out the window with a scowl on his face through the rearview mirror whilst Quinn turned back towards the front and clenched his fist in his lap. If I'd known how much trouble having the girl with us would cause, I might have argued harder against this course of action.

"Do you think she'll be okay alone with Rory?" I asked Quinn, my voice low.

"Why wouldn't she be? Not like he'll go near her or anything."

I wasn't so sure about that. Xav told me Rory seemed to be quieter than usual, which for Rory was saying something considering how he rarely spoke unless it was strictly necessary. Plus he'd given our guest a blanket.

"Xav thinks he's fascinated with Ashleigh."

He'd spoken to me about it over breakfast. Saying it was weird for Rory to be out of his room so much and he'd found him lurking outside Ash's cell when Xav had given her breakfast.

"She prefers to be called Ash…" He turned to me. "You know, I'm worried about that too."

"Has he said anything to you?"

"As if Rory fucking tells me anything other than to be careful and watch myself. I don't think he'll do anything because you know what Rory's like, but still, we need to keep an eye on it."

I grinned. Rory was just about the only one who could get away with telling Quinn what to do. As for keeping an eye on him, I wasn't sure that would be strictly necessary. Rory always kept himself in check and he hated human contact. He wasn't going to touch Ash, unlike Quinn. We all knew what he wanted to do to the girl.

"Did she explain why she was screaming earlier?"

Quinn let out a huff.

"I don't want to talk about it."

"No? Done something you shouldn't have?"

"You can fuck off too, E."

I rolled my eyes.

"I'm not judging, man. You do you."

"Well, thank you for the fucking permission."

"No need to get so tetchy, Quinn. Honestly, it's like living with fucking twelve-year-olds except it's worse because you're grown men who can beat the shit out of each other if you wanted to."

He turned away. He was pissed for some reason and I really didn't know why. Maybe he just needed to fuck Ash and be done with it. It was clear he wanted to. Not that I advocated him doing it against her will or anything, but hell, if he was going to be so bloody moody, then he needed to get her out of his system or risk jeopardising everything we'd worked so hard for.

"She's…" he started before he sighed.

"Got under your skin?"

"Yes, and I don't fucking know why."

"I do," Xav said quietly from the back.

Quinn turned his head sharply.

"Oh, you want to be included in the discussion now?"

"You know what, fuck you, Quinn. Clearly, you're too much of a cunt to be remotely civil to me right now."

"Guys, seriously, enough," I said, my hands tightening on the steering wheel. "Is it remotely helpful for either of you to be arguing over this shit? No, it isn't. So just stop it."

Both of them went quiet again. I looked back at Xav through the rearview mirror.

"Go on, why has she got under his skin then?"

Xav looked like he wasn't going to say anything then he sighed and rubbed his face.

"There's something about her. You can't tell me either of you haven't noticed. I mean fuck even Rory knows. It's like her soul is broken, but she's still trying to keep her head up despite it. Makes me wonder what the fuck Russo did to her."

"What makes you think it's Russo?" Quinn asked.

"You really think that cunt hasn't messed with her head? If she was there when you know what happened, then who's to say she wasn't there to witness other things he's done. The man is known for having a million and fucking one skeletons in his cupboards. Not to mention his fucking wife and her piece of shit brother. Isn't he due for early release or some shit?"

We knew all about that shitshow. Never thought anyone would bring down the Daniels and their sex trafficking ring. They'd been notorious amongst the crime families although they didn't deal with them much. They saw themselves as above all of that what with their billions, but really, they were just as bad if not worse.

"You mean Davenport? I heard that too. Seems like a lot of them will get out early at this rate."

"Like we're any better what with keeping a girl chained up."

"It's not like we're abusing her," I said, but even that sounded hollow to my ears.

"Because that makes it so much better. Oh, we're not hurting her so it's all fine that she's chained to the fucking wall."

"Would you shut up about that already?" Quinn said, glaring at Xav again.

"I won't shut up until you agree to let her out and give her a decent fucking room to sleep in."

"You know I kind of agree with Xav," I said. "We should at the very least give her somewhere more comfortable or we might as well give up all our morals like the people we're trying to destroy."

"He just wants to punish her for—"

"I told you not to fucking well bring that up!" Quinn practically roared.

Xav looked at me before rolling his eyes and sitting back again. We all fell silent. Quinn seethed next to me. Xav had pushed him too far, but he'd already been on edge before he even got in the car. It had something to do with Ash and her screaming earlier. Perhaps I'd get Rory to look at the footage, then we'd have a clearer idea of why Quinn was in such a foul mood. I could send him a text once we arrived. And check if everything was okay with our guest.

I could only hope things would calm down between Xav and Quinn soon because having them at each other's throats wasn't doing anyone any good whatsoever.

I looked back at Xav through the rearview mirror again, finding my heart growing tight. His eyes were dark with irritation. I knew he was frustrated with all of this. I wanted to make it better for him, but I couldn't. Not like he needed my comfort. Just my friendship, which I'd always willingly give, but I couldn't help wanting more. Wanting something I couldn't have.

I turned back to the road, knowing it was futile to be wishing for anything more between us. Xav and I would never cross that line because I would never admit to what I really felt deep down.

I'm in love with my best friend and I always have been.

CHAPTER THIRTEEN

Quinn

This day had been far too long. Dealing with the next steps in our plan had taken it out of me not to mention Ash and her bloody screaming earlier. Fuck I'd been so close to doing something I shouldn't. Her defiance intoxicated me and I couldn't help but want her in ways I shouldn't. And I couldn't forget Xav and Eric getting on my case about where I'd put her.

Sighing, I rubbed my face as I fast-forwarded through the footage of her from today. I almost missed it because I wasn't paying attention. When I rewound it, I found my eyes almost fucking bugging out of my head.

What the fuck?

I couldn't be seeing things, right? Rory had unchained her and taken her out of the room. He hadn't said anything about it when we got back earlier and I asked him how she was. I skimmed through the next hour to when he brought her back. Setting it to play, I turned the sound up.

"Thank you," she said. "I needed that."

Rory nodded at her but didn't speak. She let him put her chains back on before sitting on her cot and fiddling with the clothes she was wearing.

I'd known Xav had given her a t-shirt earlier, but this was different. She was in a smaller t-shirt and a pair of men's boxers. Narrowing my eyes, I stared at them realising Rory had given her his own fucking clothes to wear. Honestly, if I hadn't been concerned about him before, I was really fucking concerned now.

She got back under the blanket. Rory stood by the door for the longest time just watching her before he looked directly up into the camera. A small smile played across his lips for a moment before he walked out.

Was this him taunting me or some shit? What the fuck had he done with her? I didn't bother watching any further because I was pretty sure that had to be the extent of their interaction. Getting up, I stormed out of the office and stalked through the house in search of my wayward friend. I found him in the living room with Xav. They were both watching TV.

"What the actual fuck did you do with Ash earlier?"

Both of them looked up. Xav's eyebrows shot up whilst Rory's expression was blank.

"What the fuck, man? I gave her breakfast, you know that," Xav said.

"I wasn't fucking talking to you." I pointed at Rory. "Where did you take her? And why the hell was she thanking you?"

Xav looked at Rory then, his eyes wide. Rory stared at me like he wasn't going to answer any of my questions.

"I'm not fucking about, Rory. What did you do?"

The fact he wasn't answering unnerved me. Whilst Rory wasn't one for talking, he also didn't keep shit from me either. Not stuff that mattered anyway.

I did question why I was so pissed off at the thought of him making friends with her. It's not like he'd have touched her, but he'd got close enough to. He'd taken her fucking chains off.

Ash is mine. Mine.

"She was agitated so I let her have a bath," he said with his usual calm.

"You gave her your own fucking clothes."

"She doesn't have anything else, Quinn. What did you expect me to do?"

He was right. I hadn't thought about getting her anything to wear. My anger evaporated immediately. I ran my hand through my hair and stepped back. What the hell was going on with me?

"Jesus, Knox, she's not even been here two days and she's already fucked your head right up," Xav said.

If I hadn't been reeling from my own insane behaviour, I would've punched Xav in the face for that comment. Except he was right. Ash had brought out something in me I hadn't expected. I needed to possess her like I'd never needed to possess anyone.

Well, shit.

"Are you two arguing all over again?" Eric said as he strolled into the room.

"Oh no, nothing to do with me. Knox decided to rag on Rory for letting Ash have a bath."

Eric's eyes narrowed as he looked at our quiet friend.

"What the fuck is wrong with the three of you? She's just one girl. Anyone would think you're acting like jealous rivals vying for her affections right now."

"Hey, don't lump me in with Quinn. I'm not jealous of anyone."

Eric gave Xav a look which spoke volumes. The damn fool had been wanting to save Ash since the moment she got here. If that didn't indicate he had some kind of feelings towards her then I don't fucking know what did. And Rory? I had no clue what had gotten into him either. As for me? Damn right, I was jealous. I wanted Ash to submit to me and only me.

"I don't want anything from her either," Rory said quietly.

"Oh so it's just Quinn who's gone gaga for her then, is it? Could've fooled me with the way all of you have been acting since the minute she got here," Eric said, rolling his eyes. "I came in here to tell you dinner is ready, but if you're content on bickering like five-year-olds all evening then be my guest."

And with that, he walked out.

We all looked at each other. I needed to get my shit together. How could I let one girl cause this many issues between us? We'd never fought with each other so hard over another person before. Then again, none of us had encountered someone like Ash. It wasn't something we could predict or prepare for.

"I'm out," Xav said, standing up. "Eric's right, she's just a girl and quite frankly, this shit isn't worth arguing over. We got better things to be doing than ragging on each other all day."

He walked out, shaking his head. Rory eyed me for the longest moment before he stood up too.

"Consequences, Quinn, consequences."

He left too before I could formulate a response.

What the hell is happening to us? To me? I shook myself. My immediate instinct was to go have words with that girl, but it'd be a mistake. I was too fucking worked up right now to think straight. Calming down was the only option.

Maybe if we all had a civilised meal, then things would go back to normal.

Who are you fucking kidding, Quinn? Nothing is ever going to be the same again.

Not now Ash Russo was in our lives it wouldn't. She'd flipped the script entirely.

Well, fuck.

CHAPTER FOURTEEN

Quinn

As much as I wanted things to be okay between the four of us, it was clear they weren't and I couldn't help but feel responsible. They looked to me to be their leader and yet here I was losing my fucking shit. Who the hell was I right now?

Dinner between us had been difficult. Thankfully Eric had gone and given Ash her meal since I couldn't deal with seeing her. Not after earlier. Not when my fingers itched to punish her for making me feel like this. But my mouth also wanted to taste her. To feel her soft skin against mine. I shouldn't want her. Not after what she'd done. Not after what she'd been complicit in. I should hate everything she stood for, but Ash had surprised me on every single fucking level. Probably why I was standing in the doorway of her cell watching her sleep like some creepy stalker.

I've lost the fucking plot.

Yet I couldn't stop myself walking into the room and sitting down on her bed. I brushed her hair out of her face. She looked so peaceful and innocent.

"What are you doing to me, Ashleigh?" I whispered.

I slipped the keys to her chains out of my pocket. We all had a copy just in case. Carefully, I unlocked her so I didn't disturb her sleep. There would be no point questioning what I was doing right now. Merely acting on my instincts and I couldn't bring myself to care whether it was right or wrong.

I picked her up off the bed, holding her against my chest and making sure her head didn't loll all over the place. Her eyelids fluttered but she didn't wake. Her hand fell against my chest, right where my heart was thumping at her closeness.

I took her out of the cell, down the hallway and upstairs. Kicking open the door to my bedroom, I walked in and set her down on the bed where I'd already pulled the covers back. I draped them over her, making sure she was comfortable. I eyed the hallway before I shut the door and locked it but no one was about.

Rubbing my face with both hands, I didn't know what was up or down any more. For some reason, I wanted her here where I could see her and not through a fucking screen. I needed to inhale her, touch her, have her close.

"Jesus, I'm insane," I muttered.

Quietly, I stripped down to boxers, turning out the lights before I slipped in next to her. Unable to help myself, I cupped her cheek, running my thumb along her skin. When she woke up, I wasn't sure if she'd be pissed or if she'd appreciate me bringing her here. Honestly, I had no idea what Ash really thought of me. She couldn't hide how her body reacted when I was close, but that wasn't exactly telling of her real feelings inside. We could all have involuntary reactions to other people.

She shifted, letting out a quiet moan. I tensed, wondering if she was about to wake up.

"Quinn," she breathed out.

"I'm right here."

I didn't want to move my hand from her cheek, but I didn't think she'd appreciate me touching her if she did wake up. Gently, I pulled my arm back. The movement must've alerted her because her eyes flew open. She blinked, stared at me then scrambled up into sitting position, blue eyes wide. She looked around, confusion evident on her face. I could see her via the moonlight streaming in through the windows. I didn't really like the curtains closed at night.

"Where am I?"

"My bed," I replied.

Her gaze fell on me.

"What the hell, Quinn? What am I doing in your bed?"

"I brought you in here."

Her brow furrowed.

"Why?"

"I wanted you."

It seemed like the simplest explanation considering I didn't really have another one which made any sense to me.

"Wanted me? Were you going to do something to me in my sleep? That's sick. You're sick."

I sat up, looking her directly in the eyes.

"No, I was letting you sleep. No matter what you think of me, I wouldn't take advantage of an unconscious woman like that."

She glared.

"You or one of your friends stripped me bare whilst I was unconscious."

I didn't feel like having it out with her right then. Not after all the arguments I'd had today.

"And you touched me when I didn't want you to, so excuse me if I don't think very highly of your fucking moral compass."

"I've had enough shit off everyone today already without you giving me more. Lie down and go back to sleep."

"You've had enough shit? Oh well yes, it must be so hard being you. Taking women and holding them against their will is so fucking taxing."

That was fucking it. I really had no patience left. Reaching out, I grabbed her by the hair and tugged her towards me. She yelped and shoved her hands against my chest.

"Get off."

"Stop struggling."

"No!"

"For fuck's sake, Ashleigh, I'm not trying to do anything to you. Would you fucking calm down!"

I wrapped both arms around her and held her against my chest, her arms stuck between us. Her blue eyes were full of fire and she looked like she was about to bite my head off.

"Let me go."

"Do you want me to bend you over my knee again because let me tell you, I'm in no mood to be gentle."

"I don't care!"

She shoved at me uselessly before kicking out with her legs. I rolled us both over, pinning her legs to the bed with mine and holding her arms down.

"Enough. Christ, I brought you up here so you could have somewhere comfortable to sleep, but I'll quite happily put you back in the cell without a blanket and a mattress if you keep this up."

"Oh really? You literally just said you brought me here because you wanted me."

I cocked my head to the side.

"That's also true."

"What the hell, Quinn? You're so fucking weird. I don't get you. What do you want from me? I mean, seriously, what the hell do you want?"

I stared down at her. There were many things I wanted from Ash and none of them were sweet or innocent. My eyes were drawn to her mouth. Those beautiful sensuous lips of hers.

"What do I want?"

"Yes, what do you want from me? I can't deal with you flipping your moods every five minutes."

I leant closer, unable to help myself. No longer caring what this meant or the consequences Rory kept reminding me of.

"I want this."

The instant my lips met hers, fire exploded across my skin. Her mouth felt so soft even if she was currently completely still and not responding to my touch at all. Ash didn't try to turn away, she just lay there. Whether she was in shock or if she didn't want this, I had no clue. I couldn't stop myself from kissing her. I had to know what she tasted like.

Her hands flexed against mine. I was about to pull back when her body arched into me and her lips parted. Ash kissed me back, her lips moving with mine, tentatively exploring. Feeling the change in her, I let go of her hands and cupped her face. Her fingers threaded in my hair as she opened her mouth to me and let me taste her. Tongues clashed and she moaned, arching into me again.

I pressed myself between her legs, needing the friction of our bodies against each other. Needing more than just this kiss because this fucking kiss was intoxicating me further. I kissed down her jaw as I ground against her pussy, feeling her heat scorching me through our clothes. She wrapped her legs around me, her body in complete sync with mine.

"Quinn," she whimpered. "Please, god, please."

I kissed her neck, revelling in the way she tasted.

"What do you want, little girl?"

"You… please, sir."

Fuck. Fuck. Fuck.

I captured her mouth again to stop myself acting on her words. It hadn't been my intention to do anything like fuck her in my bed tonight. Even if my cock throbbed restlessly and sought her out as I ground against her harder.

She tasted minty. I'd given Xav the task of taking her to get ready for bed earlier. He'd done it without question. No matter what he said, I was pretty sure he had a thing for Ash, but who the fuck cared when she was in my bed, kissing me. Me. She wanted me.

I let go of her lips and traced a line down to her ear.

"Do you want me to touch you?"

"Yes."

"Make you come?"

"Yes, please," she panted. "Please, sir."

My resolve not to do anything further shattered.

"Are you going to touch me too, Ash? Wrap your hand around my cock. Stroke me until I come all over your tits."

"Please, I want your cock."

Jesus fucking Christ.

I pulled away so I could rip her t-shirt off followed by the boxers she was wearing. I threw them away and stared down at her naked body. Her beautiful perfectly proportioned little lithe body. The sight of her made my dick ache and leak. Shit, I wanted to fuck her so badly. I wanted to slide my cock inside her tight little pussy and fuck her so hard she screamed for me.

"Quinn, please."

"Show me where you want me to touch you."

She opened her legs for me. My mouth watered.

I'm not going to fuck her. I'm not going to fuck her. Yet.

Even as I kept repeating those words in my head, my hand went to my boxers and I pulled them off, baring myself to her completely. Ash's eyes went to my cock, widening before she reached out to me. I didn't stop her wrapping her hand around it. I couldn't help the groan escaping my lips as she started to stroke me.

I leant down and captured her mouth again as my hand trailed down her body, feeling her soft skin against my fingertips. Dipping them between her legs, I stroked her folds, finding her dripping wet. Her hand around my cock tightened.

Fuck. I want her so badly.

"You're so wet," I murmured against her lips. "He didn't fuck you the way you need, did he?"

"No."

I plunged two fingers inside her pussy, making her buck.

"I'm going to fuck you just right, little girl. Just like you need."

"Please, sir."

She was not doing my restraint any good. Her pussy was so tight around my fingers. She was so hot and wet as I thrust inside her. My thumb found her clit, rubbing it and making her mewl.

"Do you want that? Do you want me to fuck you?"

"Yes, god, please."

Her hand moved faster, almost making me lose control. But I'd told her I was going to come over her tits and that's what I intended to do. Right after I made her come all over my fingers. I inserted another one, stretching her out for me. When I did finally slide inside her, she would feel so damn good.

The only sounds in the room were her little mewls, our heated breath and me fucking her with my fingers. Such delicious noises which only fuelled the fire.

"Harder," she moaned.

I leant my forehead against hers, watching her beautiful blues, her pupils completely dilated as she panted for me.

"You want it rough. I'll make sure you know who you belong to. You liked it when I spanked you. I'll make your little arse so red, you won't be able to sit for days. Then I'll fuck you in all your tight holes. All of them. You're going to take my cock so well."

She opened her mouth but no sounds came out. I wasn't sure what she thought of what I'd said, but I didn't care either. All those things would happen, eventually. She'd take it just like she was told. Ash wanted to obey me even if she didn't know it yet.

"Quinn," she cried out. "Fuck."

I felt it hit her, her pussy clenched around my fingers and her little body jerked. The warm gush of her arousal flooded my hand. She looked so beautiful like this, coming all over me like she was made to.

When I was sure she was completely spent, I pulled my fingers out of her warmth and stuck them in my mouth, savouring each one. She watched me, her eyes wide.

"You taste delicious."

I sat up on her stomach and stared down at her hand still wrapped around my cock. She'd stopped stroking me when she came. I raised an eyebrow and waited. Ash looked at me for a long moment and then she moved her hand again. Her eyes fell on what she was doing and she bit her lip.

"I want…"

"You want what?" I grunted, revelling in the way her hand felt around me.

"I want to taste you too."

Jesus fuck.

"Are you asking if you can suck my cock?"

"Yes… sir."

She was still looking at me as if she couldn't take her eyes off my cock. Well, who was I to deny her? I shifted off her and lay back against the bed.

"Come here then."

She shifted up on her knees and crawled between my legs. Her hand wrapped around the base and she ran her tongue up my shaft. An involuntary groan left my mouth when she wrapped her lips around the head. I tangled my fingers in her hair, encouraging her to take more.

"Look at me when my cock is in your mouth, little girl."

Her eyes met mine as my cock sunk deeper in her hot, wet mouth. She hummed and I swear to god my dick got harder, pulsing against her tongue. At this rate, I wouldn't last fucking long, already pent up with lust and desire for this girl.

She used her hand to stroke me from the base as she sucked me. Christ, she was good. Whilst her fingers didn't quite fit around me, she still wanted to give me as much pleasure as she could. I could see the determination in her eyes as she kept them fixed on mine.

"You keep that up, I'm going to come in your mouth."

Her eyes darkened and she moved faster, sucking me harder. Clearly, someone wanted my cum running down their throat.

Dirty little girl.

My fingers tightened in her hair. I tensed, knowing I was so close to the edge.

"Fuck, that's it, Ash, fuck," I grunted. "Fuck, little girl."

I exploded, my cock jerking when the first wave hit. Spots formed in my vision. Her hot little mouth continued to work me as I filled it with cum until I dropped my hand from her hair. She pulled away and swallowed, catching the drops which had spilt out of her mouth.

Ash crawled up my body and lay her head on my chest with her hand resting next to it. I stroked her hair and wrapped my other arm around her, holding her close.

"Do I have to go back to the cell?" she whispered.

"No, you can go to sleep right here."

I pulled the covers over us and listened to her breathing even out before I drifted off to sleep too, knowing tomorrow would bring a whole new set of fucked up shit down on my head. She might have submitted now, but I was damn sure Ash wouldn't remain willingly submissive for me indefinitely.

CHAPTER FIFTEEN

Ash

Despite being cocooned in the warmth of the softest covers, the most comfortable bed and pinned to a very solid body, I couldn't help the rapid pulse of my heart pounding against my chest. I'd lost all sense of rational thought last night when Quinn kissed me. It was like lust flooding my veins and I could no more control or prevent my reaction to him than I could do anything but submit. And fuck had I. I'd been begging and I'd damn well called him 'sir' again. Not to mention how I'd asked for permission to put his dick in my mouth. If my arms hadn't been trapped right then, I would've slapped myself silly.

What the hell was my problem? I'd barely known this man for two days. Heat flooded my cheeks at the thought of his fingers inside me and his cock, his beautiful cock with my fingers wrapped around its length and when I'd had it in my mouth.

Seriously, Ash, he's your fucking captor! Do you think this is normal? Because girl, let me tell you, this isn't normal at all.

I shifted, trying to escape his hold, but Quinn just tightened it.

"Where do you think you're going?" came his deep voice, sending a shiver down my spine.

"Away from you."

He opened his eyes and a smirk graced his lips.

"I don't think so."

Why had I allowed this man power over me last night? I shouldn't have. It was a huge mistake no matter how good it felt. No matter that Nate had never made me come the way Quinn had. My insides clenched at the memory, wanting a repeat. I told them to hush down as there was absolutely no way I was letting Quinn kiss me or touch me like that again.

"Let me go."

He rolled his eyes.

"So we're back to that, are we?"

I shoved at him.

"Yes, we are. Consider last night a huge fucking lapse in judgement on my part."

He looked amused which annoyed me further.

"If you say so, little girl."

God, I wanted to slap him for calling me that no matter how much him saying it to me last night only made me want him more.

I swear I'm certifiable right now.

"Don't call me that."

He leant closer, running his nose up my neck and making me choke on my own breath. Heat flooded every part of me and my body screamed at me to give in. To melt and let him do whatever he pleased with it so I could experience the high he'd given me again.

"You are my little girl, Ash," he whispered, his voice like a fucking caress. "You're so small and delicate." His lips replaced his nose on my neck. "So soft." His hand splayed out along my lower back. "So warm." His tongue darted out and I couldn't help the moan escaping my lips. "So fucking wet."

I hated how right he was. Hated it so much. My body betrayed me in the worst possible way. I felt so empty, my insides clenching around nothing. And he'd barely even touched me. How did he do it? Make me putty in his hands with words and small touches.

"I'm not yours."

I refused to allow him that. I didn't belong to anyone but myself.

"You're such a pretty little liar."

I'd had enough of this. He wasn't getting what he wanted from me. I would never let him fuck me. Never. No matter how much I craved the feel of him.

So I did what I had to, I kicked out, shoved him with all my limited strength and screeched, "Get. The. Fuck. Off. Me."

And weirdly, Quinn did let go, which made me feel ridiculous. But it wasn't for long because he sat up, grabbed me and shoved me over his lap, leaving my behind very much exposed.

"Defiance won't be tolerated."

His voice was so calm and it scared the shit out of me. I tried to move, but his hand planted firmly on my back, keeping me pinned to the bed.

"You know what you need to say."

I barely got a chance to breathe when his palm connected with my behind. I whimpered as the pain blossomed. Saying it would be so damn degrading. I didn't want this. Not one bit.

"It seems you have a problem with showing respect."

Smack.

"It's really very simple, Ash."

Smack.

"You show me you can be a good little girl and I'll stop."

Smack. Smack.

I cried out as his strikes got harder each time. Hating him for doing this to me. Hating that it made my pussy wetter than it had been before.

"Quinn, please, it hurts."

Smack. Smack.

"Say it."

Why did he have to be like this? I didn't understand him whatsoever. One minute he was being gentle, next he was saying very dirty things and making me come and now he was punishing me. What did he really want?

More strikes came and I couldn't help the tears pricking in my eyes. The pain was far too intense and I couldn't stand it. No one had ever treated me like this before. And I had no idea why, despite the pain, my body craved more of it.

"No!"

Smack. Smack. Smack. Smack.

"Stop, please, stop."

My protests fell on deaf ears. I deflated, knowing there was only one way he'd give me any kind of reprieve. The tears which kept threatening to fall leaked out and ran down my cheeks.

"God damn it! Thank you, sir, thank you for your punishment," I practically screamed as his hand connected with a particularly sore spot.

He lightly rubbed my raw skin. I felt his breath tickle my shoulder before his lips connected with it.

"Good little girl."

I lay there, letting him caress me without protest. I was done. Too sore and wired to even think about moving. Every time his hand brushed over me, I felt a jolt deep in my core. My nerve endings were going haywire. My nipples were hard and rubbing against the covers slightly, the friction making me crazier. But no matter what, I wasn't going to ask him to touch me further. I was not going to ask him to fuck me even though I wanted it desperately. My body needed a release and apparently, it wanted him to be the one to give it to me.

Damn him. Damn him to hell.

"Look at you," he whispered against my skin. "Squirming in my lap. Desperate, aren't you? You don't just want me to fuck you, you need it."

"No," I choked out.

"Don't lie to me."

"I don't want you to fuck me."

Liar. Liar. Liar.

He chuckled and the sound irritated me.

"Fine, have it your way. Mark my words, in time, you'll be on your hands and knees begging for it."

"Don't make me laugh."

He lifted me off him and set me on the bed before hopping out of it. I'd felt how hard he was whilst he'd been spanking me, but now I could see and my mouth watered. My body was betraying me at every turn.

As if he knew I was staring, he palmed it, his eyes intent on mine as he stroked himself.

"You could've had this inside you, but I think perhaps you don't deserve it quite yet."

I almost screamed at him to fuck off but he disappeared into another room before I could. I heard the shower running a minute later.

Fuck you, Quinn.

CHAPTER SIXTEEN

Xavier

I whistled as I carried a tray with Ash's breakfast on it down the hallway. Today Eric had dished up waffles with syrup and berries. For some fucked up reason, I wanted to watch her eat them. How her little mouth would savour each bite. I may have told the rest of them I wasn't jealous, but that was a lie. A big fucking lie. That girl was like a siren and I think all of us bar Eric were under her spell. Though how he was unaffected I had no idea. Then again, he hadn't spent time with Ash. He'd been in and out when delivering her meals, hence why I was taking her breakfast this morning. I thought she could do with the company.

Whatever was going on with Eric, I had no fucking clue. We might be close, but sometimes I wondered why he could be so emotionally distant at times. Not that we were big on heart to heart bullshit or anything. It wasn't like with Rory who had so many emotional scars, I was surprised he even functioned as a human being any longer after what he'd suffered as a kid. Eric had his own demons, particularly regarding his family and his sexuality. It wasn't his fault they didn't understand. They assumed he was gay, but Eric didn't see genders when it came to attraction. To him, it didn't matter if you had a dick, a pussy or anything in between. And I certainly didn't give a shit who he was with as long as he was happy.

I liked both myself, though I'd been with far more women than men. I was picky about that shit. Whilst I was quite happy to stick my cock into any willing pussy I could, it was different with men. I had rules. I didn't bottom. I didn't suck cock. And I didn't get emotionally fucking attached, but that also applied to women.

I stopped in front of the door to Ash's cell, narrowing my eyes when I noticed it was wide open. Peering in, I found it empty. Her chains sat on the floor next to the bed and her blanket had been pulled back.

Where the fuck is she?

Had someone already taken her out this morning? I walked in and set the tray down on the bed before feeling the mattress. It was cold. My suspicion about where she was made my blood pound in my ears.

Quinn.

He had been on edge all day yesterday. I mean he'd had a massive go at me and Rory over Ash so why I was remotely surprised he'd taken her was beyond me.

Sighing, I took the tray back to the kitchen.

"She not hungry?" Eric asked, looking up from his own plate.

"*She* is not in her room."

Rory walked in, yawning and looked over at the two of us as he sat down. Eric started dishing him up a plate of waffles.

"What do you mean she's not in her room?"

"Exactly what I said. The mattress is cold."

Eric frowned then his eyes went wide.

"You don't think…?"

"Why do you think he isn't down here yet?"

Rory looked between us, a quizzical expression on his face. I sighed. If any of us went and interfered, would that do any good? I just didn't like this. Quinn kept changing the goalposts. What if he'd done something to her she didn't want?

"I'm going up there," I said.

"Do you think that's a good idea?" Eric asked with a frown.

"No, but I'm worried about her."

I walked out but I didn't miss his parting words.

"And here I thought you said you weren't jealous."

Not bothering to turn back and give him shit for it, I stormed upstairs and tried the handle of Quinn's door without knocking. It was locked. He never locked it.

What the fuck did you do to her, Quinn?

I banged on the door.

"Knox, you better fucking open up."

When I heard nothing, I banged again, this time harder.

"Quinn, open the fucking door."

A moment later the handle rattled, but the door didn't move. I heard a muffled female noise of frustration.

Ash.

So he did have her in there. I was fucking right.

"Ash? Are you there? Are you okay? Did he do something to you?"

There was a muffled, "Move out of the way," followed by the sound of the door unlocking and then it opened. Quinn stood there with a towel wrapped around his waist and his hair damp. Ash peered out from behind him, her eyes wide.

"What do you want, Xav?" he grunted.

I ignored him, focusing on Ash.

"Are you okay?"

She shook her head which made me frown.

"She's fine."

I put my hand out to her. Ash dashed out from behind Quinn and barrelled into me, burying her face in my chest, her hands clutching my t-shirt.

What the fuck?

I wrapped an arm around her and backed away from Quinn slightly.

"What did you do to her?"

He stared at Ash with a scowl.

"Nothing she didn't want."

I looked down at her. She was trembling and completely bare. Then I noticed just how red her behind was. My head whipped up and I glared at Quinn.

"Are you seriously telling me she wanted you to punish her?"

"I didn't," she mumbled against my chest, clutching me tighter.

Quinn did nothing but stand there, his expression going blank as if he didn't give a shit about what he'd done.

"Shh, angel, it's okay. I'll take care of you."

"Xav—" he started.

I pointed at him.

"No, you don't fucking say a word. I'm taking her to get cleaned up then down to breakfast. I knew she wasn't fucking safe anywhere near you."

I guided Ash away down the hallway towards my bedroom.

"Xavier!"

"Go fuck yourself, Quinn."

He could get mad all he wanted. I wasn't having any of it. Ash didn't deserve his shit no matter what he said.

I took her into my room. She stood trembling in front of me without covering herself.

"Will you let me see?" I asked, trying to keep my voice gentle so as not to spook her.

She nodded and turned around. I cursed when I saw just how red her arse and the tops of her thighs were. Quinn needed a lesson in restraint but now wasn't the time.

"What else did he do, Ash?"

Her shoulders sagged.

"Nothing I didn't want."

"You're beginning to sound like him."

She sighed and turned to face me again.

"Trust me, I wish it wasn't true. I mean I didn't want this." She waved behind her. "But the rest? I wanted the rest."

Her cheeks went pink and she stared at the floor. I wasn't sure whether I wanted to know what the rest meant or not.

"I want you to listen to me very carefully. If Quinn ever scares you or does something you don't want, you come to me, okay? You can come to me anytime you need, angel." I gestured to the room. "Now you know where I am."

Her head raised and she looked around at where we were. I had a desk in the corner covered in various bits of tech with my laptop open on it. There were bookcases next to it with my collection of Funko Pop characters sprawled all over them. My weights were in another corner and my bed took up the most amount of space on the back wall near the window.

"What about when Quinn keeps me locked up?"

I hadn't exactly thought about that, but if things kept going the way they were, I doubted Quinn would be keeping her in the cell for much longer.

"I'll make sure to check on you then, okay?"

"Thank you… Xav."

"You're welcome, angel. Now, let's get you something to wear."

I walked over to my wardrobes and rifled through them, finding a t-shirt with Yoda on it. I approached her and she let me slide it over her head.

"Eric's made waffles, do you like those?"

She nodded, so I took her hand and led her out of the room. Thankfully, Quinn wasn't lurking in the hallway. I'd deal with him later.

When we got into the kitchen, Eric had disappeared, but Rory was still there. His gaze fell on Ash and I could see he wanted to ask what happened but wouldn't. I got Ash settled on a stool. She winced as she sat down. I stuffed her plate in the microwave for thirty seconds to warm up before setting it down in front of her. Then I poured her some tea and took a seat beside her.

She picked up her fork and ate quietly, glancing at me every so often as if reassuring herself I was still there.

I turned to Rory who was eying us both with a frown.

"He did it again."

He knew what I meant as he tapped his fingers against the counter.

"And... other things."

Ash looked up, her face going bright red all over again.

"We didn't... I didn't... Oh god, this is so embarrassing," she mumbled.

I put a hand on her arm.

"Hey, hey, it's okay, Ash. You don't need to be embarrassed."

She stared at her plate.

"Oh yeah, totally normal to be discussing how I begged one of my kidnappers to make me come with his fingers then sucked his cock, is it?"

She slapped a hand over her mouth as her eyes went wide. I could see Rory hiding a smile and I had to admit I was too. Ash really didn't have a filter.

"Oh my god, please forget I said that."

"Too late, angel."

"Xav, leave her alone," Rory said as he hopped off his stool. "It's okay, Ash. No one is judging you for what you do with Quinn."

I stared after him as he walked out.

What the fuck?

That was the most I'd heard Rory say in a long while. I eyed Ash who was still looking like she wanted the ground to swallow her up. She'd done something to my quiet friend, I just wasn't quite sure what it was.

"I'm sorry, angel. I didn't mean it. Consider it forgotten, though, I will admit I'm wondering what it'd be like to hear you beg."

Her eyes went wide as she looked at me and her face went even redder.

"Wh… what?"

"I might have to ask Quinn what he did to make you want it so bad."

"Oh my god, Xav!"

"I'm joking… or am I?"

She bit her lip. And it made me want to bite it too. I wouldn't though. Ash wasn't mine and I had no idea what she would do if I even tried to make a pass at her for real. Quinn would be fucking mad if I did that, but I honestly didn't give a shit. He didn't get to lay claim over the girl and if Ash wanted it? Who was I to say no?

"I'm surprised none of you heard what we were doing."

I shrugged.

"Quinn had all of our bedrooms soundproofed after Eric complained about the noise."

"Eric complained?"

I grinned and nudged her shoulder.

"Well, he technically complained about the noises coming from my bedroom."

Ash raised an eyebrow and looked me over for a moment.

"Are you in the habit of making women scream then?"

I almost choked on my own breath before I laughed.

"Oh, angel, not just the ladies." I winked. "I've been known to have a few gentlemen callers too."

Her eyes widened.

"Have you ever had both at the same time?"

I couldn't help smirking though why I was even having this conversation with her was a question I'd like answered. Ash seemed innocent, but then again, she'd told me she begged Quinn to make her come, so what did I really know?

"Oh yes, a few times now. Let me tell you, some girls like watching. Turns them on."

Ash's neck and ears were red now.

"We shouldn't be talking about this," she mumbled as she grabbed her mug and held it against her chest.

I didn't want to make her uncomfortable, so I decided to drop it. Wasn't like I was suggesting I wanted a threesome with her and Quinn. That would be weird, wouldn't it? Fuck, why had that even crossed my mind? I mean if it ever came down to it, it would purely be about fucking Ash. That would be it. Nothing else. I had zero interest in that fucker and besides, Quinn was entirely straight.

"Say, how about you and I go watch some TV before Quinn comes and disrupts our fun?"

She looked up at me, her blue eyes cautious.

"Really?"

"Yeah, of course, angel. I'm sure you're bored all alone in your cell."

I hopped off my stool and helped her down off hers. She smiled up at me as I took her through into the living room. Damn, that girl's smile could light up a whole entire fucking room. Ash was as radiant as she was beautiful. Sure I had shit to get on with, but I could afford to give her some time to do something normal so she wasn't going stir crazy. Ash deserved that much.

I really tried hard not to question it when she curled up next to me with her head on my shoulder on the sofa.

Ash had said it herself, we were her kidnappers.

So what the fuck were we doing trying to get close to this girl?

And why was she letting us?

CHAPTER SEVENTEEN

Ash

oday was strange in that I didn't see Quinn once after this morning when I'd run out of his room into Xav's arms. Xav had pretty much refused to put me back in the cell so I'd ended up spending the day with him. He'd had work to do, so he'd let me stay in his bedroom with him whilst he worked on something at his desk. I'd looked over his little Funko Pop characters, realising that the man was actually a little nerdier than his appearance portrayed. He had given me a t-shirt with Yoda on it after all.

It was only come dinner time when Xav had sat me down at the dining table with the rest of the boys that Quinn made an appearance. He barely glanced at me as he sat down at the head of the table which made my stomach sink to my feet. Had I pissed him off by running away? Would he punish me for it if I had? The fact that I cared so much bothered me. A lot.

No one said a word as Eric dished up. It was chicken katsu curry with rice which tasted amazing, but with the whole Quinn thing looming over me, I couldn't enjoy it properly.

"Since there's no point in hiding this from her," Quinn started. "Russo knows we have Ash - well, he knows *Il Diavolo* has her at least."

Xav looked at him with a frown. Oh great, so he was talking about me like I wasn't here.

"What did he do?"

"Sent a message."

"Why didn't you tell me earlier?"

Quinn gave Xav a dark look.

"You were occupied."

I knew what that meant. He was pissed I'd spent the day with Xav. Wasn't exactly my fault. But wait, Papa knew I was with Quinn? Knew I was here? What was he going to do now?

"Papa knows?" I said, unable to hold my words back.

Quinn didn't even look at me or acknowledge what I said.

"We all know what needs to happen next, so tomorrow, we begin."

Xav shrugged and went back to his meal. Eric hadn't looked up from his food in the first place. And Rory? He was staring right at me with a strange expression on his face. But I didn't care about any of them right then. I cared about Quinn and what Papa had said.

I shoved my chair back, stood up and walked over to him.

"What is he going to do?"

"Finish your dinner, Ashleigh."

What the hell?

"No, what's going on?"

He looked up at me, his eyes dark with irritation.

"I won't say it again. Finish your dinner or you won't like the consequences."

"Is he coming for me? Please tell me what's happening."

He shoved his chair back, grabbed me by the arm and practically threw me down on his lap. I tried to wriggle off him, but he twisted my arm back and held it there.

"I was sure you'd had enough earlier, but apparently not," he hissed as he tugged up my t-shirt and exposed me to everyone at the table.

"Quinn!"

"Be quiet."

My heart raced in my chest. Was he going to do this in front of them? Would the guys be witness to my humiliation?

"Please, don't do this," I whimpered. "Please."

I felt his breath dusting across my neck.

"I warned you. If you'd just behaved yourself and did as I asked, I wouldn't have to discipline you."

"Not in front of them, please," I whispered. "I'll do anything."

"It's too fucking late for that."

No one else said a word. Were they going to just let this happen? Surely they knew I didn't want Quinn to do this to me. Not when I knew what would happen when he did. I didn't want them knowing it turned me on. No one but Quinn could know that.

"You're going to get thirty and you know what to say when it's over."

I almost cried because I knew nothing I said would make him stop. My face felt like it was on fire. I was glad I was hidden by the curtain of my hair. At least none of them could witness my complete and utter humiliation at the hands of the man who'd kidnapped me. Then again, they were all fucking well complicit in this, so why did I care?

The first slap came and I clamped my mouth shut, gripping Quinn's ankle with my free hand as that was the only thing available for me to latch onto. The next one arrived and he really wasn't being gentle in the slightest. I was still a little sore from this morning and this only made it sting worse.

My nerve endings were on fire with the next strikes. I tried to stop myself from making any noise, but it grew increasingly impossible. Biting down on the inside of my cheek, I started to taste blood.

Smack. Smack.

I released my cheek and whimpered. It hurt so damn much, but I was growing wet too. I fought so hard to stay still even though I could feel just how much it was turning him on doing this to me.

Fucking hell, this was the most humiliating thing to have ever happened to me and I'd been through a hell of a lot of shit from my own father.

"Quinn, please," I cried. "I'm sorry."

The only sounds in the room where my laboured breath, whimpers and the strike of his palm against my bare skin. Were they all just sitting here watching Quinn spank me?

Oh god, why is this my life?

I wriggled in his lap because I couldn't take it any longer. Needing friction between my legs because my pussy was throbbing just as much as my behind. He peppered strikes across the tops of my thighs, making it a hundred times worse.

I was dripping and it would be clear as day to anyone who looked between my legs. Considering the way I was laying across Quinn's lap, I was pretty sure at least one of them could see.

Smack. Smack.

I hadn't been counting so when Quinn laid his hand on my cheeks and stroked them gently, I almost cried in relief. My arse was on fire and all I wanted was for the ground to swallow me up.

The silence in the room suffocated me and I realised he was waiting for me. The shame of the whole ordeal drove through me. I almost couldn't bring myself to say those words, but he'd just spank me more if I didn't say them.

"Thank you, sir."

"Are you going to keep your mouth shut, sit nicely and finish your dinner?"

"Yes, sir."

"Good little girl."

He released my arm and pulled my t-shirt back down. I hissed as the fabric brushed over my sore behind. Gingerly, I climbed out of his lap and stared down at him. Quinn's eyes were dark with arousal and satisfaction. I couldn't help but be drawn in.

"Did you want something else?"

I almost told him to bend me over the table and fuck me, but then I'd already been humiliated enough by having him spank me in front of the others. Besides, getting fucked would likely be a reward so no doubt I hadn't been deemed worthy of that.

I shook my head and lowered my gaze. Shuffling back to my seat, I kept my gaze to the floor for fear of what I might see in their expressions. I whimpered when I sat back down but otherwise tried not to make a sound. My arse burnt so bad and I was so wet, my thighs felt slick. I picked up my fork and began to eat again just like I'd been told.

The rest of the meal passed silently. It was like no one wanted to acknowledge what just happened. I hated it. Hated that they hadn't come to my defence even though deep down, I hadn't expected them to. I'd told myself over and over again they weren't on my side. They were Quinn's friends.

I daintily wiped my mouth on the napkin when I was done after placing my knife and fork down and waited. I heard a chair scrape as it was pushed back. Glancing up, I found Quinn striding towards the door. My heart lurched. Would he leave me here with them?

"Ashleigh, come."

I jumped up at his command. He'd stopped by the doorway, waiting silently with his back to us. I hurried over to him. He took me by the hand and led me away. I stared down at our joined hands, wondering what the hell was going to happen to me next.

CHAPTER EIGHTEEN

Quinn

C hrist, what a fucking day. Not only was I pissed off with that damn girl for running off with Xav, but I also had her bloody father to contend with too. Fuck Frank Russo. The man thought he was a king. And like the fucking jumped up piece of shit he was, he demanded the return of his daughter.

I'd been with Rory earlier checking on our business dealings when an alert from one of our contacts came through. None of us came from money so we'd made our own, hence why we now lived in Kensington where property went for millions instead of where we'd grown up on an estate in Hackney. Violence, drugs, street gangs and crime had been some of the defining factors of our childhoods.

Geoff, who happened to work for me personally and was my liaison for the crime families, sent me a quick text followed by a photo. A white rose had been delivered to him with a message.

Return Ashleigh to me or else.

A white rose was Russo's signature. The sight of it made me ill. It was a clear threat, but I wasn't scared of him. He could try and get to me, but the reality was, no one knew who *Il Diavolo* really was. The key to creating a persona everyone feared was to stay in the shadows. To have your name whispered by those cowering away from your reputation as a man with no morals.

I knew what the 'or else' meant. Russo would kill me for having the audacity to steal his precious Ashleigh. The girl whose hand I was holding and dragging along to my office with me.

I shoved open the door and took her over to my desk. Letting go of her hand, I sat down in my chair. Her blue eyes were cautious and she fidgeted.

"Are you angry with me?" she whispered.

"No. Sit."

I patted my lap.

"I'm sore."

I gave her a look which had her gingerly perching on my knee with her legs between mine. Wrapping a hand around her waist, I tugged her against me, giving her no choice but to rest her head on my chest. I let out a breath, feeling the tension coiling in my back leave me.

"Quinn, why won't you tell me what's going on?"

"You don't need to know."

"I just want to understand."

She sounded defeated and I didn't like it. Her defiant little soul was like a drug to me but this wasn't the Ash I was coming to know.

I shifted slightly so I could tug my phone out of my pocket. Scrolling through, I clicked on the photo Geoff had sent me and showed it to her.

"Do you know what this means?"

"Papa wants you dead."

"How much do you know about your father and his activities?"

Her body tensed against mine.

I wanted to know if she remembered that day. If she understood the consequences of her actions. But somehow, I couldn't bring myself to ask her. To get her to tell me why. To understand what role she really played.

"Why?"

"I think you know more than any other daughter of a crime lord and I'm sure that has everything to do with your father never having had a son. You know your father's signature after all."

Ash was silent. I leant forward and popped my phone on the desk before settling back into my chair with her still firmly plastered to my chest.

"Papa has never hidden who he is or what he does from me, which my mother has never approved of."

"Isabella doesn't like that you know?"

Ash shook her head.

"She doesn't want me to follow in his footsteps, although really, I've had no choice in the matter. What Papa says goes."

I looked down at her.

"What do you mean follow in his footsteps?"

She traced a line down my chest with her fingers.

"I shouldn't tell you."

"No?"

"You're my father's enemy. Should I not be loyal to the man who raised me?"

I wasn't sure how Ash could be loyal to her father if she knew what he did, but they say blood is thicker than water.

"Perhaps, but by that logic, you're sleeping with the enemy."

She let out a huff.

"I'm not sleeping with you," she muttered.

I wanted to tell her it was inevitable at this point. Ash couldn't deny or hide the way her body craved me. She'd practically rubbed herself all over my cock like a needy little girl begging to be fucked raw when I'd disciplined her in the dining room. Whilst I was sure Xav, Eric and Rory weren't too pleased to be witnesses to the act, I didn't care either. I dared them to stop me with a single look and none of them had said a word.

"Are you loyal to him?"

"I don't know."

My hand around her waist tightened.

What does that mean?

"Why don't you know?"

She sighed, shifting and burying her face in my neck with her hand wrapped around the back of it. I let her stay there although her touch scorched my skin.

"Papa intends for me to be his successor in name only and marry me off to a man who will lead behind the scenes when he is gone. I don't want to be married to any of his men or their sons. I grew up with half of them. Besides, Papa didn't even care that Nate was only with me to get close to him after he practically threw me at the man."

She let out a breath which dusted across my skin.

"You'd think in this day and age your parents wouldn't get to make those sorts of decisions for you, but things don't work like that in Papa's world. His word is law and I have to obey or…"

Her hand shook and I wondered what the fuck Russo had done to her. Had Xav been right? Had he fucked with Ash's head?

"Or what?"

"Or he'll make me suffer."

Her voice was so quiet, I had to strain to hear her words. And they made me angry. I'd seen enough parents abuse their children to last a fucking lifetime. No matter what she'd done, she didn't deserve that.

"I shouldn't have told you any of that," she whispered. "If Papa knew…"

If Russo knew he'd hurt her for it. Her unspoken words were clear as day.

"Then why did you?"

She moved, curling her legs up in my lap and clutching me tighter.

"What does it matter? You're not going to let me go. I haven't told you anything you couldn't find out yourself."

She was right about that. I wouldn't allow her to leave. Not now.

I tucked my fingers under her chin and pulled her away so I could look at her. Ash's blue eyes were watery and she looked so fucking lost. And for some stupid reason, I wanted to soothe her. I brushed my thumb over her bottom lip, making it tremble.

"He can't have you back. You know why?"

She shook her head.

"I don't take kindly to anyone trying to hurt what's mine. And you, little girl, are mine now."

"Quinn," she breathed.

I couldn't help moving closer and capturing those beautiful lips of hers. She trembled and moaned when my tongue clashed with hers. Fuck, she really tasted sweet. I honestly shouldn't be doing this, but I didn't care. Ash intoxicated me on a level I couldn't begin to comprehend.

"I want to do depraved things to you, little girl," I growled against her mouth.

She twisted around, straddling me and holding my shoulders, allowing me to plunder her sweet little mouth. My hands cupped her arse, pressing her down on my cock.

"Please, sir, I'm so wet," she whimpered.

"Do you want me?"

She moaned, grinding against me.

"Say it, little girl. Tell me what you want."

"I want you to fuck me, sir."

If I had any willpower left, I would've taken her straight into her cell and locked her in so she couldn't tempt me any further. Instead, I picked her up, shoved my keyboard out the way and pressed her down on my desk. I whipped the t-shirt off her and stared down at her pretty little tits. Her nipples were hard peaks begging to be bitten.

I leant over her, kissing down her chest and swirling my tongue around one of the stiff buds. Her fingers threaded in my hair and she bucked.

"I can't," she cried out. "Please, please, god, Quinn, please fuck me."

Her words made my cock strain harder against my trousers.

"I'm not going to be gentle."

"I don't care, I need you inside me. I can't stand it."

She writhed, her body arching against me, begging me to take her. I pulled away and straightened, breathing hard. Such a fucking tempting little vixen. My hands went to my belt, practically ripping it open in my desperation to slide inside her.

"You better fucking well be on birth control, Ash."

Whilst I was always wary, I had no patience left to go in search of condoms right now. And I was pretty sure she didn't either.

"I am, I promise. Please."

I managed to free myself. My cock was so fucking hard and leaking. I tore my shirt off without bothering with the buttons and chucked it aside. I grabbed Ash's hips and tugged her to the end of the desk before standing in between her legs. Gripping my cock, I guided it to her and rubbed it up and down her slick pussy.

"So wet for me."

With one sharp thrust of my hips, I buried myself halfway inside her. Ash cried out, her hands scrambling to grip something. I grunted, trying to hold back from thrusting

Sarah Bailey

deeper without letting her adjust. She might've been wet and ready for me, but Ash was so fucking tight. Shit, she felt so good. Her hot pussy clenched around me and I just about died and went to heaven.

"Oh god," she choked out.

Her eyes were wide and her pupils dilated. I leant down, gripping her chin and forcing her to look at me.

"You're going to take every inch like a good little girl, aren't you?"

"Yes, sir," she whispered.

I smirked before I kissed her. Her hands curled around my back, her hips undulating, asking for more. I didn't deny her. Pulling back slightly, I pressed deeper, groaning in her mouth. I'd wanted her from the moment Xav carried her into our house and set her down on the cot in her cell and even more so after I'd demanded they strip her. No matter how hard I tried to convince myself otherwise, it was the fucking truth. I needed inside this damn girl. She set a fucking fire in my veins. And it had taken all of three bloody days for me to give in to temptation.

Fuck. Fuck. Fuck.

Her begging and pleading did me in. Now she was clawing my back and kissing me without restraint. I gripped her hip as an anchor before I thrust home, impaling her completely. Her pussy pulsed around my cock as she struggled to take it.

I kissed down her jaw to her ear as she whimpered.

"So fucking tight, little girl. This is just the start, you can't even begin to imagine all the things I'm going to do to you."

"Do what you want, just please, please fuck me."

"Hold on to the desk."

136

I straightened again. Ash stared up at me before she wrapped her hands around the edge of the desk. I took both her legs and shoved them up against her chest. Grabbing her hips, I pulled back and thrust inside again, watching my cock slide in and out of her tight little pussy like it was made to. I pounded into her harder and faster with each stroke, making her mewl and cry out my name. Her back arched off the desk, her body flushing a beautiful shade of red as I drove her higher.

"Fuck, Quinn."

I released one of her hips and rubbed her clit with my thumb, watching her pant and strain against me. I wasn't far off myself, all of this pent up desire I had for Ash overflowing. Her pussy was so fucking deliciously tight, just like I'd imagined it would be.

"Come, little girl."

Everything inside me tightened, but I held off, needing to watch her come apart. Needing to see her fall off the edge with me.

The moment it hit her, she cried out, her knuckles going white as she gripped the desk harder. Her pussy clamped down so hard on my cock, I lost the battle with myself. I grunted as my cock spurted inside her, coating her insides with my cum. All I could see was her, bucking and trembling around me, mewling my name in pure ecstasy and it was fucking everything.

Her legs dropped down when she was spent. I leant over her, resting my head on her chest and holding her to me. Her fingers tangled in my hair, the other hand brushing across my shoulder.

137

"Now you are sleeping with the enemy," I said, my voice quiet.

She let out a breath. Whether she wanted to agree with it or not, she was mine and I'd make her give up all her secrets about her father in time.

"I guess I am."

CHAPTER NINETEEN

Xavier

"Well, that was… fucked up," I said, shaking my head after we'd all watched Quinn take Ash out of the dining room.

"Point out the obvious, why don't you?" Eric muttered.

I looked over at Rory who had a pensive expression on his face. I'd been sitting closest to Quinn whilst he'd 'punished' Ash and well, it was certainly eye-opening. Not least because it was clear as day Ash had been rubbing herself all over his lap like she couldn't get enough. I'd tried and failed not to stare at her pussy. I mean it was right there and she was turned on as fuck by what he'd been doing.

"Yeah, I am going to point out the fucking obvious. As if you can complain, you didn't tell Quinn to stop."

"Neither did you."

"Like I'm going to get into another fight with him," I smirked. "Besides, you're just jealous you didn't get to watch the show close up."

Eric's eyebrows quirked up.

"Jesus, you're such a pervert."

I shrugged. One day he'd take that stick out of his arse and see what was staring him right in the face. Ash was a beautiful girl with a broken soul. She needed to be taken care of. And if she let me, I would take care of her in all the ways she needed.

"You try keeping your eyes averted whilst your friend spanks the shit out of a hot girl who's clearly into it."

He put his hand over his brow and shook his head. I really had no idea what his problem was. He'd been acting strange since Ash had got here. As much as he agreed with me about taking care of Ash and not letting Quinn treat her too harshly, he'd become ridiculously moody and increasingly withdrawn over the last couple of days. I should know what was going on with my best friend, but I didn't.

"It's your fucking funeral if Quinn beats the shit out of you for it. I'm done watching the three of you puff out your chests over her."

He stood up abruptly and started gathering up the dishes.

"Hey, I'll do that, you made dinner, man."

I didn't like leaving everything to him. It felt unfair considering how he always took care of the rest of us.

"Ashleigh is a human being, not an object for you to leer over. When you lot decide to start behaving like adults instead of teenage boys, come find me."

He took the dishes he was holding and walked out, leaving me staring after him.

"What the fuck is that about?"

Rory gave me a look.

"What?"

He shook his head and stood, gathering up the empty plates. Clearly, he had thoughts on it but wasn't willing to share.

"Seriously, what is Eric's problem? He knows I'm not going to do anything to her."

I got up and helped him. We walked out into the kitchen, finding it empty with the dishes Eric left on the side. He'd cleaned up everything else. I started stacking the dishwasher. Rory set about putting some of the dishes needing to be done by hand in to soak.

"You really don't know?" he asked quietly.

"Know what?"

"Open your eyes and use your brain instead of your cock for once, Xav."

I grinned and shook my head. Rory, ever the cryptic one. I suppose I'd have to take his advice and pay more attention to why the fuck Eric was acting this way. Having my best mate mad at me was the very last thing I needed.

We finished up and walked out into the hallway. I stopped dead when I heard loud noises coming from the direction of Quinn's office. Putting a finger to my lips, I nodded my head towards it. Rory followed me to the door where it became very clear what was going on. The sound of a desk rattling along with mewling noises combined with what was definitely Ash crying out Quinn's name repeatedly.

"What the hell are you two—"

I spun around and slammed a hand on Eric's mouth to stop him saying any more. If Quinn heard us, he'd be fucking pissed off at us eavesdropping. Nodding towards the door,

Eric looked over at it. We all heard "Come, little girl" loud and clear through the wood.

I dropped my hand and shuffled my feet, trying not to grin. Clearly, Quinn had finally got his way with her. Considering how Ash had writhed all over him earlier, it hardly surprised me.

"You two need to rein this shit in," Eric hissed before taking me by the arm and dragging me away towards the stairs. Rory followed, probably because he could see how frustrated our friend was.

When we were out of range, Eric dropped my arm and glared at me.

"What's your problem, man?" I said before he had a chance to open his mouth.

"My problem? My fucking problem? Christ, Xav, you really don't get it. She's Quinn's and what they get up to is none of our fucking business. Get that into your thick skull already."

"You told me we'd protect her."

His scowl deepened.

"Does she look or sound like she needs protecting? No, so stop trying to be the hero here."

"You know what Quinn is capable of. She might be dickmatised right now, doesn't mean she's going to get an easy ride with him. You know this."

I didn't trust Quinn not to fuck things up. He was keeping a heck of a lot of shit from her. We all were, but that was his doing. He made us agree not to reveal anything to her about our plans for her father and the rest of the scum like him. When she found out, how could she not hate him? He was fucking using her. Except I knew deep down it wasn't just that. Quinn had never looked at a woman the way he did her. And the fact that we were fighting over her? That was something which had never happened in all the twenty-two years of our friendship.

"Dickmatised? Are you making up words again?"

I couldn't help breaking out into a grin.

"You know, hypnotised by his dick."

I heard Rory chuckling next to me. Eric glared at him too.

"You don't take anything seriously."

"Hey, come on, Eric, that was funny."

He didn't even bother responding as he walked away up the stairs and shook his head.

"Well, at least you appreciated it," I said, turning to Rory.

He smiled and shrugged. I rubbed the back of my neck. I hadn't meant to make it into a joke and now Eric was probably more pissed than ever at me. But it was true, Quinn would hurt Ash eventually and who would be there to pick up the pieces? Well, it should be me and Eric, but it looked unlikely he would be upholding his side of our agreement. Rory wasn't capable of giving Ash comfort the way she'd need with his aversion to human contact, so it was up to me to do the honours.

"Please tell me I'm not the only one who's worried about her," I continued, unable to keep the concern out of my voice.

"You're not."

"Then what do we do?"

Rory looked pensive for a minute.

"We wait. Quinn doesn't want to heed my warnings."

I rolled my eyes.

"Quinn is a fucking liability right now."

"Yeah, he is."

At least Rory could see what was going on here unlike Eric who seemed to have blinkers on when it came to Ash. Despite knowing exactly who she was and what she'd been involved in, I couldn't bring myself to see her as anything but a girl who had the misfortune of being the daughter of a ruthless man like Frank Russo.

"You need to be careful too. She knows far more about her father's dealings than she'll ever admit, Xav. She's not innocent in this. Don't let her fool you into thinking anything otherwise. Quinn knows this even if he's lost his head right now."

And with that, he walked off, leaving me staring after him. Rory had seemed so taken by Ash, but maybe he was the most clear-headed out of all of us. He wasn't one to mince words so I should take what he said seriously. How could Ash be anything but an innocent in this war though? Quinn was using her as a pawn, true. She'd done shit for her father, also true. But did that mean she couldn't be trusted? She didn't even understand what was happening to her. Why we were doing this.

I almost growled in frustration. Who the fuck knew what to do in a situation like this? I just couldn't bring myself to see her as the enemy. Not when she needed protecting. But perhaps the people she needed protecting from the most were me, Rory, Eric and Quinn.

CHAPTER TWENTY

Ash

'd lost my damn mind. I swear to god I had. Something had snapped inside me and I couldn't take it any longer. I had to feel him. To know what it was like to have Quinn take control and give me what he'd been threatening since the beginning. He told me he was going to fuck me the way I needed and well, he'd been good to his word. It had most definitely not been like that with Nate. Not once.

When it was over, he'd barely said anything other than to clean me up and carry me back to my cell. He set me down on the floor, kissed me and told me to get some sleep. Then he'd left and locked me in. He hadn't chained me up but it didn't make it any better. I'd almost banged on the door and told him to let me out, but I knew it wouldn't do me any good. Instead, I'd curled up under my blanket with a smarting arse and a sore pussy, wondering why I'd been stupid enough to give in.

I shouldn't have told him anything about Papa but seeing that white rose made me sick to my stomach. Despite me not trusting Quinn as far as I could throw him, I didn't want Papa to kill him either. Didn't want any more bloodshed on my behalf. Papa had already shed enough in my name. Frank Russo might not be a traditionalist, but he enforced his rule without exception. He was a fourth-generation Italian by blood, but my great grandfather had self-styled himself as a British crime boss. The Russos had ruled with an iron fist ever since.

Papa could give his crown to any of his inner circle so why he'd groomed me to rule over the family in his stead was beyond me. His younger brother, Uncle Gianni, should be the next in line. But Papa didn't trust him fully despite Gianni proving his loyalty to my father over and over again. My cousins resented me for being my father's heir, especially given I was a woman. Gianni was a traditionalist, so this was a sticking point between brothers.

I hadn't told Quinn that part. Our personal family feuds were closely guarded secrets. But it was no secret I was the heir to the Russo family empire. The future queen of corruption. Raised to fulfil a role I despised. Perhaps that's why I hadn't fought harder when I'd discovered I'd been taken. Perhaps that's why I wanted to place my trust in these four men. Perhaps that's why I even let Quinn fuck me in the first place.

Sleeping with your father's enemy is wrong and you know it.

And yet no part of me regretted what I'd done yesterday.

The door to my cell opened and I sat up abruptly before I remembered I wasn't wearing anything yet again. I covered my breasts with my hands, watching Eric walk in with a plate and a cup of tea for me. His eyes roamed over me for a moment and he faltered in his steps when he realised I was naked. He seemed to visibly steel himself before walking towards me again and placing my breakfast down next to my bed. As he turned back to the door, I found myself reaching out.

"Eric…"

He stopped but didn't turn around.

"Do you not like me?"

His back stiffened. Had I said the wrong thing? I wanted to know why he didn't talk to me like the others. I mean hell, this man was just as beautiful as Quinn, Xav and Rory, but he was closed off in a way I didn't understand and a part of me wanted to.

"I don't dislike you."

He let out a long sigh and turned back, his green eyes full of conflicting emotions.

"Then why won't you talk to me at all?"

His gaze fell on where my hands were covering my breasts. My face felt hot at his perusal. He averted his gaze the next moment as if mentally chastising himself for even looking in the first place.

"Let me go get you something to wear."

Before I had a chance to protest, he left the room, shutting the door behind him. I sighed and dropped my hands so I could pick up my breakfast. A bacon sandwich with ketchup. I wondered if it was Xav who told him I liked that. Didn't matter. I took a bite, savouring the burst of flavour dancing across my tongue.

It was five minutes before Eric came back in. I'd finished off my sandwich and was sipping my tea. He approached me slowly, trying to look anywhere else but my bare chest.

"I don't care if you look at me. Not like you haven't seen it all before anyway."

It was the truth. Whilst it had bothered me the first day, I'd decided to stop worrying about it. Not like I could do anything considering it was hit or miss whether one of them would let me wear clothes or not.

"It'd be rude of me to stare."

I looked up at him as he stood over me. His green eyes were like a dark evergreen forest up close with lighter green flecks in them. Beautiful. He was beautiful with chestnut hair falling into his eyes. His navy t-shirt clung to his lean body and dark jeans hung low on his hips.

"You trying to tell me you're a gentleman?"

His lip curled up at the side.

"I'm making an attempt to be for your sake."

"My sake? Why?"

He held a t-shirt in his hands along with what looked like an oversized jumper and a pair of shorts, but he didn't hand them to me.

"My friends don't have any decorum when it comes to you and I believe you deserve better than that."

I bit my lip. That was possibly true although Rory had never given me any leering looks, unlike Quinn and Xav.

"Are you going to let me get dressed then or did you want to help me?"

He looked down at the clothes in his hands before his eyes met mine again.

"Do you want help?"

I wasn't sure whether he was teasing me or not. So I decided to play with fire because why the fuck not? I'd already thrown caution to the wind with Quinn last night.

I got up off the bed, set my mug down on the floor and stood, waiting for him. Eric looked me over with a raised eyebrow before shaking his head. He set the clothes down on the bed before taking the t-shirt and tugging it over my head after I put my arms up for him. I held onto his arm as he helped me step into the shorts. His skin was warm to the touch and my fingers tingled from it. They were far too big for me and came down past my knees, but he pulled the drawstrings tight and tied them off. Then he helped me into the jumper too. It swamped my small frame, so we had to roll up the sleeves.

"There, now you won't get cold," he said with a smile.

"Thank you."

He shrugged and rubbed his arm.

"It's okay."

I thought he might leave then, but he didn't.

"Do I have to stay in here all day?"

He looked me over and let out a sigh.

"No, I suppose not. You can watch TV, but not too loud as I need to get on with some work."

I nodded, smiling up at him.

"Did you get stuck with babysitting duty then?" I asked as he led me out of the room after collecting my breakfast things.

"You could say that."

I did wonder why Quinn hadn't come to see me this morning, but I didn't want to ask Eric. I brushed my fingers

149

over my lips, remembering the way he kissed and how I was desperate to see him again for a repeat.

Idiot.

Berating myself for what I'd done with Quinn was stupid. Not like I could take it back. I'd got caught up with everything, but I couldn't afford to forget he was still my captor. They all were. Even Eric who was looking at me strangely as we made it to the kitchen and he put my stuff in the dishwasher. There were a ton of things I wanted to ask him, but I kept my mouth shut. Whilst he was no longer being standoffish, I wasn't sure he'd appreciate me asking him questions about himself.

So I quietly followed him into the living room all the while wondering about the one man who tried to come across as having no interest in me at all, but who I'd seen have a flicker of something akin to desire in his eyes.

CHAPTER TWENTY ONE

Eric

I didn't want to find Ash remotely endearing, but the problem was, I did. She had an infectious spirit and she was bold. I hadn't expected her to outright ask me if I didn't like her. It had nothing to do with that. I didn't like the way my friends had flocked to her like she was some kind of goddess. And I had to reluctantly admit I could see exactly why.

She sat quietly next to me, eyes fixed on the screen as I went through our business financials on my laptop. Xav might run the technical side of our online gambling website as well as the other things we did, but I ran the money. Despite our shitty upbringings, Quinn had helped me get through university part-time to do accounting whilst we built our businesses from the ground up. It helped all of us in the long run.

I couldn't help glancing at her every so often. I really fucking hoped Quinn brought her back some clothes like he said he would, which reminded me, I was meant to ask her about her sizes so I could text Quinn.

"Ash…"

She looked over at me, eyes wide.

"Yeah?"

"I don't want this to sound like an intrusive question, but what sizes are you clothes-wise?"

She blinked and then twin spots of red appeared on her cheeks.

"Why?"

"Quinn is picking you up some clothes today."

She frowned.

"He is? Huh…" She crossed her arms across her chest. "He could've just asked me himself if he'd bothered to come see me this morning."

I raised an eyebrow. Was she pissed off at him? Though honestly, I could believe Quinn had irritated her for one reason or another. He didn't have a good track record when it came to the opposite sex. Quinn could be a dick as evidenced by the women who stormed out of our house throwing obscenities his way. Except it'd been a while since that had happened so I hoped he'd learnt to behave himself better. Probably not considering what he'd done to Ash last night in front of us. Then again, she hadn't exactly hated it even if I was pretty sure she was embarrassed about the rest of us being witness to such a display.

"I wouldn't take it personally. Quinn isn't exactly the best at being… well… not a dick."

"You don't say. He only wants me around when it's convenient for him."

I smiled. So perhaps Ash wasn't quite as enamoured with Quinn as Xav and Rory thought.

"You going to tell me so I can let him know or do you want to continue wearing all of our clothes?"

She sighed and rattled off a list of her sizes. I fired off a text to Quinn with the details, not expecting a response. Ash was quite petite in stature and size so I really hoped Quinn would actually get her something which fit. He did have Rory and Xav with him, so perhaps the three of them would manage. I wasn't betting on them not buying her skimpy underwear though. If I'd gone with them, I'd have made sure she had comfortable stuff as well as all the revealing outfits they no doubt wanted her to wear.

Someone had to stay and watch her though. Normally it would've been Rory who didn't like to go out much because crowds bothered him, but Quinn insisted he go to this meeting we were due to attend, much to Rory's dismay. Apparently, since I was the only one who hadn't expressed any interest in Ash, I'd been deemed worthy of taking care of her today. Quinn and his issues. Considering he'd never been jealous and possessive before, it had come as a surprise to all of us to see him acting this way about Ash. Especially given what we knew about her and her father.

"Can I ask you something?"

Ash was watching me closely, her blue eyes bright although there was a hint of hesitancy in her voice.

"Depends on what it is."

"Does Quinn normally blow hot and cold with girls?"

I frowned.

"What do you mean?"

153

"I know I probably mean nothing to him really and well, I'm his prisoner, but one minute he's, you know, all over me and the next it's like he doesn't care. I don't understand him. I tried asking, but he doesn't really give me any straight answers."

Quinn was really doing a number on her head. And I'd told Xav she didn't need protecting last night. Clearly, I'd been wrong. I shouldn't say anything to her, but I felt sorry for Ash dealing with Quinn's bullshit.

"Honestly, I don't think Quinn knows what he wants when it comes to you."

"I'm pretty sure of one thing he wants from me."

She imitated sex with her hands and I shook my head, grinning.

"Well, I can hardly blame him there, pretty sure most men would jump at the chance of that."

"Oh yeah, even you?"

I shrugged.

"Even me."

Ash's eyebrows shot up and I realised what I'd just said.
Well, fuck.

"I mean hypothetically speaking obviously since I'm a gentleman and would never think such things about you."

Liar. You've thought long and hard about what it would be like to get between Ash's legs.

Ash smirked and turned back to the TV.

"Yeah, you tell yourself that," she muttered under her breath.

I shifted in my seat wondering how on earth she'd managed to get me to admit to finding her attractive. She

154

didn't need all of us leering after her and I was trying desperately not to. I didn't want to like her in that way. We didn't need any further idiotic jealousy issues over Ash.

If I was being honest with myself, I was jealous over Xav's clear affection for the girl. And confused. My feelings were all over the place. I was trying not to dissect them because I was scared of what I might find.

Besides, it's not like there was any danger of Xav getting involved with Ash when she was Quinn's... was there?

CHAPTER TWENTY TWO

Quinn

ory was sulking like a petulant child as we left the house. He might hate being around people, but I needed him. I also wasn't sure I entirely trusted him with Ash any longer. I'd seen the dark look in his eyes when I'd had her over my knee last night at the dinner table. Knowing all about my friend's fucked up past and the things he enjoyed doing to women made me wary. When it came to Ash, all bets were off because Rory had never deliberately sought out the company of a girl just to be around her before. And if I left him at home today, I was sure he would've.

Yes, I was acting crazy, jealous and paranoid, but Ash was goddamn mine and I wouldn't allow anyone else to have her.

"Why did you agree to this fucking meeting again?" Xav said, crossing his arms over his chest as we all sat in a member's only club that went by the name of Black Night. Neutral territory for us.

"You think I want to deal with these fuckers?" I retorted.

"No, which is why I was asking."

Rory stared out of the window, his brow furrowed and his whole body tense.

"And I've only explained like a hundred times we can't take down Russo by ourselves."

"But you want these idiots gone too."

I sighed. Xav really didn't understand diplomacy. He was an all guns blazing guy which is why I was the brains behind our operation.

"I'd quite like all the idiots who think they can rule over the city like top dogs gone, but that's not going to happen."

I wasn't stupid enough to think I could destroy every single person linked to the crime families of London, but I could take down the worst of them. The ones I had a personal fucking vendetta against along with Rory, Eric and Xav.

Xav didn't get a chance to respond as Colm Moran and his men walked in. I stood up to greet them.

"Morning boys," Moran said with a grin, showing the gap in his teeth from a bar fight where someone had knocked it out with a pool cue. Something he seemed to be quite proud of.

I shook his hand and watched him seat himself with his two men standing behind him before taking a seat myself. Rory watched them quietly and Xav sat up straighter, his hand resting on his thigh.

"So, Mr Knox, what can I do for you?"

Colm Moran was an Irish gangster and quite frankly a complete cunt, but he hated Russo so I figured the enemy of my enemy could be my ally. Not that I wouldn't double-cross him the first opportunity I got.

"I've heard a rumour Russo's daughter has been taken."

Deceived

Moran's eyebrow raised and a sly smile appeared on his face.

"Is that so? Ach, that fucker needed taking down a peg or two."

He looked up at his two guards and nodded. One of them tugged a phone out and started fiddling with it whilst keeping his gaze fixed on Xav and Rory. They wouldn't do anything without my signal.

"Of course, it's unconfirmed. Russo wouldn't want to appear weak to the families."

Moran's grin got wider. I'm sure he'd take pride in destroying Russo, but he didn't have the resources. Messing with Frank's business, however, that he could do.

"Ballsy move. Tell me, what twat thought fuckin' with Frank Russo would be smart?"

I shrugged. Moran had no idea who I was outside of the casino I owned with the boys. A very exclusive venue. You had to know someone to get in as we didn't just allow any old fucker membership into the Syndicate.

His man leant down and whispered in Moran's ear before straightening.

"You've got to be shitting me." He shook his head and leant forward. "Word is it's the man those cunts call *Il Diavolo*. No one has even seen the fucker. Why they're all so scared of him…" He rolled his eyes and leant back again. "Ach, it's all just fuckin' rumours."

I tried not to smile. My reputation always preceded me. Little did they know most of it was a complete fabrication. I wouldn't deny I'd killed just as Rory, Eric and Xav had, but it'd been necessary for our own survival. Those three were the

159

only people I gave a shit about in this world. The three I'd do anything for.

"What if they're true? Wouldn't that be something you could use?"

He looked thoughtful for a moment though the man likely only had two brain cells he could string together after the number of blows to the head he'd had. Moran enjoyed underground fighting to prove his mettle. The kind where there were no rules. Some of them ended up being bloodbaths or so I'd been told by Xav who'd attended a few on my say so, but never participated.

"Russo dotes on his little girl. If she's really gone, he's going to come after this *Il Diavolo* hard, possibly leave his other assets unprotected."

I tried not to clench my fists at him calling her Russo's little girl. Only I was allowed to call her that. She was my fucking little girl, not Russo's. God, I wanted her right now. I needed to inhale her. Feel her taut body trembling for me.

My little girl. Mine. All fucking mine.

"Ach, what do you want for this information?"

He knew I wasn't the kind of man to give things freely.

"Nothing… for now."

"You want me to owe you a favour."

I inclined my head.

"Just a little hint here and there to the others. You know what they say about vultures circling."

Moran smiled and stood.

"Aye. Nice seeing you, Mr Knox."

We both knew that was a lie, but I stood and shook his hand. Moran and his men walked out.

"That man is a cunt," Xav muttered.

"So are you, but you don't see Rory or me complaining."

"Ha-fucking-ha, fuck off, Quinn."

Rory didn't look amused either, but he was still sulking. I checked my phone, finding Eric had messaged me with Ash's clothing sizes.

"Come on, we have other things to do."

The two of them stood and we walked out of the club together.

"The casino, or are we going to be a group of girls squealing over clothes shopping?" Xav asked as we got in the car.

"The casino."

"You got it."

Rory sat in the back, scowling as he stared out of the window.

"Would you fucking cheer up?" I said, turning back to him as Xav pulled away from the curb.

He looked at me. Being outside, yeah that bothered the shit out of Rory.

"If I let you pick out her clothes, would you at least stop looking like you're going to kill me and Xav?"

"Hey, I didn't force him out of the house," Xav interjected. "If Rory's going to kill anyone, it's you."

"I'm not going to kill either of you," Rory muttered, although his expression was still dark.

"Praise the fucking Lord, he speaks," I said with a grin.

"I already told you I don't want anything from her. Why would I want to pick out her clothes?"

161

I raised an eyebrow. As if I believed a word which came out of his mouth regarding Ash. Xav rolled his eyes and tapped his fingers on the steering wheel.

"You like Ash, Rory. Stop trying to deny it."

He scowled at Xav, clearly not impressed at the two of us ganging up on him.

"I do not like anyone, especially not you two right now."

"Aww man, that's so sweet, I've always wanted to be on your hate list."

I swear a vein was popping in Rory's forehead. We usually tried not to wind him up because we all knew what he'd been through. But honestly, sometimes I really did think Rory needed to lighten up a little. He was much too serious.

"Do you plan on pissing off everyone in our household, Xav? You've already managed to make Eric stop talking to you."

Xav's smile dropped and he gripped the steering wheel. I had no idea what was going on between him and Eric. Rory insisted nothing had happened between the two of them, but who knew.

"What do you mean, Eric's not talking to Xav?" I asked.

Rory rolled his eyes and looked out of the window.

"He's not happy with Xav perving over Ash twenty-four seven."

"I am not perving over… You know what, fuck you, Rory, and fuck Eric and his uptight bullshit," Xav growled.

Silence fell over us. I glanced at Xav who looked like he wanted to rip the steering wheel out of the car. If Xav was leering over Ash, then it wasn't surprising Eric was pissed off given the way he felt about Xav. Rory and I thought it was obvious, but our friend was clueless. They should just fuck and get it over with. I'm sure everyone would be happy when all that repressed sexual tension was no longer hanging in the air.

Then again, I wasn't exactly happy with Xav wanting Ash either. He wouldn't do anything because they all knew she was mine, but that didn't stop the need to make sure she was aware of it pulsing through my veins. She kept telling me she wasn't and that really fucking got on my nerves. And I was still pretty unhappy about her running off to Xav after she spent the night in my bed. Didn't matter that she'd begged me to fuck her last night. She shouldn't want another man to comfort her.

You're not exactly comforting her either, Quinn. Did you forget you locked her in the cell last night instead of taking her up to bed with you?

I almost growled in frustration. If I'd had her in my bed, I wouldn't have got any sleep. The things I'd have done to her... I shut down those thoughts before my cock got hard all over again. It'd been a fucking nuisance when I was alone without her last night and this morning. Maybe if I'd taken her with me, I wouldn't be suffering with the urge to pound her tight little pussy right now. I might have fucked her out of my system.

Who are you kidding? You couldn't fuck Ash out of your system if you tried.

I was a fucking mess over this bloody girl. If I didn't want her going to one of the others, then I'd have to make sure I gave her what she needed. I just had to find out what that was.

Jesus, I was beginning to sound fucking pussy-whipped. I couldn't afford to forget who Ash was and what she represented. She should be my fucking enemy. But she wasn't. She was far from it. In fact, she was the key to everything.

And I couldn't for the life of me bring myself to hate her for it.

CHAPTER TWENTY THREE

Ash

ric put me back in the cell long before the others came home. I was bored out of my mind staring at the four bare walls. I'd paced the room several times and wondered when one of them would come to see me. Well, honestly, it was Quinn I wanted to see the most. I felt like I was starved of his presence which was utterly ridiculous. I'd never sought out a dominating man before since I knew too many in my father's inner circle, but even as I rebelled against Quinn, I submitted too. Submitted to his voice. His touch. His need to make me obey him.

So when the door to the cell opened and he stood there with a bag in his hand, I almost ran and threw myself at him. It took all my willpower to stay where I was in the middle of the room, hands clenching and unclenching at my sides.

"I have something for you," he said, his dark eyes traversing the length of me. "Strip."

"Excuse me?"

He took a step into the room.

"I said strip."

I crossed my arms over my chest. He didn't get to leave me alone for almost an entire day and then order me to strip for him.

"Why should I?"

"I suggest you don't try my patience today, Ashleigh."

I glowered. When he used my full name, it reminded me of Papa and I hated it. I didn't want my father mixed up with Quinn. He didn't get to ruin this for me. Whatever the fuck this even was between us because I sure as hell didn't know what Quinn actually wanted from me.

"Don't call me that."

"It's your name."

I looked away.

"Only my parents use it."

I don't know why it triggered me so much. Just did. Perhaps because Papa repeatedly used it when he was making sure I understood my place and my future role.

"You will hurt him, Ashleigh. You will do it because you're going to take my place one day. You need to be ruthless."

"I don't want to, Papa."

"A Russo does not show weakness. You are going to be strong and resolute. Do you want to disappoint me, Ashleigh? Do you want to bring shame on this family?"

I shuddered as the memory threatened to spill out, my arms falling to my sides. Warmth radiated off him as he walked over to me and tucked a finger under my chin, forcing my face up to his.

"What's wrong?"

166

"N… N… Nothing."

He gave me an incredulous look which had me trying to shy away from him. Quinn wouldn't let me escape, his fingers curled around my face, keeping me in place. Could I really rely on this man in front of me? I didn't know anything about Quinn, but I wanted to. I needed to understand him and why he seemed so insistent on keeping me. Why he wanted me in the first place.

"Quinn… I…"

It's not like I could tell him what my father had made me do. It shamed me to know he'd forced me. The head of our family shouldn't hesitate to do what was necessary. That was the lesson he was trying to teach me, except I didn't want to learn it. I didn't want to be that person. Being like my father filled me with dread because he'd lost so much of his humanity along the way.

"Tell me what's wrong, little girl."

My legs almost buckled at him using what I was coming to think of as his term of endearment for me. Who knew if it really was that or not. I couldn't take this. My soul hurt. All I wanted was to have someone else take away my pain.

I reached up and pulled his hand away from my chin before stepping forward and wrapping my arms around him, burying my face in his solid chest. He stood still for a long moment before he dropped the bag he was holding and put his arms around me. His hand tangled in my hair, stroking down the strands.

"You left me alone," I whispered. "Please don't do that again."

I wasn't talking about today, but last night when he'd brought me back in here after we'd had sex. It'd felt like a dismissal after he'd got what he wanted from me.

His back stiffened at my words but I didn't care. So what if I'd only known him all of four days? It felt like it'd been weeks.

"What exactly are you asking for?"

"Just you."

He let out a breath.

"You don't want the others?"

"I honestly don't know what I want, but I do know I'm lonely when you're not here so take from that what you will."

The thing is, I liked all of them despite myself. I felt things for all of them which confused the hell out of me. They were my captors and it was so fucked up on so many levels. I couldn't tell Quinn I didn't want them as it would be a lie.

He pulled my face away from his chest. His eyes were dark as he leant down and captured my mouth with his. My body thrummed from that touch. I felt so small in his arms. Perhaps it's why Quinn kept calling me his little girl because I was tiny in comparison to him. I'd always been short despite both my parents being tall. Papa sometimes called me his little teapot princess, a nickname I hated more than him calling me Ashleigh.

"Take your clothes off, little girl," he whispered against my lips before pulling away and taking a step back.

I felt bereft without him right there and I could barely hide my disappointment. His eyes were almost black as he watched me fidget, teetering on the decision of whether to obey him or not.

"Don't make me wait."

His hand flexed at his side. Not wanting to provoke him into punishing me, I tugged at the jumper I was wearing, pulling it off followed by the shorts and t-shirt. When I stood bare before him, his lip curled up at the side in a smirk. My face heated up as his eyes roamed over my skin as if branding every inch into his memory.

He leant down, picked up the bag he'd brought in and handed it to me.

"Put these on. I'll be outside the door."

And with that, he turned and strolled away, leaving me staring after him.

What. The. Hell.

Shaking my head, I set the bag on the cot and tugged out what he'd brought me. My eyes widened at the underwear set. White see-through lace. I took out the dress next. It was the same colour blue as my eyes and would fit tight against my body, coming down to just above my knees. I put each piece on, staring down at myself when I was done. The dress was like a glove, showing off all my limited curves and pushing up my breasts. I couldn't deny whoever picked this out had good taste even if I'd never felt more on show in my entire life. The last thing in the bag was a pair of nude heels. I slid my feet into them and took a few steps. They were comfortable enough.

I couldn't do anything with my hair so I just ran my fingers through it to detangle it before I took a breath. Quinn said he'd be waiting. For the first time since I'd got here, I actually felt like a woman rather than the girl they'd chained up.

I held my head up as I walked out. Quinn leant up against the wall with his hands shoved in his pockets but he straightened when he saw me. His eyes darkened significantly as they roamed over my figure. He put a hand out to me and I took it, finding myself tugged up against him. He tucked a finger under my chin, tipping it upwards.

"Stunning."

"You didn't happen to get me a hairbrush or anything like that, did you?"

He smirked.

"Perhaps I did."

He didn't let me answer, his mouth descended on mine again and I found myself spun around. Quinn pressed me against the wall and took his fill of me, his hands roaming across my body, making me melt. I moaned, clutching him as his tongue tangled with mine.

There was a slight cough to our right. Quinn pulled back and stared down at me.

"I'm looking forward to unwrapping my present later," he whispered, his eyes making it clear he meant me.

I shivered, the anticipation of what Quinn would do to me almost making me want to beg him to unwrap me now.

He pulled away entirely and took my hand, turning to look at who'd interrupted us. Rory stood there, his hazel eyes roaming over me. My heart lurched at the emotion swelling in them. I'd never seen him look so… miserable and I wondered if it had anything to do with him catching Quinn and I kissing. But why would it? Rory didn't like me that way, at least I was relatively sure he didn't. He never once indicated he wanted anything from me so why did he look like that? I fought against my instinct to go to him and ask him what was wrong. I'd paid attention when he told me human contact scared him.

His expression shut down the next moment, his face becoming entirely blank. That made my heart ache and I had no clue why. What the hell was happening to me and these four men?

"Dinner's ready," he stated before turning and walking away from us.

Quinn tugged me along after him, smiling down at me which made my body heat up, but I was still worried about Rory. Worried about what was going on in his head. I had to find a way to talk to him. I could ask myself again and again why I even cared since I was a prisoner of these men, but in the four days they'd had me, all the lines had become blurred.

Xav whistled when we entered the dining room.

"Well, look at you."

Eric's eyes roamed over me with clear discomfort burning in them, but I was pretty sure it had to do with him not wanting to find me attractive.

Quinn made me sit next to Eric, directly across from Rory whilst he took a seat at the head of the table to my right. His hand caught mine on the table, making it very clear who I belonged to. Except I'd told Quinn enough times I wasn't his. I'd spent long enough being beholden to my father, I wasn't going to allow another to force me into a role I hated.

I tried to catch Rory's eye, but his gaze was firmly fixed on his plate. I suppressed a sigh, my fingers tightening in Quinn's. This was going to be one awkward dinner at this rate. Not that last night hadn't been either. At least I hoped this time Quinn wouldn't have any reason to discipline me in front of everyone. That would make an already bad situation far worse.

CHAPTER TWENTY FOUR

RORY

I couldn't do it. I couldn't look at her. I couldn't.

Everything about her was damning. Soul destroying. Ruining. I couldn't.

Seeing her kiss him. Seeing him touch her. Seeing anything to do with her. I couldn't.

Why had he brought her into our lives? She was the source of all the conflict between the four of us and I hated it. I hated every moment of every second she'd been here.

And what I hated the most, was how she made me feel something after I'd closed myself off from the world. I wasn't meant to feel, not after… everything. The one person who understood. Who knew why I couldn't deal with people, well, *he* was the reason *she* was here.

The worst part of all of this was I didn't even hate her. I couldn't bring myself to say her name because that would make it real. All these feelings would be real and I couldn't allow them to be.

I kept trying to tell myself I didn't want anything from her, but that was a lie. A lie I told myself to make this easier. No.

I wanted everything from her. Her. Ash. Ashleigh. Ashleigh Vittoria Russo. I wanted her more than I wanted to be free of my burdens. My pain. Because Ash, beautiful Ash who was the brightest fucking star in the sky, she'd be the balm to it all. She'd make it okay. Make me okay. But I couldn't have her. Because she was his.

His. His. His.

The word fucking echoed around my skull. Tormenting me. Torturing me in ways I'd not been subject to for years.

I'd never betray my best friend. Never. Not least because Quinn was the only person in this whole entire world who saw me. Who cared. Who saved me. I had Eric and Xav, but Quinn knew more than them. He knew everything. Every. Single. Thing. He was my safety net. He was the one who listened. He held me when everything was dark. He gave me a reason to live again. And Quinn had given me my revenge.

I looked up from my plate when I heard her laugh. Her head was thrown back and the beautiful rich sound tinkled out of those perfect lips. Her blue eyes were bright with amusement and it could've only been Xav who made her laugh like that because it was what he did. The knife lodged in my chest twisted, making it harder for me to keep breathing.

I couldn't stop looking at her. Taking in each and every one of her features. From the small freckle above her right eyebrow to the way her messy blonde hair cascaded down her back. Hair I wanted to run my fingers through. Hair I wanted bunched in my fist whilst she cried underneath me, begging me to stop all the while her body pleaded with me to continue. I almost groaned at the vivid images plaguing my every waking moment. It wasn't often I even craved human contact but with her, I'd risk everything to feel her skin against mine.

And that fucking dress I'd chosen for her? Well, that was ruining me on a level I couldn't even begin to comprehend. Highlighting each and every one of her subtle curves just like I'd known it would. Quinn wouldn't have told her who picked it out, but I chose it because of her eyes. Her beautiful crystal blue eyes. Everything about Ash was beautiful. Xav called her an angel, but to me, she was the northern star. The one which would guide me home.

Ash dropped her head back down, her eyes met mine and my heart stopped in my chest. There she was, pleading with me silently not to shut down on her. Not to run away. I was caught in her snare and there was no fucking way I could free myself. But the reminder of who she was. What she was. What she'd done. All of that made me look away.

Because no matter what I felt inside, there were glaring issues I couldn't ignore.

Ash was Russo's daughter.

Russo had hurt someone who meant everything to me.

And Ash belonged to him.

CHAPTER TWENTY FIVE

Ash

Quinn whisked me out of the dining room the moment we were finished with dinner so I didn't get a chance to talk to Rory. Though honestly, I couldn't think about that right now because the way Quinn was looking at me set my blood on fire. Like he was imagining all the dark and dirty things he wanted to do to me.

He took me upstairs to his bedroom and this time I actually looked around the room. The walls were midnight blue. There was a huge abstract painting above his bed, red paint fading into black. It felt rather fitting. Quinn. The man who'd walked out of hell itself. The Devil.

His bed was huge with a mahogany headboard interspersed with long black metal bars. The rest of his furniture, two bedside tables, a chest of drawers and an ottoman at the end of the bed matched it.

Quinn's breath dusted across my neck as he moved my hair to the side. He kissed my bare shoulder, his hand banding around my waist. I shivered at his touch.

"Little girl," he whispered. "Tonight you're going to call me sir and only sir, do you understand?"

"Yes."

"Yes, what?"

"Yes, sir."

He kissed my shoulder again. I had no wish to defy Quinn. I wanted the pleasure he'd bring. My body craved it. The anticipation had killed me all through dinner even though I was also worried about Rory. But right now, I couldn't afford to think about him. This moment was about me and Quinn. No one else.

Quinn slowly unzipped the dress and peeled it off me, letting it pool at my feet. His hands ran across my bare stomach. I swallowed, trying to keep my knees locked because I was in danger of melting into him.

"Lie down in the middle of the bed for me."

"Yes, sir."

He groaned, releasing me. I stepped out of my heels and walked over to the bed. Crawling up on to it, I laid down on my back and waited.

"Put your hands up by the headboard, little girl."

"Yes, sir."

I did as he said. He smirked and moved over to his chest of drawers, opening the top one and pulling out several things I couldn't see properly. Shutting it, he brought them over and laid them down next to me. He got on the bed and crawled up over me, picking up a length of a soft-looking rope.

178

Looping it around each of my wrists, he secured me to the headboard in a series of intricate knots. I stared up at my bound wrists wondering what exactly Quinn had planned for me. This clearly meant he didn't want me to try and escape.

He picked up something else next. It took me a minute to realise what they were and by that time, he was already running his thumb over one of my lace-clad nipples. It stiffened under his touch. When he was satisfied, he attached the little rubber ended clamp over it and tightened the screw until I let out a little gasp. It was on the borderline of being painful. He proceeded to give the same treatment to my other one before attaching the clamp on the other end of the chain.

I moaned. It hurt but it felt good at the same time.

"Such a good little girl," he murmured, leaning down and running his tongue over where my nipple peeked out from the clamp. I bucked and he tugged on the chain between them. My nipples blossomed with pain.

"Ah, fuck!"

He grinned which made me want to tell him off, but then again, I didn't want Quinn to punish me either.

"Is this what you meant by doing depraved things to me?"

"Just one of many things I'll do to you."

I shivered. He'd not asked me if I wanted any of this, but I'd come to expect that from him.

"What if it gets too much?"

His dark eyes glittered as he shifted lower.

"Pick a word, Ash."

"A word?"

"A safe word. You say it if you want to stop, although I guarantee you won't want me to stop."

He kissed down my stomach whilst his hand still rested around the chain between my breasts.

"What if I called one of the other guys' names?"

Quinn tugged on the chain hard and I yelped.

"You better be fucking joking, little girl. I don't want their names on your lips, understood?"

I whimpered at the pain, biting down on my lip. Maybe that wasn't the wisest thing for me to joke about considering how possessive he seemed to be of me. But I didn't belong to him.

"Yes, sir."

He continued kissing down my stomach, meeting the line of my knickers. Releasing his hold on the chain, he tugged my knickers down my legs and threw them off the side of the bed.

"The word, Ash."

I tried to think of something suitable but it was hard when he was stroking my inner thighs with the pads of his fingertips and staring up at me with such an intense expression I thought I might combust on the spot. It had to be something I wouldn't cry out randomly during sex.

"Jelly."

He smirked but gave me a single nod. His head dipped between my legs and he ran his tongue along my pussy, delving in between my lips and finding my clit.

"You taste so fucking good. Going to make you nice and wet for me."

His fingers teased my entrance, circling it as his tongue flicked over my clit. My eyes practically rolled back in my head. My hands shifted above me, but I was barely able to move my arms because of the way he'd restrained me. I whined as his tongue grew more insistent, relatively sure whilst he wanted to make me wet, he wouldn't let me come.

His fingers slid inside me, hooking upwards and rubbing just the right spot which made me buck and strain against my bonds. The chain shifted, tugging on the clamps a little. All the sensations hit me at once, leaving me moaning and begging him not to stop.

He pulled away slightly, keeping his fingers buried inside me and kissing my inner thigh.

"Please, sir, please."

"Patience. We've barely even started."

I almost cried when he withdrew his fingers, dragging them down lower until they met my other entrance.

"I'm going to fuck you here, little girl, not tonight, but soon."

I tensed as his fingers circled puckered skin.

"No one has touched me there before," I whispered unsure if I even wanted him to or not.

I stared down at him, unable to comprehend how it was possible for his eyes to get so dark they were practically black.

"Are you curious?"

I had no idea what to expect with Quinn. He'd given me so many new experiences already and perhaps this one would be okay too. It's like he knew what I needed before I did. Knew how to play my body just right.

"Maybe I am."

His smirk set my blood on fire. He sat up and tugged off his shirt, leaving me staring at his beautiful physique. All lean muscle and perfect abs. I couldn't believe my eyes. He had a dusting of dark hair across his chest and a happy trail. Nate had been attractive, but Quinn? Quinn was like a fucking dark fallen angel and it was all I could do to swallow back the gathering moisture in my mouth.

"Do you like what you see, little girl?"

I nodded because speaking right now would be impossible. His smirk got impossibly smug, but honestly? He definitely had something to be fucking smug about. I hadn't been paying much attention when he'd fucked me last night, so desperate to have him inside me, but now I could thoroughly appreciate the view.

He slipped off the bed and quickly disposed of the rest of his clothing. I swear I just about died when he crawled back on the bed, grabbed my hips and flipped me over, dragging me up on my knees. The way I was bound made it impossible for me to do anything but lean on my elbows with my hands raised above my head. The chain hung heavily, making my nipples ache as each movement caused it to swing.

He used his hand to spread me wide open before dragging the head of his cock along my folds. I felt very exposed and completely unable to do anything about it. Quinn had me at his mercy. I should hate it. I shouldn't want this from him, but I did.

"Please," I whimpered. "Please fuck me, sir."

He seemed content to continue teasing me. I was pretty sure his gaze was locked on my pussy and it made me shiver with need.

"I want your cock, sir. I want to be fucked hard, please."

He slapped me across my arse and it made me jolt. The next time he did it, I moaned, pressing myself against him the best I could. I wanted to cry out of sheer desperation.

"Please, sir, please. I need you."

The fact he wasn't even saying anything made it worse. I couldn't tell what he was thinking or about to do because I couldn't look back at him. I ached all over, relatively sure the moment he pressed inside me, I'd be hard-pressed to hold back from coming. So on edge with the overwhelming sensations coursing through my body.

"Damn it, please, it's too much. I know I promised to call you sir, but seriously, Quinn, I need you to fuck me before I lose my mind."

He leant over me, his hand reaching underneath me to wrap around the chain. He tugged and I cried out, tears pricking at the corners of my eyes. Sex had never been this intense before. I didn't know what to do with myself other than beg him for mercy because he was the one in control. He had the power to make this go away.

"Are you going to scream for me, little girl?" he whispered in my ear, sending shivers down my spine.

"Yes, sir."

He straightened, held onto both my hips and jerked forward, impaling me in one brutal thrust. I choked on my own breath as my body lurched and tears fell down my cheeks. Quinn didn't give me a second to adjust, he pulled back and slammed into me again. I cried, the intensity of it all making me come apart at the seams. On the edge of the precipice and wondering how long it would take me to free fall.

His hands tightened around my hips as a low grunt escaped his lips. The pounding he gave me was unlike anything else I'd ever experienced, fucking me like a man possessed. I had no choice but to let him. My nipples ached. My clit throbbed. My body so tightly wound, I wasn't sure what would happen when I let go finally.

It was too much. All too much. So when he reached around and strummed my clit once, I detonated, screaming as I strained against my bonds. Arching back when wave after wave of explosive bliss radiated across my skin.

I was almost limp when I came down, but Quinn was in no way done yet. He leant over me and tugged on the chain again, making me whimper with his fingers still on my clit.

"I can't, please, no more."

He kissed my shoulder, his pace slower but still punishing.

"Good little girls take what's given to them."

I couldn't escape him even if I tried. He was determined to torture my body with pleasure. No matter how my face was streaked with tears or I cried out at his fingers driving me towards another explosive ending, he kept fucking me without any sort of mercy.

"Please, please, no more," I practically sobbed because it was too overwhelming. My whole body was on fire, my nerve endings going haywire and all I wanted was to curl up in a ball until my body stopped trembling.

I arched my back as my second climax hit me, crashing down on me like a tidal wave and making me cry out his name. He grunted and cursed, his fingers digging in hard on my hip as he ruthlessly fucked me until I felt him let go too.

When he caught his breath, he flipped me over on my back after pulling out of me. I lay there, utterly spent and unable to move. His dark eyes glittered as he leant over me and kissed me. When he pulled back, his eyes roamed across my chest.

"This may hurt."

Deceived

He reached down and unclamped each nipple. I moaned as they started to throb uncomfortably now they were free. He unbound my wrists next, rubbing them as he brought them down to my chest. I hissed when he reached around my back, unhooked my bra and peeled it off me.

He left me on the bed and slipped into the en-suite. I heard the water running. When he came back out, he picked me up and carried me into his bathroom. I didn't even get a chance to protest as he stepped into the bath with me and sat down, settling me between his legs. When the hot water hit my sore nipples, I whimpered.

"Shh, little girl," he whispered in my ear. "Let me take care of you."

I lay my head back on his shoulder and closed my eyes, too exhausted to move an inch. It wasn't long before I drifted off to the soothing noise of him humming in my ear whilst he gently washed me with a soft cloth. And I wondered what had happened to the devil who'd kidnapped and fucked me because this man right here, I wasn't quite so scared of him any longer.

CHAPTER TWENTY SIX

Ash

ery little happened over the course of the next week. I spent most days with either Eric or Xav and my nights in Quinn's bed. Rory was avoiding me like the plague. The only time I saw him was at mealtimes and even then, he'd give me the cold shoulder. I had no idea what I'd done. So when the day finally came around where the others had to go out and leave me alone with him, I decided I was going to take full advantage of it. Except currently I was stuck in the damn cell because Quinn didn't trust me to roam the house alone. Not that I blamed him. I could quite easily attempt to escape.

I sat on the cot, twiddling my thumbs. It was times like these I actually felt like a prisoner. During the past week, I'd been allowed out pretty much the whole time so to be trapped again didn't sit well with me.

Was Rory really that averse to being around me that he'd make me spend all day in here?

I looked up at the cameras, wondering if he was watching me. I stood up, knowing this would be recorded but no longer caring.

"Are you mad at me?"

I wrung my hands out in front of me.

"Because if you are, I'm sorry even though I don't know what I did."

I paced away, dragging a hand through my hair before twirling some errant strands around my fingers.

"I know you don't like talking and that's okay. I don't need you to talk. Hell, I don't even need you to listen, but I don't like being alone. Did you know I've felt that way my whole life? Alone. Being a Russo comes with a thousand and one expectations, none of which I've ever lived up to. I'm not my father. Hell, I'm not even my mother. So I don't know why you, Quinn, Eric and Xav took me, but I'm not them... I'm not a..."

I looked at my hands, remembering the blood coating them after I tried to stop *him* bleeding out. Blood I felt as though I could never wash off. I'd scrubbed and scrubbed and scrubbed, but it was still there, haunting me.

"A monster."

But I was.

My father had made me one that day. Turned me into someone I didn't recognise when I stared at myself in the mirror.

I didn't want Papa to find me. I didn't want to go back to that life. I didn't want to be Ashleigh Vittoria Russo, heir to the family throne. Corruption and greed ran through my veins, but I didn't want those things to define me. I wasn't my father's daughter. Not in the way he wanted or needed me to be. I think Papa knew that deep down, but he was too stubborn to see he couldn't mould me into the woman fit to rule the Russo family.

The door to my cell swung open. I turned abruptly at the sound. Rory leant against the doorframe, his beautiful hazel eyes sad. It made me want to go over to him and wrap my arms around his back, but I wouldn't.

"I know you aren't," he said quietly.

"I'm not what?"

"A monster."

I fidgeted, unsure of what to say now he was here. Turns out, I didn't need to because he stepped back and indicated with his head I should follow him. He didn't lead me into the kitchen or living room. No, he took me towards the back of the house and through two large patio doors. We stood in what I initially thought was a conservatory, but it was more like a hothouse since the room was warm and full of tropical-looking plants growing up towards the glass ceiling.

Rory shut the patio door behind me and we walked further in until we came to a small seating area with two huge comfortable looking chairs and a coffee table with a stack of comics on it. He put his hand out, indicating I should sit down.

"What is this place?" I asked, looking around instead.

We were surrounded by ferns and other wide leaved plants.

"My... sanctuary."

My head whipped around and I stared at him. His expression was blank, but he shrugged a little at me.

"And you brought me in here?"

He looked away from me, his eyes roaming around the room.

"Quinn had this built so I could have the outside, inside. I have someone help me look after the plants regularly. I thought you might like to see it."

I took a step towards him despite knowing to do so would perhaps make him uncomfortable.

"You and Quinn are very close."

He didn't acknowledge me verbally but I could see his agreement in his expression. Could I gather enough courage to ask him why he'd been avoiding me? I wasn't exactly the hesitant type, but something about Rory made me wary of pushing him. Like there was a darkness inside him, seeping out of his pores and making him so... lonely.

"You never answered my question."

"Am I angry with you?"

I nodded. Somehow he knew what I was talking about.

"No, Ash. I'm not."

I took another step towards him. What was I even doing right now? I had no idea. It was like a pull between me and these four men I couldn't deny or understand.

"Then why have you been avoiding me?"

He flinched. I'd been told I could be blunt on occasion, but I didn't believe in beating about the bush, having had enough convoluted bullshit within my family as it was.

"You're Quinn's."

I curled my hand into a fist. Quinn might like to think that since I'd spent my nights in his bed having the best sex of my life, but he'd be wrong.

"Is that what you think? I don't belong to anyone but myself. Besides, what does it matter? Does it mean you can't talk to me?"

The thing is, whilst Quinn might satisfy me in a way I never knew I needed, we didn't exactly talk very much. Quinn was far more interested in getting between my legs than having an actual conversation with me. That was on me too since I hadn't pushed to get to know him further. It felt as though it would be opening up a can of worms. And most of the questions I'd want to ask him like *why had he taken me* and *what was my role in all of this*, he wouldn't answer.

Rory looked bewildered for all of thirty seconds, then his eyes darted away from me.

"You don't understand."

Another step almost closed the distance between us. His body tensed and he looked prime for flight.

"Do I make you nervous?"

"No."

"Then why do you look like you want to be anywhere but here right now?"

He swallowed visibly. Rory could certainly run if he wanted to, but I had a feeling it didn't have anything to do with my closeness even if he'd told me he was scared of other people touching him.

"I don't understand why I feel drawn to you, Rory. I don't understand any of this."

I stepped forward and stared up at him. There were inches between us. Rory's body heat seeped into me. The urge to touch him made my muscles twitch in protest as I kept my hands by my sides.

"Are you scared of me?" I whispered.

"Yes."

I don't know why it made my heart ache so much to hear him admit that.

"Why?"

"You make me feel, Ash," he said, his voice barely above a whisper. "And I don't like to feel. That's why I stay away."

He tipped his head down and stared at me, his hazel eyes darkening.

"Feel what?"

"Everything."

I didn't know what that meant. Nothing in his expression gave away what he was really feeling at me being so close to him. I acted on instinct, reaching out and leaving my hand hovering over his as if asking for permission to touch him.

"Ash…"

"I won't if you don't want me to."

"We can't do this."

"We aren't doing anything."

He shook his head.

"We are and you know it."

Was it so wrong for me to want to be closer to him? It's not like I'd be betraying Quinn by being Rory's friend.

You don't just want to be his friend, Ash. Don't lie to yourself.

Quinn and I weren't even anything. He was my captor and whatever was going on between us didn't mean he felt anything else for me. I felt things for him, but I felt those things for the others too.

"I don't belong to anyone but myself," I whispered. "Let me make my own choices."

192

CHAPTER TWENTY SEVEN

RORY

If I could've stopped looking at her right then, I would've. She was so damn close to me. I didn't let anyone but Quinn, Xav and Eric near me like this. My skin itched all over, but not with revulsion like it normally would when someone I didn't know very well was near me.

"What do you want from me, Ash?"

Her blue eyes closed momentarily and she took a breath.

"To know you."

"Nothing else?"

I had to ask because I had no idea what was happening right here. I'd told her she was Quinn's and that still stood no matter what she said. She slept in his bed. He'd made it very clear to the rest of us we weren't to lay a hand on her. He'd become weirdly possessive. It wasn't like him which is why I wanted to respect his wishes.

Whether I thought it was a good idea for him to get close to her or not was neither here nor there. Quinn would always do what he wanted despite my warnings. And yet here I was wanting to get close to her too.

"I wouldn't ask you for anything you weren't willing to give." She peered up at me as if seeing straight into my soul. "Can't we be friends?"

As if that was possible. She kept referring to us as her captors. Her wanting to know us wasn't normal, but nothing about this situation could be called normal.

"Why do you want that?"

"It might come as a surprise, but I don't actually have many friends, at least not real ones. Anyone who I thought was my friend only hung around me because I'm Frank Russo's daughter and they had to or face... well, you know." She waved her hand around. "I was nineteen when I met Nate and my life pretty much revolved around him and my family. Attending Papa's parties, doing as he told me to. Then Nate broke up with me and now I'm here with you four. Is it so wrong that I don't want to feel alone anymore?" She cocked her head to the side. "Quinn won't let me go so shouldn't I make the best of my circumstances?"

My chest felt tight hearing her tell me those things about her life. A girl like Ash didn't deserve to be locked up in an ivory tower. She should be free. I couldn't set her free though. Not least because she would be in danger now and I couldn't have that. Even though I'd stayed away, it didn't mean I didn't care what happened to her. In a lot of ways, I cared far too much for someone I barely knew which wasn't like me at all.

"Why me? Xav and Eric would be far better choices."

Her lips quirked up at the sides.

"This isn't about them but since you brought it up... I want to know all of you and I'm done pretending I don't. I don't care if it's wrong or fucked up. Everything about my life has been fucked up from start to finish. You think being kidnapped is the worst thing that's happened to me? Think again. You don't grow up as the daughter of Frank Russo having a normal, easy life."

I wanted to ask her to tell me everything. Explain what she meant by it all. Of course, I never thought she'd grown up having it easy. I'd never compare her upbringing to mine since she'd come from privilege whereas Quinn, Xav and Eric and I had lived barely above the breadline. But Ash came from a criminal family known for its ruthlessness too. One which had expectations she wasn't happy about fulfilling.

"All of us?"

"Yes, but we're talking about you and me right now."

When she looked up at me like that, with those damning crystal blue eyes of hers, I didn't want to deny her anything. I wanted to give her exactly what she was asking for. She'd dropped her hand from where it had been hovering over mine, but I wanted to show her it was okay. Though I had no clue how I'd really feel when her skin met mine.

I lifted my hand until it was level with her face. Ash watched me silently, just waiting. The pads of my fingertips dusted over her cheek. She sucked in a breath and I let one out. Her skin was so soft. Human contact had always been repellent because of what I'd been through, but Ash... Ash was different.

"Okay, you win. Friends."

I dropped my hand, knowing I'd likely made a stupid error of judgement but not being able to resist Ash at all. No matter if she was Quinn's. No matter if she was Russo's daughter.

There was just something about her. Something I needed in my life.

She smiled and it nearly made my heart stop. How did this girl manage to shine so bright?

"Yeah?"

I nodded, completely unable to take it back. I didn't want to upset Ash. She'd already been through enough.

She bit her lip and then stepped away from me, putting her hands behind her back and rocking on her feet. Happiness radiated off her and I found myself smiling.

"You should smile more."

I raised an eyebrow but didn't let my smile fall.

"You're cute when you smile."

Before I had a chance to respond, she skipped away from me and planted herself in one of my oversized chairs. I didn't tell her it was the one I normally sat in because she'd got herself comfortable, tucking her legs up underneath her.

She thinks I'm cute. No one has ever called me that before.

"Are those yours?" she asked, pointing at my comics.

I rubbed the back of my neck.

"Yes."

She leant forward and picked one up.

"Batman, eh?"

I had shelves of them in my room, but I regularly brought down a few to read when I was in my conservatory. Quinn took the piss out of my comic obsession, but he'd always gone out of his way to buy me them when we'd been kids and he had extra pocket money, which wasn't often. They were my escapism from my reality. I'd kept them hidden under a loose floorboard in my bedroom, trying desperately to keep them in pristine condition where I could.

I sat down in the other chair and took it from her.

"These are from a limited series crossover with the Teenage Mutant Ninja Turtles. I also read a lot of indie comics, but Batman is my favourite."

"Do you have a lot of comics then?"

I nodded, a little embarrassed about admitting it to someone like Ash. It was something I'd been teased relentlessly for when I was a kid, but I didn't care.

"Can I read one?"

I couldn't help staring at her, confused as to why she'd want to.

"I want to see why they interest you." She put her hand out, but I didn't give her the comic. "Am I not allowed?"

I set the comic down and picked up the rest because I had one here that she might like. Finding it in the stack, I handed it to her. She looked down at it and smiled.

"Catwoman?"

I shrugged.

"I think it might appeal to you more than Batman."

She raised an eyebrow but sat back and opened it up to the first page, eyes scanning over it. I watched her read it, smiling every time she smiled, watching her brow furrow in places and when she bit her lip.

I want to know what her lips feel like… against mine.

I couldn't help it. Wanting to kiss Ash was wrong, but my life wasn't exactly black and white. It never had been. I still wouldn't act on my feelings or desires. What I wanted from Ash, she likely would find reprehensible. What I liked would scare people if they knew. And whilst I knew the things Quinn liked, he hadn't told me if he'd done any of that with her. So who really knew what she'd think.

Didn't matter. Ash was with Quinn. So I had to keep those thoughts to myself even if they tormented me.

But if I could, Ash, I'd demand everything from you. Your heart, your body and your soul. And in return, I'd give you me if you'd have me, broken parts and all.

I'd make Ash my northern star... but given how tiny she was, I'd settle for her being a little star. She'd still shine the brightest of all.

CHAPTER TWENTY EIGHT

Xavier

When we got back from the casino, I went looking for Ash to make sure she was okay. Not like I didn't trust Rory with her, but he had told Quinn to put her in the cell before we left. I wanted to let her out.

When I reached it, she wasn't there. I tapped my fingers against my thigh. That meant Rory had let her out and there were only three places she could be. Quinn's office, but Rory wouldn't take her in there and he most definitely wouldn't have taken her to his room. So there was only one logical place left.

I stalked down the hall, into the dining room and down another hall, reaching a second living room. Opening the patio doors, I stepped into what I'd dubbed Rory's Tropical Paradise, not that he appreciated the name. I walked further in, past one of the large palms before finding Rory and Ash in his little seating area. Ash was curled up in the oversized armchair Rory usually sat in, her head resting on the arm, her eyes closed with one of his comics laying in her lap. He had his nose buried in a comic, but he lowered it when he heard me, putting a finger over his lips and nodding his head towards Ash.

He got up, placing his comic down carefully on the coffee table before silently moving towards the patio doors so we wouldn't disturb Ash. I followed him, stopping when he did.

"Is she okay?" I asked in a low voice.

He nodded but then shook his head.

"I'm worried about her," he admitted after a moment.

"Why?"

He shifted on his feet, looking towards where she was still sleeping.

"What she said today… it's concerned me."

I cocked my head to the side, waiting for him to elaborate. He looked distinctly uncomfortable, but then again, Rory preferred not to speak unless it was necessary.

"She wants to know all of us, Xav. We're keeping her here against her will, but she wants to know us." He rubbed his face. "She said she doesn't have any real friends. I get the feeling her whole life has revolved around her family and doing her father's bidding. It's like she's broken inside. What normal girl would want to spend time with their captors or… sleep with one of them."

"We're not exactly normal either."

He gave me a look which said he didn't appreciate my joke.

"I'm serious, I think Russo coerced her into the role he's set out for her. She had this weird look in her eyes earlier and said she wasn't a monster, but her voice, it sounded like she didn't believe her own words."

If that was true, then what happened that day… she might not have wanted to be a part of it. And that made me feel sick. What father forces his daughter into a life of bloodshed and destruction? A fucked up one who lacked morals.

"Why are you telling me this rather than Quinn?"

He sighed, his eyes hardening.

"I should tell him."

"You're worried about his reaction since he's pretty much obsessed with her, right? Don't blame you. But you are the one who said we should be careful with her since she knows far more than she's let on."

He nodded once and looked down at the floor.

"I know what I said, but I'm not so sure any longer."

I shifted on my feet, looking over at Ash on the chair. She was still sleeping, her chest rising and falling at a steady pace.

"You like her."

"So do you."

I wasn't going to deny it. When I looked at Ash, my instincts were overwhelmingly geared towards protecting her. And after what Rory had said, the one person she needed protecting from the most was her own father. Quinn was right. Russo couldn't have her back, but not because of what she'd done. My angel didn't deserve to have her wings clipped by her own father. I wasn't going to stand by and allow anyone to break her further.

My angel.

Jesus, she wasn't mine. I needed to get a grip.

"And?"

"She insisted she's not Quinn's. He won't like that."

I scoffed.

"Of course not, he thinks she's his possession."

"She doesn't. That makes her dangerous to all of us."

I frowned.

"Why?"

His lip quirked up at the side.

"One day Ash might ask for things we can't give her. If we do, we'd be opening a can of worms. Do you think Quinn would ever be okay with it? I don't."

I stared at him. Was he suggesting Ash would want more than one of us?

"I don't have an issue with sharing as you well know."

"If it meant I could have her…" He looked over at Ash again. "…neither would I."

"I won't tell Quinn you said that."

For Rory to admit to wanting someone, that was a huge fucking deal. Especially since he was admitting it to me and not Quinn.

"I'm not going to act on it and neither should you. Not unless you want to bring down a world of problems on our heads. We're already in enough shit as it is."

He was right. Of course, he was. Didn't mean I had to like it.

"If she asks for it, Rory, how am I going to say no?"

He shrugged.

"I suggest you think long and hard about whether you want to throw away twenty-two years of friendship over a girl. I know the answer to that question, but do you?"

I gritted my teeth, absolutely hating the thought of ruining what we had with each other. We weren't just friends, we were a family of four forged in blood. I'd die for them and they would for me. That's how our friendship worked. So no, I couldn't do it. Not even when I wanted to throw Quinn through a window for being a prick.

"She's not just a girl."

His lip twitched.

"I know."

In those moments, Rory and I forged an understanding with each other. Ash wasn't just some girl to either of us. And she never would be.

"Stay with her... I should go speak to Quinn."

I grinned.

"No need to tell me twice."

Rory slipped from the conservatory as I walked over and sat down in his vacated armchair. My little blonde angel looked so fucking cute when she was asleep. I wanted to touch her, but I didn't. Instead, I reached out and took the comic out of her lap, setting it down on the rest of the ones on the coffee table. As I pulled back, she blinked and raised her head off the arm.

"Xav? Where's Rory?"

She yawned and stretched.

"Speaking to Quinn, so I'm afraid you're stuck with me."

"Oh well, that's not so bad." She smiled and gave me a wink. "You talk more than him."

I chuckled and shook my head. Next thing I knew, she was out of her seat and in my lap, her blue eyes filled with mirth.

"And you don't mind this."

I wrapped a hand around her waist.

"What?"

"Touching."

I raised an eyebrow.

"You like that, eh?"

What the hell are you doing? You know you shouldn't touch her.

Wasn't my fault she'd sat on me. I should put her back in her own chair, but now she was close, I didn't want to.

Twin spots of red appeared on her cheeks as she walked her fingers up my bare arm. She'd never asked about my tattoos even though Ash was one of the most curious girls I'd ever met.

"I don't have a touchy-feely family. You could say I was starved of affection." Her voice was quiet and hesitant. "Sometimes I just want to be held, you know."

Her eyes were sad and it tugged at my heartstrings.

"Quinn doesn't give you that?"

She sighed and looked away.

"He does and he doesn't. I feel like he wants me around to fuck and that's it."

Quinn had no fucking clue how to treat women properly. I mean, shit, I didn't have the best track record either. I wasn't a relationship guy, but I always tried to treat women with respect. They deserved that much.

"Come here."

I tugged her closer and let her rest her head on my shoulder, wrapping both my arms around her. She let out a little contented sigh of appreciation.

"I'll hold you anytime you want, angel. No strings attached."

And I meant it. No matter how much I'd like to do more with her, I would never take advantage of the situation. I just wasn't that type of guy.

"You make being here more bearable," she whispered, her fingers trailing down my chest.

When she said stuff like that, it made it that much harder to keep my distance from this girl. To not want to give in.

"I try."

"I'm not saying I don't want to be with Quinn, but I don't know if he's capable of giving me everything I need. I barely even know anything about him. He won't talk to me. He treats me like I belong to him, fucking caveman behaviour if you ask me." She stilled her hand on my chest above my heart. "None of this is normal, Xav. None. What kind of girl sleeps with the man who kidnapped her?"

This is why none of us should've touched her in the first place. Ash was only ever supposed to be a means to an end. From the moment we brought her here, our lives had been irrevocably changed by her presence. She'd brought fire and fury in her wake, refusing to be anything but herself. She gave Quinn shit only to be punished for it, got Rory talking, which was no mean feat, and had me and Eric falling out over my crush on her. All in less than two weeks. If that didn't tell us exactly what type of trouble we'd gotten ourselves into over kidnapping this girl, I didn't know what would.

She wasn't what anyone had expected. Not only had she messed with our heads, but we'd also messed with hers too. Especially Quinn.

"The kind who has lived under the rule of her father for too long and wants to be free to do as she chooses."

She lifted her head and looked at me.

"How do you know that?"

"Rory does talk on occasion."

"He told you what I said to him?"

I nodded, not wishing to lie to her. She laid her head back down.

"You're right. Papa has kept me in line. Not just within the family but pushing me into a relationship with a man who was only with me to ingratiate himself into Papa's inner circle." Her fingers started tracing lines across my chest again. "I didn't sleep with Quinn as an act of rebellion against my father, I did it because I wanted to."

I couldn't help but place a kiss on the top of her head.

"And that's all that matters. You do you, Ash. Don't let anyone else's opinions get in the way. Trust me, Eric and I have been given enough shit in our lives over our sexuality, but we don't let that stop us being with who we want. It doesn't define who we are as people so whatever. If you want to sleep with Quinn, that's your choice to make."

She looked up at me.

"I gathered you're bi, but Eric?"

I smiled.

"I should let him tell you himself."

"Because that's totally not a weird conversation to have."

"Eric doesn't see gender, he sees people."

She looked thoughtful for a moment before smiling.

"You know I got him to admit he thinks I'm attractive."

I cocked my head to the side.

"You did?"

She nodded, her smile widening.

"But he said he wouldn't leer at me because I deserved better."

I threw back my head and laughed. That was such an Eric response. Always trying to be the good guy.

"Hey, it's kind of nice that he's trying to be a gentleman."

I settled back down and stroked her hair.

"I know, angel. It's just Eric being Eric. He's always been the peacemaker."

"Why do you call me angel?"

So many reasons, but most of them I can't tell you.

"Because you are one... to me anyway."

Ash settled her hand over my heart, which was steadily thumping in my chest.

"I don't think I am one," she whispered. "But I'm honoured you see me that way."

The sadness in her voice almost threatened to undo me. It made me realise that Rory could be right. Ash could see herself as a monster. The question was... why?

CHAPTER TWENTY NINE

Quinn

he longer Rory spoke, the more enraged I became. Why the thought of Ash confiding in him did that to me was a fucking wonder. I couldn't stand it. She was mine. Fucking well mine and they weren't allowed to have her. My fists clenched under the table as he paced in front of me. Rory didn't pace which left me feeling unnerved as well as frustrated and pissed off.

"It concerns me, Quinn, she shouldn't want to get to know us. She's our prisoner. It's not normal. I don't think she's doing it out of wanting us to sympathise with her so we'll let her go either. She's lived a lonely and sheltered life."

I watched him growing ever more agitated, keeping my jaw clenched shut lest I said something I didn't mean. Right now, anything could come out of my mouth.

"She thinks she's a monster. What twenty-one-year-old girl would ever think that about herself? It makes me question what Russo did to her to make her feel that way."

"What the fuck makes you think it was him?"

He stopped and stared at me, eyes narrowed.

"You're telling me you think she did that to herself?"

I didn't know what to think any longer. Ash and I hadn't really talked about her father any further since the first night she'd let me fuck her on the very desk I was sitting at right now. I'd meant to, but I'd been too busy burying my cock in her at every opportunity I had. She did that to me. Made me so fucking crazy with lust, I couldn't think straight. I had to have her taut little body writhing under me. Controlling her pleasure and pain. Fuck she was so beautiful and responsive. She came alive underneath my touch.

I rose from my desk slowly, tension coiling inside me.

"What I think? What I fucking think?"

His expression didn't change, but Rory knew I was angry.

"Quinn…"

I walked around my desk towards the door.

"Whatever you're thinking of doing, don't. You know this won't end well."

I stopped and looked at him over my shoulder.

"You can shut the fuck up, stop lecturing me and stay the fuck away from Ashleigh. You hear me? All of you can. If I get so much of a fucking whiff that any of you have touched her…"

Rory stiffened, his eyes going wide.

"You'll what, Quinn? Kill us? Do you realise how insane you sound right now?"

I didn't give a shit what I sounded like. No one else was having her. Like a drug, she intoxicated me, tangling me up in a twisted web of hatred and desire. I'd lost my fucking mind and it was all her fault. Except it was mine too for allowing this. For even touching her in the first place. I was in no fucking rational frame of mind to look in the mirror and face what I'd done.

Rory didn't stop me leaving. He'd already told me where she was. I stalked through the house until I reached his conservatory and threw the door open. What I saw made my blood pound in my ears.

"Ashleigh, come here right now," I said with an unnatural calm which I most definitely was not feeling right then.

She looked up from where she was curled up in Xav's lap like it was fucking normal and completely acceptable for her to be cuddling another man.

"Quinn?"

"Don't make me repeat myself."

Xav stared at me, his eyes growing hard. He didn't move to let go of her.

"You don't have to go with him, Ash."

Ash looked between us, confusion written all over her features.

"Oh yes, she fucking well does."

Her face fell and she stared at me.

"I'm not your lapdog, Quinn. You can't just tell me to come heel."

I gritted my teeth. If she was going to act like a brat, then she'd be treated like one. I advanced on her, grabbed her by the arm and dragged her out of Xav's lap. She squeaked and her hand went to mine, trying to pull me off her as I tugged her towards the doors.

"Get off me!"

I ignored her. She could protest all she wanted. The girl was about to get a fucking lesson and one she wouldn't quickly forget.

"Quinn, stop it. Why are you doing this? I didn't do anything."

I almost stopped dead in the hallway, but the need to make her understand who she belonged to drove me. She screeched and protested the whole way upstairs to my bedroom. I shoved her in and locked the door behind us.

"What is wrong with you?" she demanded, planting her hands on her hips. "You're acting like a caveman."

"I'll show you a fucking caveman."

She took one look at my face as I advanced on her and started to back away. Grabbing her by the arm, I marched her over to the bed. I'd left out the ropes I'd used on her the night before, but this time she wouldn't be getting any fucking pleasure out of them. She wriggled in my grasp, trying to get away from me, but I held fast.

"You forget your place, little girl. This wilful nature of yours does you no favours. Clearly, you need to be shown what happens when you misbehave."

"What are you talking about? I don't understand."

I grabbed the rope and started knotting her wrists together.

"What part of you're mine do you not understand?"

She stared up at me, her blue eyes dark. Even though her hands were now tied together, she ripped them away from me and stumbled backwards into the bed.

"I'm not your fucking possession, Quinn."

"All of them know fucking well better than to touch you."

She righted herself and moved away from me, trying to wriggle out of the ropes.

"Oh really? Why? Because you told them not to? Fuck you. You don't get to dictate that. You don't get to dictate anything. He was giving me a fucking hug because I asked him to. He fucking well listens unlike you." Her chest heaved with each breath she took, her eyes wild with anger. "All you want is to fuck me. And guess what? I need more than that. I need to feel like more than just a warm hole for you to stick your dick in. So don't you dare tell me I did something wrong because I wanted some affection for once in my fucking life. Lord fucking knows I never got it from my parents or my arsehole ex-boyfriend. Not one of them cared about what I needed. And neither do you."

Her words knocked all the wind out of my sails. I watched my little girl stamp her foot and let out a frustrated noise when she couldn't get the ropes off her wrists. Then tears welled in her eyes and the sight of it made my chest ache and my stomach churn.

"Damn it, Quinn. Is it that bloody hard to understand I want you? Not just sex, but you. All of you. I want you to talk to me. I want you to care. I just plain fucking well want you, but right now, I don't even know why because all you do is treat me like shit. And I don't know what else I fucking well expected considering you're my fucking kidnapper. So yeah, jokes on me I guess. Ha-fucking-ha. Look at poor Ash wanting the person who's actively trying to destroy her father and ruin her life."

She choked back a sob as tears started falling down her cheeks.

"I'm so tired of being the pawn in everyone else's games. First my father, then Nate and now you. So fine, punish me for wanting to know you and your friends. Punish me for wanting to understand. Just go ahead and fucking punish me for wanting anything but the fucking shit lot in life I was handed. I don't care anymore."

All of her words felt like a punch to the gut. Xav was right. Rory was right. Ash was broken on the inside. And me getting angry with her wasn't helping matters.

I stepped towards her, not wanting to spook her in the slightest, but she stood there, tears streaming down her cheeks with abject misery on her face. She flinched when I got close to her and reached out, but I ignored it. Carefully, I undid the knots around her wrists and threw the rope away. Then I gathered her up against my chest and held her. After a moment, she gripped my shirt and sobbed, her small frame shaking with the effort.

"Shh, little girl," I murmured. "It's okay."

It wasn't like I didn't know how to comfort someone, I just didn't do it very often. In fact, the only people I'd ever offered it to were Xav, Eric and Rory. Those three meant more to me than anyone in this world. And I'd been acting like a complete tool since Ash had arrived in our house. Since we'd taken her.

What I was doing wouldn't give me the information I needed from her. It wasn't doing any of us any good whatsoever. I might not be a good man, but I certainly didn't want Ash to think I was completely heartless. I did own one. It just happened to be closed off to anyone but my three best friends. My family. I no longer had anyone else to speak of.

My gut twisted. My blood family. I couldn't afford thoughts about them. They weren't welcome.

"Why are you doing this to me?" she sobbed.

I stroked her hair, wondering how to answer that. My reasons were simple before I'd taken her, but now they were complicated because I'd blurred the lines. As much as I hated her, I didn't at the same time. The constant battle between the two opposing sides raged inside of me.

"I took you because you're Russo's most prized possession."

Her body shook harder.

"And I want him to suffer." *Suffer as I have.*

"The only one who's suffering here is me," she whispered. "My father doesn't care about me. He only cares about his reputation, that I'm there to succeed him as head of the family and destroying everything I am so I become like him. I don't want to be my father. I don't want to be a monster."

A part of me wanted her to suffer, but the larger part didn't. The part of me which actually still had a soul worth salvaging. The part which still had feelings.

"Do you want me to take your pain away, little girl?"

She shuddered, clutching my shirt tighter in her fists.

"No," she sobbed. "The pain reminds me I'm still breathing. Just give me you, Quinn. I just want you."

Could I give her that? No woman had really ever asked that from me before. I mean sure, they'd wanted a relationship from me, but no one had said it with such desperation and conviction. No one until Ash. And I'd never wanted to give a woman an insight into me until her. How could a girl I'd known barely two weeks have such a profound effect on me?

It had to be Ashleigh Russo of all people. The one girl I'd been determined to hate for what she'd been complicit in.

Where the fuck was my ruthlessness? It'd fled the building the moment she arrived. This girl was my weakness. One I wasn't aware I possessed until now.

"I'm right here."

She shook her head against my chest.

"No, you're not. Not in the way I need. Doesn't matter anyway, it's not like you care."

"You think I don't care?"

"How can you when you treat me like I'm your own personal fucktoy? I'm a human being, Quinn, not a possession."

If that's what she thought of me why did I even fucking bother? Maybe I should give her that man. The one who cared so little about the world. Maybe Ashleigh should really meet the one they all called *Il Diavolo* because he sure as shit wouldn't care one iota about her feelings. Her needs. Her emotions.

Except I wasn't him. Not inside. And when it came to Ash, it was impossible to be him. Because the truth was… I did care. Far more than I ever should.

CHAPTER THIRTY

Ash

I felt pathetic crying on Quinn and practically begging him for more like those weren't the actions of someone who'd lost the plot. This man had taken me away from my family and held me against my will. So why did I want him? Why had I let him get inside my head like this? Inside me at all.

Quinn let go of me only to pull my face away from his chest and cup it between his hands. A fresh set of tears ran down my cheeks. His eyes were so dark and full of emotion.

Sometimes I hated how attractive his features were. From his perfect high cheekbones, tanned skin and dark hair to his strong, athletic body, Quinn was devastating. And I'd fallen under his spell.

"I care, little girl," he said, his voice low and quiet. "I don't enjoy making you cry like this."

He wiped away my tears with the pad of his thumb, making me feel so small and helpless under his intense gaze.

"You don't?" I whispered.

He shook his head, dropping his hands from my face. Pulling me over to the bed, he slipped out of his shoes, got on the bed and put his hand out to me as he sat up against the headboard. I took it, allowing him to pull me into his lap and wrap his arms around me like I was a small child in need of comfort. And I suppose right then, I was.

"I don't want to upset you," he said softly. "Perhaps when you first arrived, but not now, little girl."

He kissed the top of my head before settling his cheek on it. I trembled, not because I was scared but I hadn't expected him to be so… soft with me. Admittedly he always took care of me after he'd thoroughly ravaged me, but this was different.

"Did Rory tell you what I said to him? Is that why you're angry with me?"

"Yes."

So Quinn was jealous. I wasn't sure how I felt about that. The intensity of his possessiveness towards me was actually a little terrifying.

"Has it occurred to you the only person I'm intimate with is you?" I put my hand on his chest. "I like the others, but I want you."

"Then why won't you admit you're mine?"

"Is that what you need to hear me say? Will it stop you getting so pissed off about me being around the others?"

I didn't want to say it. I didn't like the connotations associated with ownership. But if it got him to stop acting so crazy, then I would.

"Don't say it if you don't mean it."

"I only want to be with you."

Liar. You want the others.

It didn't matter what I wanted. Wanting more than one person didn't sit right with me. Wasn't that greedy? How could I expect them to be okay with it? Especially when even the thought of me with anyone else did this to Quinn. I didn't think he'd ever agree and if I wanted Quinn, which I did, then I had to keep my desire to know what it was like to be touched by the other three under wraps.

I wasn't even sure why I wanted more than one man in the first place. This had never happened to me before but I had limited experience with boys. Nate was the first real man I'd ever been with although I hadn't lost my virginity to him. No, that had been Fabio, the son of one of my father's friends who was also my first kiss. I'd been sixteen and him, twenty. I'd asked him to since I trusted him. Fabio was married with a baby now and still very much affiliated with my father's empire.

I'd always assumed I'd be monogamous but meeting these four men had me questioning everything about myself. Wanting Quinn didn't mean I stopped wanting to know and be close to Xav, Rory and perhaps even Eric.

I looked up at Quinn. His eyes were dark and his expression grim. I wasn't sure if he believed me or not.

"I don't know how else I can convince you," I whispered.

He shifted and reached over to the bedside table, pulling out some tissues. He proceeded to clean up my tear-streaked face and encouraged me to blow my nose. I must've looked

Sarah Bailey

like a right state but Quinn didn't shy away from me. In fact, he looked at me like I was still beautiful to him.

He dropped the tissues on the bedside table and turned his head back to mine. I reached up and ran my fingers along his jaw, which ticked. Not caring if he was still mad at me, I started to unbutton his shirt, watching him carefully for any indication that he wanted me to stop. When I reached the last buttons, I ran my fingers along his bare chest under his shirt, revelling in the feel of his hard muscles against the pads of my fingertips.

I leant towards him and kissed his jaw, desperately wanting to reassure him. He didn't stop me kissing my way down to his ear.

"If I take off my clothes and lay across your lap so you can punish me, would you like that? Do you want to hurt me for the way I've made you feel, sir?"

I sucked his earlobe into my mouth, grazing my teeth down it and causing him to let out a groan. Honestly, I craved the way he handled me. I loved the sting of his palm. The high was unlike anything else I'd ever experienced.

"Yes," he hissed as I sucked harder. "Yes, little girl."

I needed no further encouragement. Pulling away, I slipped off the bed. I undressed slowly, adoring the way his heated gaze lingered over me. When I dropped my underwear, I crawled back on the bed and settled myself face down over his lap. Quinn's fingers ran down my bare spine. This would be the first time I'd willingly submitted to being punished by him.

"So beautiful," he murmured. "Such perfect skin."

He adjusted me so I was in just the right place before the first strike came. The pain shot through me, but I didn't flinch or cry out. The rapid succession of the next ones made me squirm in his lap. Why this type of pain turned me on was beyond me. All I knew is I wanted him never to stop punishing me like this.

I could feel him growing harder by the second under me. I arched into each strike, small whimpers and pants escaping my lips.

"So good for me, little girl."

"I want to be, sir."

He let out a grunt of approval, peppering me with more strikes. By the time he was done, I was a mess, desperate for his cock inside me.

"Thank you, sir."

Quinn stroked his fingers across my sore behind. I couldn't see his face so had no idea what he was thinking or planning to do next. As long as he fucked me, I didn't care. His fingers dipped between my cheeks and stroked over my other entrance. I tensed, but his fingers brushed lower to my pussy.

"So wet and wanting."

He seemed to coat his fingers in my arousal before dragging them back up and circling around. I squirmed. The sensation was different but not unpleasant.

"Quinn…"

"Shh, little girl." He stroked my back with his other hand. "I told you I wanted this."

His touch left me and he leant away. The sound of a drawer opening and closing followed before his hands were back on me. Then I felt a cool gel-like substance settle between my cheeks and I knew I wasn't getting out of this.

He took it slow, teasing my entrance until I was panting and squirming in his lap, rubbing against his cock which made him grunt. When he pressed the tip of his finger inside me, I cried out a little at the strangeness of it, but I didn't tell him to stop. Quinn worked me with one finger for a few minutes. It stung when he inserted two. I whimpered, unable to help the sound spilling from my mouth.

"It hurts."

"I know, little girl."

His voice was so soft and reassuring. I couldn't help but relax a fraction. He wasn't doing this to make me feel pain. He wanted it to be pleasurable for me. That's why he was gentle as he touched and prepared me.

He leant over me, I could feel his warmth and his breath against my shoulder.

"I won't fuck you here today. You're not ready."

His assertion made me relax further. Quinn could just take this from me if he chose and I would let him. But I wasn't prepared for it. To have his cock inside me like that.

His fingers disappeared. I let out a breath but it wasn't a long reprieve. Something pressed against me which definitely wasn't his fingers.

"Quinn, wha—"

My words were stolen as the object was unceremoniously thrust inside me. The stretch and burn made me shift, hands scrabbling at the covers.

"Fuck! What the hell?"

Quinn didn't answer nor did he let up, deeper it went until I felt it bottom out. I lay there, trying to comprehend what just happened, my hands buried in the covers and my breathing erratic.

"What did you put in me?" I whispered, choking out the words.

"A plug, so you can get used to being filled."

I felt filled all right. The sensation was quite unlike anything else I'd experienced before.

"Sit up, little girl."

Gingerly, I shifted into sitting position on his lap. Each movement shifted the plug inside me. Quinn was wiping his fingers with a tissue, a smug and satisfied look on his face.

"Take my cock out."

My eyes widened but I did as he said. He looked harder than he had ever done. It pulsed in my hand as if desperate to feel me. I stroked my hand up and down his shaft, adoring the softness of his skin in contrast with the hardness of his engorged cock.

"Fuck me."

It wasn't that I'd never been on top before, but I stared at Quinn like he was crazy. Did he really think I was going to let him fuck me with a plug in my arse right now?

"I can't."

He gripped my hip and tugged me closer. His eyes darkened as if irritated by my response.

"Don't displease me, little girl."

I didn't stop him when he forced me over his cock and started to press me down on it, but my eyes pleaded with him. How would I take him and the plug at the same time? His cock breached me and I cried out, the intensity and the stretch making all my nerve endings fire. It didn't exactly hurt but it ached in a way which had me flinching.

"It's too much."

He neither acknowledged me nor stopped in his endeavour to penetrate me up to the hilt. I'd never been stretched so much in my life. Each inch made the ache worse. I tried to breathe through it, my heart rate pounding in my ears. I gripped his shoulders to steady myself as he continued to press me down on his cock.

"Quinn," I whimpered. "Please."

I reminded myself I had a safe word if this was really too much for me to cope with, but I didn't want to say it. Didn't want to be defeated by this. I had a sick need to prove myself to Quinn. To show him he had no reason to suspect I would allow any of the others to touch me no matter how much I craved them.

When he was finally fully seated inside me, his eyes met mine. His pupils were fully dilated and there was a dark smile on his face. Both of his hands wrapped around my sore behind, making me wince. Even though I was struggling with his cock and the plug inside me, I leant towards him, planting my lips on his and kissing him because I needed something else to concentrate on. I cupped his face, feeling his stubble graze my fingers.

After a few minutes, I started to move a little, feeling more comfortable with his cock and the plug in me at the same time. I rocked back and forth on his cock. Quinn groaned in my mouth, spurring me on. Pulling away, I bit my lip as he stared at me with desire and lust sparking in his eyes.

"You feel so fucking good," he growled. "So tight. Fuck."

He encouraged me to rise and fall on him. I obliged, wanting to please him. He tipped his head back against the headboard, watching me as his fingers ran down the centre of my chest.

"You want me to fuck you harder, sir."

"Take your pleasure from me. Show me how much you want my cock, little girl."

I planted both hands on his chest, arching my back as I rode him harder and revelling in the way it felt to be in control. To have him watch me take what I needed from him. His expression made me feel like a queen. The way his eyes roamed over my chest. How he watched me with rapt attention like he was stuck and couldn't look away.

"Touch me please, sir. I want to come on your cock."

He smiled wickedly before his hand fell between my legs and his fingers found my clit, stroking the little swollen bud. Each brush of his finger drove me higher, making me ride him faster until I was on the edge. I was so full and my body so taut, I couldn't hold back.

The dam broke and the waves battered me. I cried out his name over and over, my body shaking and trembling above him. My fingers dug into his chest and everything in that moment faded away to just me and Quinn. Just this moment of pure ecstasy where I forgot who I was and all the shit in my life.

I slumped against his chest, my head on his shoulder as I tried to catch my breath. My hand wrapped around his neck, anchoring me to him. He stroked my back and kissed the top of my head. I never knew sex could be like this. Not until I met Quinn and realised there was so much more my body craved and desired.

"You were right, you know," I whispered.

"About what?"

"I needed you to fuck me right."

His chest rumbled with his amusement. I was only half-serious. Nate definitely did not fuck the way Quinn did and well, there was no comparison in terms of who was better. Quinn won hands down without all the added extras of discipline, being tied up and now… learning that I might actually enjoy anal. Although, I had yet to experience his cock there, so I would reserve judgement on it until then.

"I'm not done fucking you yet," he said when he settled down.

Next thing I knew, he'd flipped me on my back and was driving into me without mercy. I held onto his back, letting him ravage me just the way he wanted. I watched his face screw up in bliss, his thrusts growing ever more erratic by the second. He let out a guttural moan, burying his face in my neck as his body twitched and shuddered above me.

We lay there in complete silence for several long minutes, Quinn stroking my face gently and me holding him tightly.

"I won't let you go, little girl," he whispered in my ear.

"I don't want you to."

"Perhaps not now, but I won't rest until I bring down your father."

I didn't flinch at his words. I'd known from the start he hated Papa. It's just now, I wasn't so sure I cared if Quinn took him down. I might love my father, but the role he'd forced me to play was intolerable and I couldn't forgive him for it. Here and now, I had no idea where my loyalties really lay. Funny that in such a short space of time, your whole life could be thrown into disarray and the path you thought was set in stone could change so drastically.

"I know you won't," I whispered back.

If there was one thing I knew about Quinn, that was his determination to get his own way. And I doubted even my father could withstand a man like Quinn, but perhaps he was made of stronger stuff than me. Papa was a cold-blooded killer after all. I'd seen him in his element and it scared me.

The thing is Quinn scared me too, but for different reasons.

It scared me just how much I was growing to care for someone I didn't really know.

And how much I'd throw away just to stay right here by his side.

Because the truth was… I belonged here with him, Eric, Xavier and Rory.

CHAPTER THIRTY ONE

Xavier

All evening I'd worried about Ash after Quinn dragged her away yesterday afternoon. She didn't resurface for dinner. He'd come down and taken stuff up for the two of them. When I questioned him, Quinn told us she was sleeping. He had this gleam in his eyes as if he'd finally got what he wanted. And considering what Quinn wanted was Ash all to himself, that concerned me. What happened between the two of them?

Now morning had come around and there was still no sign of them. Rory, Eric and I sat up at the breakfast bar in the kitchen. Normally I'd be wolfing my food down considering Eric had made a full English, but my stomach was in knots. The way Ash had talked about her relationship with Quinn yesterday set me on edge. She needed more than he was offering her. Needed the affection she'd never grown up with and someone to listen to her.

Normally Eric would ask me what was wrong but he wasn't talking to me. Still, he kept glancing my way with a frown as if he wanted to say something about my lack of appetite. Rory was quieter than usual, his whole demeanour off. Ash had really done a number on the four of us.

We all turned our heads towards the door at the sound of laughter down the hallway. Her laugh. The sound was like music to my ears. I hadn't honestly realised how much she lit up our household until now. Longing ripped through me. Knowing I shouldn't disrupt everything between us made me tamp down on it. Didn't stop me wanting her. Needing her. Feeling starved of her presence in a way I'd never felt with anyone before.

You're a fucking mess, Xavier. A big fucking mess.

Ash was practically wrapped around him as she and Quinn entered the kitchen. Her blue eyes were bright and her face void of any worries. My stomach sunk down to my feet. Did our conversation yesterday mean nothing to her? She looked up at Quinn like he was some kind of fucking god. I wasn't too proud to admit jealousy coated my veins.

"Morning boys," she said as she looked over at us.

Rory glanced at them, Eric gave her a smile and me? I stared, wanting to tear her away from Quinn's side and ask her what the fuck was going on.

If the less than warm reception bothered Ash, she didn't show it as Quinn and her sat down. Eric got up and sorted out two piled high plates along with coffee for Quinn and tea for Ash. She thanked him with a grin. I noticed Eric's neck flush slightly as he turned away and sat back down. My eyes narrowed. So, Ash was right. Eric did like her. After all the shit he'd given us over Ash, it pissed me off further.

Fuck, I was in such a shitty mood.

The whole way through the rest of breakfast I had to watch her whispering and giggling with Quinn which only soured my mood further. Rory left abruptly halfway through, his eyes cold and his body tense as if he was just as irritated as I was by the display in front of us. I had no idea what happened between him and Quinn yesterday. Rory wouldn't talk about it even if I did ask him so I hadn't bothered. Ash stared after him with furrowed brows, but her face cleared when she looked up at Quinn again.

I stared down at my second cup of tea, having long finished breakfast, but reluctant to leave the room. Honestly, I didn't know how to feel other than frustrated with the whole situation. Eric kept staring at me which also didn't help. I wish he'd just spit out what he wanted to say so we could get over this ridiculous argument between the two of us. It plain fucking sucked I couldn't talk to my best friend about my idiotic feelings towards someone I should never seek to have. Eric's perspective would've been pretty fucking welcome right about now.

Quinn stood up abruptly and put his hand on Ash's shoulder, keeping her planted on her chair.

"One of you needs to watch her today."

It wasn't a request, it was an order.

He leant down and kissed Ash, his hand tangling in her hair. Seeing this display of affection made me ill.

Idiot. Fucking idiot.

"See you later, little girl," he said to her quietly before he pulled away and left the room.

She stared after him before turning back to me and Eric.

"Who's turn is it?"

233

Eric got up and looked pointedly at me.

"I have to go out."

I almost told him to stay in so I didn't have to get lumbered with Ash all day since Rory was off somewhere doing god knows fucking what. Except Eric and I weren't talking, so I kept my mouth shut, inwardly seething at the prospect of being around the cause of my issues.

He started to walk away towards the door when I stood and followed him, catching his arm before he escaped completely. Something inside me snapped. I couldn't allow this to go on any longer. He stiffened at the contact before looking at me.

"E…" I started, my voice low. "I'm sorry."

He looked down at my hand on his arm before raising his eyes back up to mine. The pain in them startled me into severing the contact between us.

"Me too."

I shifted, rubbing the back of my neck and feeling incredibly awkward.

"We okay?"

The pain in his eyes was still there and it unnerved me.

"Yeah, Xavi, we're okay."

My insides flipped when he called me that. As adults, he rarely referred to me as Xavi, but when we'd been kids, it's the only name he used. I missed those days even though they were hell. There weren't these complications between the four of us brought on by the presence of one girl.

There were so many things on the tip of my tongue, but I knew I had to watch Ash today which made me hold back my words.

234

"Good."

He gave me a tense smile before he walked out, leaving me alone with the girl who'd turned my world inside out. I trudged back over to the breakfast bar and started cleaning up everything. Ash slipped off her stool and silently helped me with it. When the dishwasher was full and turned on, I walked out and upstairs, assuming she was following. I sat down at my desk in my bedroom and turned my laptop on. I heard Ash behind me, her breathing uneven, but I ignored it. I tried to convince myself I didn't care if she was confused by my behaviour.

"Are you upset with me?"

My heart sank.

"No," I grunted.

The moment her hand landed on my shoulder I flinched and shifted away as if her touch burnt me. And really, it had. I wanted her with an intensity which threatened to consume me. After our conversation yesterday, I thought we'd grown closer, but her behaviour towards Quinn this morning said otherwise. She'd decided he was the more worthy option and that was that. Quinn didn't fucking well deserve her.

"Xav…"

"Don't, Ash, just don't."

She retracted her hand and I could feel the confusion and hurt radiating off her in waves. I rubbed my face, wishing everything was different. Wishing I didn't feel this way towards her. Wishing I could just get over it. But I couldn't because I fucking well cared. And caring had only ever left me with devastation and regrets.

"You are mad at me."

Her statement rocked through me. I span around in my chair and faced her. Those blue eyes were full of hurt and it killed me.

"What do you expect? I was fucking worried about you. He came in and dragged you away like a ragdoll, you didn't even come down last night and this morning you're acting like everything is fine. So tell me, Ash, what the fuck else did you expect?"

She flinched back, her hands curling around her waist as if my words physically pained her. I shouldn't have spoken to her like that but my hold on my temper was fraying at the seams. I no longer had it in me to pretend for her sake.

I looked over at the door, realising it was wide open and almost cursing. No one else needed to hear this. Ash's eyes followed mine. The next moment, she walked over to it and shut it firmly before turning back to face me again.

"Do you think this is easy for me?" Her voice shook on the words. "Do you think any of this is easy?" She waved her hand around the room. "Because it isn't. None of it. None of what I'm feeling inside is easy." Pressing her hand to her chest, she took a step towards me. "Xav… I like you, but I can't do anything about it. I don't want to cause problems between the four of you."

She liked me. What did that even mean?

"What are you saying?"

Her body shook and her hand went to her mouth.

"I can't."

"No, you don't get to say that and then take it back, angel. What do you mean?"

She shook her head. I got up and went over to her, resting my hands on her shoulders. She looked so small, staring up at me with abject misery on her face.

"Ash... please, what is going on? What happened last night? What aren't you saying?"

She dropped her hand from her mouth and her shoulders deflated.

"Quinn would lose his shit if he knew. I don't want that. You don't understand. I can't act on any of these feelings."

"What feelings? You're not making any sense."

Reaching out, she put her hand on my chest, right where my heart was thumping. Her touch made my skin prickle all over.

"This, Xav, this right here." She took one of my hands and placed it on her breastbone right where her heart was pounding too. "This happens whenever I'm near one of you. Not just Quinn, but you, Rory and Eric. I don't understand it nor can I help it. All I know is how it feels. How I yearn for something more than friends with all of you."

Her words were the very last ones I expected to hear out of her mouth. She wanted all of us. Not just Quinn, not just me but all of us.

She dropped her hand from my chest and took a step back. My hands fell and I had no clue what to say to her. No clue she felt that way.

"I can't explore that possibility. I can't ask any of you to be okay with it. And I won't do that to Quinn when it's clear he would never entertain the idea. He's not perfect, I know that, but I still want him. That hasn't changed even though he dragged me away yesterday. I told him how I felt about him...

how I wanted more and I think he heard me. I think he listened. So whatever I feel, whatever else I want, it doesn't matter. Besides, you guys might think I'm attractive, but that's as far as it goes."

Ash was fucking blind if she didn't see how much me, Rory and, I was beginning to see, Eric, liked her. Wanted her. But I understood her concerns about Quinn. I understood because he'd gone fucking mental over the thought of the rest of us getting close to her. Taking what he saw as his.

I suddenly needed to be away from her because the fact she'd admitted she wanted me made it infinitely harder not to reach out, pull her to me and kiss her senseless. I paced back to my chair and sat down, tapping my fingers on the arm and wondering how on earth to approach the rest of this conversation. And instead of seriously considering my words, I blurted out the first thing which came to mind.

"The truth is I'd share you with all of them, angel."

Ash's eyes widened at my admission.

"What?"

"You have no idea how incredible you are, do you? You light up every room with your very presence and every time I see you, I'm reminded of just how beautiful and radiant you are. An angel sent to fucking save us from this misery and shit we've been living our entire lives. I've never had an issue with sharing and if that's how it had to be so I could touch you in all the ways I've imagined, then so fucking be it. I'd give anything just to feel your lips against mine."

She stood there for a long moment before she stepped towards me.

"You mean that?" she whispered.

"I wouldn't say it if I didn't."

"You know I can't, Xav. Can you imagine what Quinn would do?"

"I don't have to imagine. He'd kick the shit out of me, plain and simple. Well, he could try. I have about fifty pounds on him." I flexed my arms. "Though Quinn is tough as nails so I doubt either of us would go down easily."

She shook her head.

"I don't want that. Coming between any of you is the very last thing I want. I mean, fuck, I don't even know why I want more than one of you in the first place. I've never had these sorts of urges before. It's not normal, is it?"

I smiled.

"Nothing about this shit is normal, angel. It doesn't matter. You do what's right for you, fuck the rest of the world and their opinions on what's normal."

She fidgeted, hopping from one foot to the other, her hands clenching and unclenching at her sides. I put a hand out to her.

"Come here."

Her feet carried her over even if she looked sceptical. I grabbed her hand when she neared me and tugged her into the chair. Her knees were either side of mine and her hands rested on my chest to steady herself.

"Xav…"

"Shh, I won't do anything… What happened between you and Quinn yesterday?"

She looked away, her cheeks flushing.

"I just want to know if everything is okay between you, that's all."

Ash took a breath, her hands trembling against my chest.

"We argued. I told him he didn't get to dictate whether or not I was friends with you guys, which I'm still adamant about. I accused him of not caring, but he assured me he did. He was so… tender with me after I started crying."

My heart tightened at the thought of tears in her eyes.

"And I wanted to convince him he had nothing to worry about. That I was only intimate with him so I let him, uh, punish me and then we… well… you know. And after that, we talked until I fell asleep. He woke me up to eat, then we hid under the covers together and I told him about my childhood a little. I guess we managed to sleep late this morning."

I didn't know why I wanted to hear more details, but I did. I wanted to know everything because if I wasn't going to get to touch her, then I just needed something more.

"Punish you how, angel?"

Her face went redder and her neck flushed. She looked away. I reached up and gripped her chin, making her face me again.

"Tell me."

"You surely don't want to hear about that."

"You forget I watched him punish you. I saw how much it turned you on."

"Xav…"

"You don't have to be embarrassed with me, angel. Seeing you like that… fuck, it was hot."

She shifted in my lap, almost making me groan because her proximity had made my cock rock hard. She wasn't quite resting on it so she had no idea, but fuck did I want to press her down so I could feel her.

"Okay," she whispered. "But I can't look at you when I say it."

I released her chin and she leant towards me, skimming past my face. Her breath dusted across my ear as her hands moved up to my shoulders.

"I lay across his lap naked. He didn't need to hold me down this time. I wanted it. There's something about the pain which brings me pleasure."

I curled my hands around her hips, my thumb brushing over her stomach which made her breath hitch.

"Each time his palm met my skin, it was like fire flooding my behind, but in a good way. It makes me…"

"Makes you what, angel?" My voice was gruff and low.

"Wet. So wet. And I ache to be… fucked."

I stifled a groan at her words. My cock throbbed. Shit, I wanted to fuck her so much. Bury my cock deep inside her wet little pussy and know exactly what it was like to have her lose control.

"I couldn't help but rub myself all over him, wanting so much more."

"Was he hard for you?"

"Yes, so hard. Like he was desperate to be nestled inside me."

"Fuck, Ash."

Her fingers on my shoulders tightened and she shifted in my lap as if talking about this was turning her on too.

"When he was done, I needed more, but Quinn had ideas of his own."

My fingers dug into her sides because I was holding back from doing anything further.

"What did he want, angel?"

"I can't…"

"You can. Tell me… tell me what he did to you."

She let out a long breath, her mouth moving closer and brushing across my ear.

"He touched my… Oh god, he touched my…"

I sucked in a breath.

"He touched my other hole."

This time I couldn't stifle a groan. This was so fucking hot and only made the fire inside me burn hotter.

"No one has ever touched me there before," she confessed. "But I liked it… well, I liked it until he stuffed a plug inside me without warning after he fingered me."

"Did you ask him to stop?"

I hoped she fucking hadn't. God, I wanted to know what it felt like to be nestled inside her tight little arse as well as her pussy. The fact that Quinn had got her to allow him to made me covet this girl even more.

"No… He said I wasn't ready to have him fuck me there yet… it didn't stop him wanting to fuck me whilst I had it inside me though. I didn't think I could take it, but he made me sit on his cock." I could feel her trembling in my hands. "It stretched me so much but not in a bad way. He knew I could do it even if I didn't. Then he made me fuck him, told me he wanted to see me take my pleasure from him. So I did. I rode his cock hard because it felt so good."

I groaned again, my thumb stroking her harder. God, I was almost at breaking point. My cock pressed against my jeans, making it almost impossible to think about anything else. It ached in a way it never had before.

"Did you come?"

"Yes," she hissed, shifting in my lap again. "I made him touch me and when I came, it was ecstasy. The intensity was unlike anything else. I forgot about everything for those few seconds."

I released her only to grab one of her hands off my shoulder and shove it in between us. I let it hover over my cock, testing her.

"I want you, angel. I want you so fucking much."

"I can't," she whimpered. "Fuck knows I want to, but I can't… I shouldn't have even told you any of this. Fuck… fuck… I want you too."

"Did he come?"

"Xav…"

I shoved her hand against her pussy and she moaned.

"Tell me."

"He flipped me on my back, fucked me without mercy and then he came."

I rubbed her hand against pussy, knowing this was entirely playing with fire, but we'd been doing that since the moment I'd tugged her in my lap. Not even Rory's words about the consequences of taking Ash to my bed pierced through my lust-filled haze. Quinn would well and truly fucking kill me and punish Ash severely, but none of that mattered. Not when having her would be worth it all.

"Here's what's going to happen, angel. I'm going to put you on my bed and you're going to touch yourself whilst I go into my bathroom and do the same. Fuck knows we need to because you're right, if I touch you and you touch me, Quinn won't forgive us."

She shuddered and let out another breath.

"Okay."

"I'm going to think about you making yourself come on my sheets when I lay in bed tonight. I'll fist my cock and beat one out to your voice telling me exactly what Quinn did to you last night. I don't want anyone else but you, angel. No one else gets my cock so hard. Even your voice makes me twitch."

Her grip on me tightened.

"This isn't fair," she whispered. "How can I go back to him when I'm going to be thinking of you doing that?"

A part of me felt smug satisfaction I could affect her in this way.

"I want you to think about me. I want you to crave it, Ash. To know what it'd be like to have me between your legs."

"Xav," she whimpered.

If I didn't put her on my bed and walk away right now, I might never do it. Not when her voice sounded so needy with my fucking name on her lips. So I did just that, I got up with her in my arms placed her on the bed and walked away, unable to look back because I knew if I did, I would be fucked. I locked myself in my bathroom, leaning against the door and breathing in and out. What I'd done and what Ash had admitted had irrevocably changed everything.

There was no fucking way I could stay away from her now.

And if it ruined my friendship with Quinn...

So fucking be it.

CHAPTER THIRTY TWO

Ash

As I huddled under the covers in Quinn's bed, unsure of when he'd arrive back after he'd locked me in here, I remembered how I'd wantonly writhed on Xav's bed with my hand down my knickers knowing full well only a wall separated me and him. What the fuck had gotten into me? Only last night I'd been assuring Quinn I only wanted him and then today I'm readily admitting to Xav I'd quite happily open my legs for all four of them if they were on board with sharing me.

I groaned, digging my palms into my eyes. The thought of Quinn coming up here and wanting sex made me tense. All I'd be thinking about whilst he touched me was Xav. What his hands felt like. What would his kisses ignite in me? How would he pleasure me? And all of those thoughts whilst I was with Quinn would be very unwelcome. Not least because I still craved Quinn's touch like nothing else.

When Xav had come out of his bathroom with a cheeky glint in his eyes, I'd almost hidden under his covers, cheeks flaming with embarrassment. I'd been unable to hold back from crying out when I came. I knew he'd been listening since I heard him grunting through the door too. Neither of us had mentioned what had just occurred or brought up what I'd admitted again but the tension in the air was thick with desire for the rest of the day. And I just about managed to compose myself when we went down for dinner in the evening.

I had no idea if Quinn noticed me acting strangely or not. He hadn't talked much. In fact, he'd pretty much just wolfed down his meal and gone back to his office so I'd spent the evening in front of the TV with the other boys watching a film. He'd come to collect me an hour ago, telling me he'd be up late after kissing me on the forehead. Something was clearly distracting him and I was sure he wouldn't tell me if I asked.

I rolled on my back and stared up at the ceiling, not wanting to be here at all. My mind kept wandering back to Xav. Was he doing what he'd told me he would right now? Was he thinking about me too? Did he mean it when he said he'd share me? He had mentioned having threesomes before so maybe it wasn't as big of a deal to him as it was to Quinn. It wasn't just about the sex side of things although I really wanted to explore that. I genuinely liked Xav, at least what I knew of him. He listened and wanted to know me. And he'd tried his best to protect me from Quinn although honestly, I didn't need protecting. Quinn might be able to overpower me physically, but I gave him as good as I got.

That was the other thing. Quinn might make me feel so small in comparison to him, but with Xav, I felt tiny. Wrapped up in his arms, his huge hands cradling me close, I felt safe for the first time in my life. Like he'd walk through fire just to keep me whole and unharmed. Stupid to think that of someone who'd stolen me from my life, but I couldn't exactly see him that way any longer. Quinn was the mastermind behind this even if the others had gone along with it. I placed most of the blame for my predicament on him which was crazy considering I was sleeping with him.

The sound of the lock turning in the door and it opening startled me from my thoughts. Not daring to peek out of the covers, I curled up on my side and listened to Quinn move about the room. He disappeared into the bathroom for a time before coming back out and slipping into bed next to me. I felt his warmth before his touch. He curled himself around my back with his arm slung over my side. I almost tensed but he made no move to touch me further as his breath tickled the back of my neck.

"I know you're awake, little girl," he whispered.

I shifted, snuggling back against him and threading my fingers through his.

"I couldn't sleep."

As much as thoughts of Xav had permeated my brain, I still wanted this closeness with Quinn. To be held by him and it be more than just him wanting to get into my knickers. This is the part which confused me the most. It wasn't a case of desiring one more than the other. I wanted Quinn equal parts as much as I wanted Xav. Shouldn't I want one more than the other? But Xav had told me nothing about this was normal so

249

I should stop trying to rationalise it and accept it for what it was. I desired a relationship with more than one man. But I couldn't resign myself to it no matter how hard I tried because it simply didn't make enough sense to me.

I'd been taught my whole life that monogamy was the only way. When you come from a family like mine, other views weren't allowed. They were frowned upon. I was brought up to marry a man of my father's choosing because that's just how it is in our world. He'd not stopped me being with Nate, but then again, my father treated me more like his son than he ever did his daughter. So sowing my wild oats? He'd barely bat an eyelid. Me wanting a relationship with two men or, if I was truthful with myself, four of them? Yeah, he'd have real issues with that. Not least because Quinn, Xav, Rory and Eric were not men he'd choose for me. They were Papa's enemies.

"I have to take you out of the house tomorrow evening."

I stiffened.

"Why?"

"We all have to be at the casino and I don't want to leave you here alone."

He could just leave me in the cell. Not like I could escape.

"Casino?"

"Mmm hmm, we own the Syndicate."

The name rang a bell, but I couldn't put my finger on why. Papa had probably mentioned it.

"Oh."

"You know it?"

I shook my head.

"It's the most exclusive casino in London. Only the richest of the rich are granted membership."

"So that's how you lot make your money."

He chuckled, holding me tighter.

"Only one of the ways, little girl."

I wasn't going to ask what else Quinn was involved in. He wouldn't tell me and I wasn't sure I even wanted to know. Growing up in the criminal underworld gives you a rather jaded view of life and humanity. Especially when your own father never shielded you from the worst of the worst. I'd seen men maimed, tortured and even killed at the hands of him and his men. Papa believed in being the harbinger of his own brand of justice. Anyone who betrayed him would be seen to by Frank Russo personally. Something he'd tried to instil in me, but I'd never wanted to learn his lessons. I'd never killed. And that was one of the biggest things which separated me from my father. I still didn't have that black mark on my soul.

Not wanting to think about that shit any further, my mind went back to what happened between me and Xav today. Guilt flooded me. Not because of what I'd done, somehow I didn't regret that. It was being here with Quinn and thinking about another man. I shouldn't feel okay with the whole thing. I felt guilty because I didn't really feel guilty for wanting Xav at all. And that was just plain fucked up.

"I'm tired," I whispered.

"Then go to sleep."

"You don't want to…"

His fingers tightened in mine.

"You asked me to treat you better, little girl. Is this not what you wanted? I'm perfectly content to hold you like this and it be nothing more."

I relaxed fully against him, all the tension leaving my body. I honestly had expected him to want sex since he'd been very adamant about it before. Maybe our argument yesterday was a turning point. He'd not tried to fuck me this morning although he had kissed me thoroughly, making my toes curl.

"Can I still have a kiss goodnight?"

He let go of my hand and used his to turn my face towards him. In the low light, his dark eyes glittered with amusement.

"Only if you ask nicely."

"Please can I have a kiss… sir?"

He leant towards me and captured my lips in a searing kiss which left my limbs jellified. When he pulled away, the gleam in his eyes made me shiver. He knew the effect he had on me and it pleased him no end.

"Sleep, little girl. I can wait until morning to take my fill of you."

I burrowed deeper into his embrace and settled down. Whilst my body felt warm all over from his touch, my eyelids were growing heavy. Today had proved well and truly mentally exhausting for me. Despite wanting to be here next to Quinn, I still wondered what it would be like to drift off in a different pair of arms. Much bigger arms covered in intricate ink. And whether I would feel just as content with him as I did with Quinn.

CHAPTER THIRTY THREE

Eric

The four of us stood at the bottom of the stairs by the front door. Quinn was on his phone, Xav was leaning up against the wall drumming his fingers on it and Rory was staring at the door like it would physically harm him. I was closest to the stairs so noticed Ash coming down first. The sight of her took my breath away. I knew this girl was attractive, but something about the cut of the dress she had on made my skin prickle with awareness. It clung to her small but shapely frame in all the right places, the red fabric fitting tight across her bust. Her black heels peeped out through the slit in her dress rising to mid-thigh. Her blonde hair was curled, pinned and draped down one shoulder. Her face was mostly free of make-up, showing off her youthful glow. In essence, Ash was stunning.

She saw me watching her descend the stairs and gave me a smile which lit up all of her features. I had a hard time keeping a straight face when she stopped next to me. Quinn glanced up from his phone, gave her the once over before nodding and turning towards the front door. Xav pushed off the wall, gave Ash a wink and followed Quinn out. Rory just looked uncomfortable. He hated wearing a suit and being out of the house so this trip didn't sit well with him. And judging by the way his eyes glided over Ash, her appearance wasn't helping either. He walked out too, not saying a word, but no one expected him to.

Ash looked up at me as I put my arm out to her. None of the others had decided to be a gentleman, so it was down to me. Again.

"You look handsome this evening, not that you don't normally, but I like your suit," she said quietly as I led her out of the front door.

I almost stopped dead, startled at her words. I looked down at myself. We were all dressed up for this evening. I had a navy suit on with a matching waistcoat, dark brown shoes and a dark green tie. Turning, I shut the door, making sure to lock it, thoroughly unsettled by her complimenting me, but not wishing to make Ash feel uncomfortable either.

"Thank you, Ash. I know those jokers haven't said it, but you look beautiful."

Ash flushed and fidgeted before I took her hand again and led her down the steps to the car.

"Thanks. I didn't know if this was appropriate or not."

"More than appropriate. It's perfect."

We stopped by the open car door where Rory was waiting to let Ash sit in the middle. She stared up at me.

"I meant it, you know… green suits you."

She dusted a piece of lint off my lapel before letting go of my arm and climbing in, leaving me staring after her. Rory quirked an eyebrow but said nothing before he got in and shut the door. I shook myself and opened the driver's door, wondering what the fuck just happened.

Xav was in the front seat, staring out of the window. Normally Quinn sat there, but it seemed he wanted to be in the back with Ash this evening. I glanced in the rearview mirror. Ash was right up against Quinn, his hand resting on her knee in what could only be described as a possessive gesture. Rory didn't look exactly comfortable being next to her, but I was pretty sure it had more to do with his aversion to any sort of human contact than anything else.

I started the car and pulled away, wondering what the fuck we were even doing bringing her to our casino. Quinn wouldn't want her on the floor considering the world knew *Il Diavolo* had her rather than us. Not many people knew Quinn and *Il Diavolo* were the same man. Any who did, let's just say they weren't breathing for much longer. Snitches weren't welcome in our world. That was how Quinn had earnt his reputation in the first place. Despatching our enemies with ruthless efficiency and leaving only whispers of his name in his wake.

Usually, I'd have strongly objected to bringing a woman into all of this, but Ash had come from our world. She'd grown up in it. Heir to her father's criminal empire and the Russo family. We had a queen in waiting in our midst, except Quinn didn't intend to allow Ash to wear the crown. He wanted to erode Russo's power base piece by piece until there was nothing left but ashes and dust for the girl at his side to rule over.

What he hadn't accounted for was his own reaction to Ash. His need for her which we could all see as clear as day from the moment we brought her here. She'd thrown us all for a loop and now Quinn was trying to regain control. To stick to the plan. Which is why we all knew if Ash witnessed what happened next, it would devastate her. Rory, Xav and I all agreed we didn't want her here, but Quinn insisted. Things were the way they'd always been. What Quinn said goes.

The journey to the Syndicate was silent and by the time I pulled up in the back alley, you could cut the tension in the car with a knife. Quinn had likely not told Ash a thing about why we were coming here. I turned off the engine and we all got out. Quinn didn't bother taking Ash's hand, striding towards the back door and keying in the code.

I sighed, watching the other two follow him. It was down to me to act like the gentlemen yet again. I stepped up to Ash and took her hand, placing it in the crook of my elbow and leading her towards where Xav was holding the door for us. His gaze heated as he looked Ash over. Glancing at her, I saw a similar look in her eyes which made me suspicious about what occurred between them yesterday. Xav had been acting strangely in the morning and whilst I'd told him we were cool, we weren't. I still hated the way he looked at her. Hated how it made me feel. And most of all I hated that perhaps Ash felt the same way about him as he did her. Because whilst I wanted Xav, I also wanted Ash to look at me like that too. Fucked up as all of that was. It's why her compliment earlier threw me off balance. Ash had looked at me like a man and not the person who was complicit in holding her captive.

"Do you always come here around the back?" she asked.

"Quinn doesn't like to draw attention. The members might know we own the casino, but we mostly prefer to stay out of the day to day running of things."

I nodded at Xav as we went in and drew her towards where the lift to the top floor was waiting with Rory and Quinn inside. Silence descended over us as we rode up together. Ash was tense next to me. I could tell she wanted to ask me further questions, but there were only certain things I could even tell her about our operations here.

The Syndicate was our baby. We'd opened the place after our online gambling site had taken off in a big way. We catered to the rich and powerful wanting somewhere to relax and gamble in peace away from the public eye. The amount of money which changed hands in this building would be eye-watering to some. We ran a completely legal operation here unlike some of the other ventures we had a hand in.

We all stepped out when the lift doors opened and Quinn led us along to the big office at the end of the corridor. It had huge windows with views of the city skyline. On one of the walls was a bank of monitors which had angles on most of the casino floor as well as the private rooms. The desk sat in the middle of the room, dominating the space with an imposing black and chrome finish.

I led Ash over to it and made her sit down behind it since all of us bar Rory would be busy. He always stayed in the office when we came here since he outright refused to be on the floor with people milling around everywhere. He said the atmosphere of the over-privileged elite suffocated him. Honestly, I hated rich pricks too, but it didn't bother me in the same way.

She put a hand on my arm when I tried to walk away as if scared to be left alone in here.

"Will you be back?" she whispered.

I stared down at her, wondering why she sought reassurance from me rather than Quinn. Then again, Quinn had practically ignored her the whole way here other than to mark his territory and he certainly wasn't looking at her now.

"Rory's staying with you."

She glanced at him before turning her gaze back to me, her blue eyes almost pleading.

"Why am I here?"

I leant down towards her, putting a hand on hers.

"Quinn didn't want you to be alone at home. It's okay, Ash. Nothing is going to happen to you."

I felt sick telling her that considering it wasn't entirely the truth but needing her to let me go so I could get on with things. As much as I wanted to calm her down, we weren't here for pleasure. Business took precedent. And Ash was collateral damage in this war. Not that I wanted her to be, but facts were facts. We had to stay the course and that meant hurting her in the process as much as that didn't sit comfortably with me at all.

"Okay."

I could tell by her tone she didn't believe me, but there wasn't much else I could do. I patted her hand and straightened. She let me go, staring down at the desk. I glanced at Quinn as I walked away, but he hadn't been paying any attention to our exchange. His eyes were on the monitors.

"It's time," he said with a grim smile.

Xav shoved off the wall he was leaning against and disappeared out of the door. We all had our parts to play this evening.

"Shall we?"

Quinn nodded once then walked over to Ash, leaning down to place a kiss on her forehead.

"Be good for Rory, little girl."

Before she had a chance to reply, he strode out of the room. I looked over at Rory who was watching the monitors closely next to me.

"Look after her," I told him in a low voice.

His hazel eyes met mine. There was no need for words, Rory would make sure Ash was okay and stayed in here whilst we dealt with everything else. I hoped she didn't see what was about to go down but knowing there would be no hiding it.

I glanced at her before I slipped out of the room. Her blue eyes had clouded over and there was an atmosphere of dread surrounding her. Ash knew something was wrong. The aftermath resulting from this evening wouldn't be pretty.

I just hoped Quinn knew what he was doing and what he stood to lose when things came crashing down around her.

CHAPTER THIRTY FOUR

RORY

I could feel Ash's eyes boring into the back of my head, but I didn't turn around to look at her. Instead, I watched Xav walk across the main floor of the casino. I didn't want to be here anymore than Ash probably did. It was worse for me as I knew what would happen. And making sure she didn't run out of the room the instant she realised, well, I wasn't looking forward to that at all.

We had security who also monitored the floor, but Quinn didn't trust anyone else watching over him, Eric and Xav. That's why I was here. To make sure if anything went wrong, we could get out of it unscathed.

I felt her before I even looked to my left. She'd left ample space between us, but I was always aware of where she was in relation to me. Something I could neither deny nor hide. Ash affected me in ways I never imagined another person could.

She stared at the monitors, her eyes darting to each one in turn.

"What's going on?"

I'd known the question was coming before she even asked it. Ash's innate curiosity would get the better of her if she wasn't careful.

"Nothing you need to worry about."

The lie stuck in my throat.

Ash didn't look at me. Her eyes were firmly stuck on one of the monitors which displayed Xav sitting at a blackjack table whilst the dealer dealt him in.

"Does he liked to gamble?"

"Xav? No, he hates it."

"Then why is he?"

I almost sighed. Quinn told us all not to explain things to her, but I found myself wanting to so she wouldn't get the shock of her life.

"He's not there to gamble, Ash, he's watching the floor."

She glanced at me then, her crystal blue eyes wide.

"So it's a ruse. Does the dealer know?"

I almost smiled.

"They all know who we are."

She bit her lip.

"You talk to me more than you do anyone else."

I stared at her then. Whilst I talked to Quinn a lot, she rarely saw that. In many ways, Ash was right though. I didn't like talking to other people, but I didn't mind so much with her. In fact, I almost wanted to talk to her so she could know me like she wanted.

"I mean I know you and Quinn are close, but you don't talk to Eric and Xav as much."

"Xav's childish and Eric's too preachy about right and wrong."

I smiled to let her know I was joking. She grinned back.

"I bet they'd give you shit if they knew you thought that about them."

I shrugged.

"Xav's proud of it and Eric thinks I'm being deliberately obtuse when I don't listen to him lecturing all of us."

"How long have you known each other?"

I shifted on my feet, looking back up at the monitors.

"I've known Quinn practically all my life. Been twenty-two years or so for Eric and Xav."

I felt her take a step closer to me rather than saw it.

"How old are you?"

"Quinn didn't tell you?"

"No, he doesn't tell me very much at all."

It hardly surprised me since Quinn was determined to keep her at arm's length whilst still getting between her legs. His reasoning was all kinds of fucked up, but I respected it. Respected his boundaries because this was Quinn. The one person who I'd walk through fucking fire for.

"He's thirty, Xav and Eric are twenty-nine and I'm twenty-seven."

"I knew you were the baby."

I glanced at her again.

"You did?"

She nodded, biting her lip.

"You look like the youngest, the dimples give it away."

I frowned.

"What?"

"When you smile, you get dimples in your cheeks… that's why I said you look cute when you're smiling and why I think you should do it more often. Not that you aren't cute when you're not smiling or anything, it's just more pronounced then."

Her crystal blue eyes glittered as she spoke, her lips tugged upwards. It had me leaning closer to her.

"If you really knew me, you wouldn't describe me as cute, Ash."

She shrugged and smiled wider.

"Can't stop me, it's a free country, but don't worry, you still retain your dark and twisty crown underneath the attractive outer package."

She waved a hand at me. Her words made my chest tighten.

"What makes you think I'm dark and twisty?"

"I see it behind your eyes and you said you don't like to feel. I grew up surrounded by monsters, Rory. I'm not blind to men who've witnessed things they shouldn't have and even less so to children. Whatever happened to you… it marked you permanently. And I think you're loyal to Quinn because he saved you from it. That's why all of you follow him."

It was as if I'd been sucker-punched to the gut. Ash saw right through me and it unnerved me to a point I had to step away from her. My skin prickled all over with awareness. No one had ever looked at me the way she did. No one had ever wanted to see past the façade I put up. No one until her.

If my retreat bothered her, she didn't show it. Ash peered up at me with understanding written all over her features. This girl really was something else.

I wasn't meant to be having this kind of discourse with her right now. My focus should be on what the others were doing.

I stared up at the monitors, unsure of how to answer Ash at all. That's when I heard a squeak of surprise next to me.

"What the fuck? Why is he here?"

My eyes followed hers, finding her attention on a monitor showing a tallish man with blonde hair styled in a quiff striding through the main gambling room. My stomach sank all the way to my feet. There was no hiding this now. Not when he crossed the room and was nodded on through into the VIP area. And definitely not when Quinn met him in the lobby with Eric behind him. Nate and Quinn shook hands as if they were business partners. And I suppose in many ways they were.

Ash's face went deathly pale and her fists clenched at her sides.

"Rory, why is Nate here?"

"Ash…"

She turned to me, confusion and anger flooding her features.

"Why. Is. He. Here?"

"I can't tell you."

The truth of the matter was I couldn't. We'd all promised Quinn. If she wanted to know, she'd have to ask him.

Her expression darkened further.

"He told you not to, didn't he?" She raised a clenched fist and lowered it again. "I'm so stupid. I should've never trusted a word he said. Never." Her blue eyes burned with hatred. "Is this why I'm here? So I can bear witness to even more of his lies? Does Quinn have any idea how much Nate devastated me when he broke it off? I thought we were going to get engaged. I thought he was who Papa had chosen for me, but no, he was just using me." And as if I thought it couldn't get any worse, Ash looked up at me with no small amount of disgust. "Tell me why he's here. Tell me what the fuck Quinn is doing with him."

I shook my head, taking a step back and putting my hands up.

"I'm sorry, Ash. I can't."

"You're sorry? You're fucking well covering for him."

Her eyes flashed with hatred directed solely at me and it just about killed me. No matter how much I cared about Ash, I'd never betray Quinn. It didn't matter if I didn't agree with his methods, he deserved my loyalty. He'd earnt it over and over again.

"If you're not going to fucking well tell me, then I'll ask him myself."

She started to walk towards the door. The instinct to protect my best friend flared within me. I reached out, grabbing her by the arm and stopping her in her tracks. Ash sucked in a breath at the same time I did. The air around us crackled. Her skin burnt into mine, making me feel ten times hotter than I had done before. And my need for her intensified. The need to have her pinned down and taught exactly how dark and fucked up I was inside. The need for her to know what kind of beast she'd awoken inside me and I'd had trouble leashing again.

She turned and looked down at where I held her, a mixture of confusion and anger flittering across her face.

"Let me go."

As much as this killed me, I couldn't do as she asked. As much as touching her went against all my instincts and was disconcerting as fuck, I couldn't allow her to leave this room.

"No, little star. I can't let you go. You have to stay right here."

Ash's mouth fell open and I realised what I'd said. What I'd called her.

"What did you just call me?" she whispered.

I clamped my mouth shut. No way in hell could I say that again. She couldn't know how I felt about her. How I saw her. My little star shining so brightly she almost blinded me with her beauty on the inside and out.

She didn't even attempt to tug her arm out of my grasp, just stared at me with conflicting emotions flittering across her features.

"Rory…" My heart squeezed painfully at the way she said my name. "Why did you call me that? What aren't you telling me? What's going on?"

CHAPTER THIRTY FIVE

Quinn

I had to hold back from ripping this cunt a new one. He'd spent two years with *my* little girl. Whilst I hadn't known back then just how important Ash would be, it didn't lessen my need to end him. Except that wouldn't do. Not when I still had need of him.

"Is he on his way?" I asked with narrowed eyes after I shook the cunt's hand.

"He'll arrive shortly. The promise of distraction and new contacts proved too alluring."

"Good."

"He's not happy."

"Why would he be? His most prized possession has disappeared."

Nate shrugged. I gritted my teeth.

"You call her a possession. She's still a human being, Knox."

So, maybe he did care about the girl he'd spent two years with. Not wanting to show my hand, I rolled my eyes. Better he thought I didn't care than reveal the truth.

"He doesn't seem to think so."

"You know as well as I all he cares about is power and how he can use his assets. If it hadn't made him look weak for being unable to protect his own, he wouldn't care if she was dead or alive. She may be his heir, but make no mistake, he will cut her loose if she threatens his position."

As much as I despised the man in front of me, he knew what he was talking about. He'd spent two years getting close to the one person I wanted to destroy.

I gave him one sharp nod before I stepped away and turned to Eric. He'd be overseeing the game tonight whilst I played. Attending her father's party the night we took Ash was a risk, but a calculated one. Tonight was another.

"Keep an eye on him," I said, keeping my voice low.

Eric nodded, his expression neutral. He didn't like this any more than I did. I sat down on one of the large sofas dotted around the room, laying my arm across the back of it. One of the waitresses came over and handed me a tumbler filled with whisky. I nodded my thanks.

Nate might suspect I had Ash, but he didn't know for sure, nor would I enlighten him. He was merely an asset in my arsenal. I didn't trust him nor did he trust me. Probably wise since I had no qualms about throwing whoever I needed to under the bus. That was the way of this world. Learn to survive or you wouldn't live to see the next day. It had always been kill or be killed. I preferred to stay alive. Only three people had my utmost trust and that wouldn't change any time soon.

My skin prickled with awareness the moment they walked in. Flanked by two well-built men, the king and his queen stood side by side. Frank looked relaxed although his eyes said he was anything but. His dark grey suit was pristine. He wore no tie, preferring to have his shirt collar open. Beside him was Isabella. Her purple chiffon dress clung to her shapely figure and fell to her knees reminding me of her daughter, but her eyes were cold and calculating, the complete opposite of the open honesty of Ash's crystalline baby blues. It made my chest tighten because I knew she'd be witness to this and my emotions towards my little girl were so conflicted, I barely recognised myself any longer.

The two men with the Russos wouldn't be the only ones, hence why I'd stationed Xav on the floor. He needed to keep an eye on the rest. And Rory would oversee us all. At least that was the plan. He also needed to watch Ash and make sure she didn't disrupt the evening. I didn't exactly trust her not to get riled up by everything. I had little choice but to bring her. She wouldn't be safe where we couldn't keep an eye on her and no one would be getting their hands on my little girl.

Nate spoke in low tones to Russo before leading them over to a set of comfortable chairs nearby. I watched them in the periphery of my vision, not wanting to draw attention to myself. Other members of various crime families filtered into the room, each served drinks by our staff. None of them approached me, which I was grateful for. The final participant was Colm Moran. He tipped his head at me as he strolled in with his two men.

The Syndicate was neutral ground, but none of the families would attend anywhere without protection. They were right to be worried. Some of them might not walk away from this game unscathed.

Eric clapped his hands together and announced it was time. Everyone began to file into the room, leaving their bodyguards to keep watch outside. I hung back with Eric, feeling my skin crawling at the sight of all these men and women I despised. They were drenched in dirty money. Their fancy outfits were bought with blood and exploitation.

"Stop looking like you want to kill everyone," Eric hissed.

I modified my expression.

"But I do."

I watched his lip quirk up for a few seconds before falling again.

"This is going to go very wrong, you know that, right?"

"I'm counting on it."

He gave me a sharp nod before I walked into the high-stakes poker room knowing everything was about to implode and feeling rather fucking smug about it.

It wasn't just Russo I wanted dead. It was everyone in that room. However, you couldn't go around knocking off the sons of the mafia kings and crime families without causing an uproar. That was why I was playing this game. You pit them against each other and watch as they squabble before they destroy each other. Those who are left, well I'd pick off the dregs.

I smiled as I took my seat. I'd made the strongest of men look weak by taking his daughter from right under his nose and now it was time to watch the cards fall into place.

CHAPTER THIRTY SIX

RORY

How could I answer her questions? She couldn't find out how I felt about her and I couldn't tell her what Quinn's plans were either. Ash continued to stare at me, her blue eyes wide with confusion. My skin was still burning where I was holding her. Everything about this had me struggling for control. The thing I prided myself on. Restraint and control were the only things which got me through the day. Ash kept bulldozing over all of it again and again, leaving me without a clue of how to protect her from me.

"I can't tell you," I said quietly.

The pain in her eyes almost damn near killed me.

"Was I wrong to think you cared?" she whispered. "Your actions and your words don't add up, Rory. So forgive me if I don't understand what you want from me. Forgive me if I've misread everything because I really did think you might actually care about me."

I almost let her go because her words stung. Of course I fucking well cared about her. That was why I had to stop her running downstairs and getting herself hurt. She didn't understand and I couldn't enlighten her. I'd known Ash for two weeks. That didn't negate a lifetime of friendship with Quinn.

Ash's eyes drifted away from me as something clearly caught her eye. All the blood drained from her face. I turned my head to see what she was looking at. Well, that was just great. I thought her seeing Nate would be bad, but this was worse. Ash looked like she was about to faint.

"Why are my parents here?"

Her eyes met mine again. So much confusion and pain. All of it gutted me.

"Ash…"

"No… he can't have them here. Why? Why is Quinn doing this? I thought he hated them. I thought…" she faltered as she noticed more people appearing in the VIP area. "What… why is Vincenzo here? And is that Mr Bykov? Rory, what the fuck is going on? Why would Quinn invite the fucking Mafia and Bratva here? Is he crazy?"

Vincenzo Villetti was the son of a prominent member of the Mafia and Gregor Bykov was the older brother of the Russian mogul, Viktor. Both had ties to the Russian Bratva. Of course, Ash would know who they were. She was her father's heir after all.

"Quinn knows what he's doing."

"Does he? Papa hates Mr Bykov. Did Quinn consider what kind of animosity he'd ignite by bringing them all together?"

"The Syndicate is neutral ground."

She threw up her free hand.

276

"Don't you tell me it's just a game. Nothing is just a game. This is Quinn's idea of pitting everyone against each other, isn't it? I'm not stupid, Rory."

I tried not to flinch. Quinn didn't realise just how smart Ash was. She saw past all the bullshit and went straight to the heart of things. Quinn was going to be in for an earful by the end of tonight. Ash looked riled up and ready to explode.

"You're not going to talk, are you? See, I was right, you don't care."

I stared at her. Maybe it would be better if she thought I didn't care. Maybe it would make this thing between us go away because fuck knows I needed it to. She was Quinn's and I couldn't have her.

Ash tried to pull herself out of my grasp but I held on tighter. I couldn't keep this up. If I didn't find a way to restrain her, I would do something I regretted. Her skin against mine tortured me. I wanted her and the urges inside me were rattling against their chains.

I tugged her away from the door. Ash tried to dig her heels in, but I was too strong for her. I brought her back over to the desk chair and pressed her down onto it. She struggled against me, but I held her down with a hand on her shoulder.

"Stay."

"No. Let go of me."

Reaching back, I tugged open one of the drawers and grabbed the set of handcuffs Quinn kept in there. Next thing Ash knew, her wrist was wrapped in metal and the other side attached to the chair. I stepped back. Ash looked down, her eyes wide.

"What the fuck, Rory?"

"I told you, you can't leave. It's not safe for you."

"But my parents are there!"

"And they can't know you're here."

Little star, stop making this harder on both of us.

Every part of me wanted to crawl onto that chair and teach her a fucking lesson, but I wouldn't. Quinn might like to spank girls for defying him, but me? I wouldn't let any of her disobedience go unpunished. She'd learn the true meaning of pain. Then she wouldn't dare do a fucking thing to defy me ever again.

Christ, rein your shit the fuck in, Rory. Now is not the time.

I couldn't think like that. Ash wasn't mine to discipline. And she didn't need me getting those ideas in my head either. I understood why she was upset, but I didn't have it in me to comfort her or give her words of reassurance. I could never give Ash what she truly needed so even if she wasn't Quinn's, I wouldn't be enough for her. I was too broken and damaged inside to have anything real to offer a woman, especially not one like Ash who shone so damn brightly.

"This isn't fair. You can't just handcuff me to a fucking chair."

I didn't answer her, instead, walked away to the monitors again. She could try and escape now, but she wouldn't get very far whilst she was attached to that chair. The game was about to start now everyone had taken their places. It was time.

"Let me go. I need to go to them."

The pleading note in her voice made my chest ache. I didn't turn around.

"Please, I need to see my parents."

278

She might think that, but it wouldn't do her any good. Besides, Russo didn't know Quinn was *Il Diavolo*. Now was not the time to show our hand.

"No, Ash, you're not leaving and if you don't sit there and shut up, you won't like the consequences."

I glanced back at her. Ash's eyes were wide, her expression betraying her shock at my tone. Stern and broking no objections. I didn't usually talk to anyone like that but my patience with her was fraying and I didn't have time to deal with her when I was meant to be watching the others on the monitors. Her head dropped to her chest and a small sound of distress emitted from her lips. I swear my fucking world dropped out from under me in those moments. I'd done that to her. Not even seeing her parents or Nate had made her sound so… broken.

What the fuck did you just do?

I'd shown her a part of me I kept hidden. The part of me which I never allowed out. But Ash dragged it to the forefront with every word she spoke, every moment she was near me.

Her fingers gripped the arms of the chair, going white and her whole body caved in on itself. I wasn't good for Ash. I'd never be good for her. She needed someone else other than me right now. She needed someone who'd take care of her in the ways she needed.

So I pulled out my phone and fired off a single word. I just had to hope I'd made the right decision here because hurting Ash was the very last thing I ever intended to do.

CHAPTER THIRTY SEVEN

Xavier

God, I was fucking bored. Quinn had tasked me with the least interesting job of all. Watching the floor. Nothing was happening and pretending to gamble grated on me. He knew I hated being out here, but I realised the necessity of it all. Russo's men surrounded the tables around me. Quinn knew he'd never attend anywhere with only two personal bodyguards. Russo was nothing if not paranoid and that served him well.

I drummed my fingers on the table, watching the dealer. Tierra knew I wasn't here to play. The staff were well aware of who I was and what to expect when I was on the floor. She was a pretty dark-haired girl who'd made the eyes at me on more than one occasion. She'd probably be a good lay, but I didn't dabble with the staff. You don't shit where you eat. Besides, Quinn would have a fucking field day if he found out. I was already walking on thin ice after what occurred between me and Ash yesterday. Not that he knew about it.

I didn't want the pretty dark-haired Tierra. I wanted the blonde angel who'd taken our lives by storm.

My phone buzzed in my pocket. I tugged it out and looked down at the display before clicking onto the message.

RORY: SOS

What the fuck?

"I need to cash out," I said to Tierra who immediately finished up the hand before dealing me out.

I picked up the chips, stuffing them in my pocket and not giving a shit about the other players as I strode away. Whilst Quinn would be pissed I left my post, Rory sending me an SOS was more pressing. Had everything gone wrong already? Quinn was sure things would end with blood spilt this evening.

I was through the staff door and into the lift to the top floor within minutes, growing ever more agitated. There wasn't any point asking Rory what was wrong. I was sure I'd see soon enough.

I rammed my shoulder through the door to the main office, expecting some kind of madness to have taken place. Instead, I found Rory pacing in front of the monitors with Ash sitting at the desk, her head bowed. As I looked closer, I realised she'd been handcuffed to the chair and her hands were gripping the arms, knuckles completely white.

I approached Rory who stilled when he saw me.

"You want to tell me what's going on?"

"She needs you," he said in hushed tones. "I can't do this, Xav. She needs someone who can hold her and I can't."

I glanced over at Ash again. She seemed almost catatonic. Her eyes were vacant as she stared down at her lap.

"What happened?"

"She got mad when she saw Nate and tried to leave, I had to stop her. She almost lost it when I refused to answer her questions so…" He waved at her. "Then she saw her parents and now I don't know what to do."

I nodded as if I understood, but I really didn't. What the fuck had caused her to shut down?

"Are you sure nothing else happened?"

"I promise."

There were things he wasn't telling me, but knowing Rory, he wouldn't talk about it any further. Clearly, something had gone wrong. I rubbed the back of my neck and wondered what the hell I was meant to do. Ash had told me I made things more bearable for her so maybe I could get her to talk. Maybe I could pull her out of this. I knew why Rory had messaged me. Eric was overseeing the game and Quinn was playing. They couldn't leave or they'd risk everything falling apart.

"Watch them, I'll deal with her."

I didn't wait to get his response. Walking over to the desk, I squatted down next to Ash and put my hand on her knee.

"Angel, can you look at me?" I asked softly.

She didn't immediately respond. I could feel her leg shaking under my touch. Why had seeing them done this to her? Was it because Quinn had been so adamant he hated her family? That wasn't far from the truth, but even he knew he couldn't just walk into Russo's compound all guns blazing. That was a sure-fire way to get yourself killed.

Was it her parents or was it something Rory had done? My money was on the latter. I didn't know why, but something about this whole thing was off.

"I know it's confusing, angel. Your whole life has been turned upside down and it's normal to be overwhelmed, but I need you to look at me."

Her blue eyes raised and met mine. Tears pooled in them and I couldn't help but want to gather her up in my arms and keep her safe.

"Why?" she whispered. "I don't understand."

"I wish I could tell you, angel, but you're going to have to wait until this is over."

Two tears made tracks down her cheeks. I couldn't stand it. Not caring she was still handcuffed to the chair, I reached up and tugged her off it, sitting down with her in my lap. Her arm was stretched up to the chair, but she didn't seem to mind. She wrapped her free hand around my neck and buried her face in it.

"You're okay, angel. I've got you. I promise I'll keep you safe."

I didn't care if I couldn't keep that fucking promise. Ash was all that mattered right then. Making sure she was okay. That she got through this no thanks to fucking Quinn for subjecting her to it. For making it clear we'd been planning this for longer than she could comprehend. A way to bring down her father and his empire. A way to destroy them all.

It hadn't always been this way. We used to only care about dragging ourselves out of the depths of hell we'd been born into. Then everything had changed and Quinn had become so single-minded in his need to end the cycle of corruption, greed and death. If you betrayed any of the families, you would wind up maimed or worse, dead. So we'd been careful in our approach. Quinn might think I didn't understand his methods. I did. I just didn't like all of them.

"Is he going to kill them?"

I stiffened.

"No. Not tonight."

Lord knows I shouldn't fucking tell her that, but I couldn't bring myself to care about what I should and shouldn't do any longer.

"He's still my father."

"I know, angel."

The thing about parents was even when you knew they were evil, corrupt and immoral, you still loved them regardless. I understood Ash's predicament far more than the others because I had the same problem.

Ash clutched me tighter, crying but trying not to make too much noise.

"Is it just your parents and Nate?" I whispered.

She shook her head.

"What else, angel?"

I wasn't sure whether she'd actually tell me or not.

"I can't," she sobbed. "I can't do this anymore."

The pitiful note in her voice broke my heart. I looked up at Rory who was staring at the both of us rather than what was going on in the VIP room. He looked stricken.

"What did you do?" I mouthed at him.

He waved a hand at her helplessly. I didn't know what to think any longer. Everything was a complete and utter mess. I was meant to be downstairs taking care of shit and yet here I was with Ash because Rory had fucked up.

"I've got you. I'm right here, okay? You can do this, angel."

Ash didn't respond, she just held onto me as if I was the only thing keeping her from drowning.

This whole thing is utterly fucked.

I just fucking well hoped Quinn's quest for revenge was worth tearing all of us apart.

CHAPTER THIRTY EIGHT

Eric

I n the moments before you think it's all over, your life really does flash before your eyes. Only mine was seeped in regrets of what could have been if I'd made different choices. I never believed the saying. Never thought it would happen to me. Something about having a gun shoved against your temple makes you question what the fuck you're even doing with your life. Makes you wonder why you've been so scared of admitting the truths you've kept buried for so long. Makes you think about everything and nothing.

The room had gone deadly silent the moment the hulking blonde Russian to my left whipped out a pistol and pressed it to my head.

"Cheat," he ground out in a thick accent which set me on edge. "You let them cheat."

Knowing showing fear would get me killed, I stayed as still as possible. Quinn told us there'd be bloodshed, I just didn't think it'd be my own.

"Gregor," Villetti, the Italian purred. "What is the meaning of this?"

"This man knows his friend cheats."

My eyes fell on Quinn. His jaw ticked with his annoyance and concern, the only outward sign this affected him.

No one was cheating. I'd know. I happened to be the sole dealer and could count cards like nobody's business. That little fact would not be revealed otherwise it would be certain death.

"If you're accusing me of cheating, point the gun in my direction," Quinn said almost casually. "Besides, I've not won a single hand. If I was cheating, surely I'd have more chips in front of me."

He waved a hand at the table before sitting back, his eyes narrowed on the Russian. Gregor didn't lower his gun nor did he turn it on Quinn. He leant forward slightly.

"You are throwing each hand. And the rest, the rest are cheats."

Was he seriously suggesting everyone at this table had cheated their way through this poker tournament? We knew the members of this game would be on high alert considering they were either rivals or enemies, but this wasn't planned for. At least, none of us expected anyone to shove a gun in our faces.

"You fucking accusing us of cheating?" Colm Moran piped up, his eyes almost bulging out of their sockets as he leant forward and slammed his hand down on the table.

Gregor turned on him.

"*Da, irlandtsy.*"

"What the fuck you saying to me?"

Gregor smirked and I swallowed hard.

"Gentlemen," Quinn interrupted before this could take a turn for the worse. "I would remind you this is neutral ground. Spill blood here, you will face the consequences."

Moran glared at the Russian, but sat back, crossing his arms over his chest. Quinn had made his threat very clear. This was our casino. Although it didn't give me a breather, Gregor Bykov still had his fucking gun against my temple.

"Gregor, put the gun down," Villetti said, drumming his fingers on the table.

"I do not take orders from you, little man."

He shoved the gun more firmly against my head. I flinched involuntarily, but I'm not sure he noticed considering his eyes were on Villetti. I wasn't sure if me saying anything would help so I kept my mouth shut. I looked at Quinn again, but his eyes were darting between Gregor and Villetti. At least he didn't have a fucking gun in his face.

I wondered briefly if Rory had seen this and was going to do something about it. He was meant to be watching as after all and he always took his responsibilities seriously. The fact there'd been no immediate response made me suspicious. What was the holdup?

Villetti shook his head, his fingers still drumming and the noise beginning to grate on my ears. How everyone could be so calm was a mystery to me, but then again, all of these men had seen violence in their lives. It marred every single person involved in crime. No one escaped it. No one got out unscathed. That was the way of these things. Coming from a life of poverty, I knew all too well the consequences of living below the breadline and resorting to stealing to survive. Life hadn't been kind to me or my family growing up. The only saving grace was my three friends who kept me sane.

"You are merely losing heavily. Accusing everyone of cheating is being a sore loser. Do you want me to tell your brother you started a war between the families over a poker game on neutral ground?" Quinn said, his dark eyes betraying none of the inner turmoil I knew he was experiencing.

Quinn was loyal to a fault. When one of his own was threatened, he'd walk through fire to save us. He might say Xav had a saviour complex and he really did, but Quinn, whilst smart about it, wouldn't allow anything to happen to the four of us. It didn't, however, fill me with confidence right now.

Gregor's brother, Viktor, wouldn't be impressed with his behaviour. Whilst Gregor was older, Viktor had money and clout within the financial industries and ties to the Russian Bratva, whom his brother was a member of. It didn't matter, Gregor was very much beholden to his younger brother.

"Viktor cares not what I do."

We all knew that was a lie, but no one spoke up. Antagonising the Russian wouldn't be a smart move.

My heart pounded in my ears as sweat beaded around my hairline and at the back of my neck. I trusted Quinn to find a way out of this, but it didn't make it any less disconcerting. And all I could think of was how many regrets I had. How I really wanted to change that. How I wanted to live so fucking badly, it made my chest ache with longing.

If I got out of this, I'd do it. I'd tell him. All these years I'd kept my feelings to myself, but life was short and you never knew when it would be ripped away from you. Now more than ever I was aware of that fact.

Quinn was about to open his mouth again when the door to the room flew open and someone stepped in. They instantly raised their hand and pointed the gun in it towards Gregor Bykov's head.

"Drop your fucking weapon before I blow your brains out across the fucking table," Xavier growled.

CHAPTER THIRTY NINE

Xavier

sh had gone silent, her body relaxing under my touch. I was about to pull her away from my neck so I could look at her when Rory let out a weird choking sound.

"Xav…"

I looked over at him.

"What?"

"You need to come here."

"A little busy."

Partly his fault I was here taking care of our girl in the first fucking place.

Our girl? What the fuck?

"It's E."

Those two words had me stiffening. What did he mean it's Eric? What the fuck was happening to my best friend?

Not wanting to scare Ash, I gently tugged her away from me. Her blue eyes fixed on mine, sadness radiating from her.

I stroked her cheek, wanting her to know she was still important to me but I needed to know what Rory was seeing.

"I need to get up, angel."

She nodded slowly before edging out of my lap. I got up and helped her to her feet, getting my girl seated again. Dropping a kiss to her forehead, I stroked her hair and breathed her in. God, she smelt so fucking good. I pulled away and turned to the monitors. What I saw there made my stomach drop and rage course through my veins simultaneously. The first thing I did was pull open the top drawer of the desk and whip out the gun we kept loaded in there. Next, I stormed over to Rory before taking a closer look at just who had a gun pointed at my best friend's head.

"That Russian bastard."

Rory looked down at my hand then back up at me.

"What are you doing with that?"

I locked eyes with him.

"This?" I shook the gun a little. "Going to splatter some Bratva brains out all over our nice clean green felt."

Before Rory had a chance to respond, I strode towards the door.

"Don't do something stupid, Xav!"

"You're a fine one to talk. You couldn't handle our girl for five minutes without running to me," I threw over my shoulder.

If he had a retort, I didn't hear it as I slammed my shoulder into the door and walked out along the corridor into the lift which was still sitting on this floor. The whole way down, I fought against the urge to punch the wall. Eric was my fucking lifeline. If he was gone, what the fuck would I do? Without him, I had no one who just understood everything without me needing to say a single word. He knew me inside out. It had been us against the world for as long as I could remember. Sure, Quinn and Rory were my family, but Eric was the closest thing I had to a brother. I would kill to keep him safe.

I didn't bother to hide the gun as I stepped out of the lift and strode down the hall. This was my fucking casino. I could walk around naked if I wanted. I walked through the door to the VIP area. If anyone was shocked by my presence, they didn't say anything. And no one stopped me slamming open the door to the room where they were holding this ruse of a fucking poker tournament. I raised my hand and pointed the gun at the motherfucker who had the audacity to shove his own in my best friend's face and threatened to blow his brains out.

Gregor Bykov's eyes swung to me but my gaze fixed on Eric. I could see fear in his green eyes and it just about fucking killed me. He was trying not to show it but I saw right through him just as he always did me.

"Xavier, that—"

"Shut up, Quinn," I ground out, silencing him.

I took another step into the room, my eyes flicking over to the man who had Eric's life in his hands.

"Listen very carefully you Russian cunt, if you even so much as squeeze that trigger, you'll be face down on the table faster than the bullet will take to leave the chamber of your pistol. I don't fuck around and I certainly don't miss. If you think I'm afraid of what your friends will do to me, think again. You don't fuck with me and my own. Lower. Your. Gun."

The Russian's eyes hardened.

"Your friend is a cheat."

I almost laughed. Eric was the most straitlaced of the four of us. He believed in right and wrong. He'd never cheat as the dealer. Not even when Quinn suggested we should to piss everyone else off. Turns out we didn't need to. Trouble had found us all by itself. My skin prickled. Was this fucking karma for us taking Ash? The world didn't want her to get sucked into our mess. The world could go fuck itself. Ash was ours. I was with Quinn. We couldn't let her go.

"Everyone is fucking cheating if you ask this guy," Colm Moran muttered.

My trigger finger was feeling happy but I knew if I shot Gregor, he would shoot Eric. That couldn't happen. Eric wouldn't survive a bullet to the head at point-blank range. The very thought of losing him left a huge gaping wound in the centre of my chest. My body burnt with the need to keep him safe no matter the cost.

"Enough."

Everyone turned at the sound of Frank Russo's voice. He rose from his chair very slowly, his dark eyes assessing each and every person around that table. He placed one hand on it and leant towards Gregor.

"Put it down."

His deadly but firm tone had the hairs on the back of my neck prickling. No fucking wonder his own daughter was obedient to him. The man's very presence made me want to bolt. He reeked of death and destruction, seeping from his pores like he was forged in hellfire itself.

Gregor lowered his gun very slowly, placing it on the table. Eric didn't relax. I indicated with my head he needed to get behind me. The sooner I got him out of harm's way, the better. He rose from his chair and stiffly walked towards me, his eyes betraying his gratitude and fear at the same time. When he was behind me, I lowered my weapon too, turning my attention to Quinn. The rage and anger radiating off him almost made me flinch. He wasn't happy with me coming in all guns blazing, but he was seriously pissed at Russo for having the ability to rein Gregor in.

Frank sat down and his wife put a hand on his arm. Isabella looked like an older version of her daughter. That's when I noticed my girl had nothing of her father in her features, but the thought was fleeting as Quinn turned his attention to me and Eric.

"Get another dealer and Rory."

I wasn't about to leave him alone here so I looked back and nodded at Eric. He almost bolted from the room but I could hardly blame him. Every part of me burnt to seek him out and make sure he was okay. Give him whatever he needed to get through this.

No one spoke. The tension in the room made my skin itch. Time seemed to pass infinitely slow until Rory walked in with one of the staff. They immediately took Eric's place but did not look happy about it. Rory stood off to the side of the door. I walked over to him and slapped the gun into his hand.

"Watch Quinn, he's not himself," I muttered.

Rory gave me a nod and then I left because no one was keeping me from my best friend.

CHAPTER FORTY

Eric

I leant against the desk with Ash staring up at me. Panic still coursed through my veins at just how much danger I'd been in, but the adrenaline was fading leaving me to feel the full force of those emotions.

"Are you okay?" she asked, her blue eyes wide, betraying her concern for me.

When I'd got up here, I'd tried not to think too hard about what just happened. My first instinct was to tell Rory Quinn needed him and another dealer. He hadn't stopped to explain why Ash was handcuffed to the chair. His only parting words were to look after her. It made me wonder what the fuck happened, but then again, shit had just happened to me too.

As soon as I'd got close to Ash, I realised she'd been crying so I got her some tissues and cleaned her face up, preferring to care for her than deal with my own emotions.

"I should be asking you that."

She shrugged, giving me a half smile.

"I'm not the one who had a gun in their face."

I'd rather not be reminded of it, but it happened. The Russian had threatened my life over a poker game. That made all of my worries and problems seem so insignificant.

I'm going to tell him. I have to.

"You want to explain why you're attached to that chair?"

"I tried to run when I saw my parents... Rory..."

I stared at her.

"Rory handcuffed you to it."

Her cheeks flushed and she looked away.

"Yeah."

That meant he'd willingly touched her. For someone who hated all human contact, it was a turn up for the books.

I sighed and opened the desk drawer, pulling out the key. I uncuffed her and dropped both back in the drawer, closing it. She rubbed her wrist which had red marks on it from where the cuff had been pulled too tight. I took her hand and pulled it towards me on instinct. My eyes met hers as I leant over her wrist and placed one single kiss in the centre of it. She trembled, her pupils dilating. I don't know why I did it. Perhaps it was her expression or the need to make her feel better. Either way, it was fucking stupid, but something about Ash drew me in. I hadn't felt that sort of pull towards someone since the day I met Xavier.

"Eric—"

The door to the office slammed open. I dropped her wrist, pulling back slightly. Ash's eyes flicked to the door. The odd moment between us was gone. A moment which disconcerted me more than having a gun shoved against my temple. Whatever was between Ash and me didn't change my feelings towards my best friend. If anything, they burnt stronger since

300

he'd rescued me. He hadn't hesitated. The idiot would get himself killed just to save me. But he was my idiot.

I felt his presence before I saw him. He came around the desk and pulled me towards him without even glancing Ash's way. My face was shoved up against his chest and his arms were around me before I had a chance to blink.

"I was so fucking scared I'd lose you," he whispered.

His chin rested against my head and I breathed out, the tension and anxiety leaving me instantly. Xav had a way of calming me just as I did him.

"I'm still here."

"No fucking thanks to Quinn and his stupid schemes."

I grinned despite myself. Quinn and his schemes had got us this far even if his methods were completely unorthodox.

That's when I felt it, a soft, delicate hand clinging to me before a body pressed itself firmly against both of us. A feminine scent surrounded me, mixing with the familiarity of Xav's distinctive smell of sandalwood, making my mouth water. One of Xav's arms left me and wrapped around her, bringing her closer to us.

"Want in on the action, angel?"

"I'm glad both of you are okay," she whispered, her soft voice filling my ears and warming me from the inside out.

Her words were unexpected, to say the least. Why did she care about us when we were the ones who'd stolen her from her life?

"As if I'd let some Russian fucker take this dopey shit from me."

"You're the dopey shit," I muttered.

I knew he was grinning. I knew my best friend like the back of my hand. All his reactions. All his moods. I'd studied him for years, branding each and every one of his expressions into my retinas in case he was torn away from me abruptly. That was the way of our lives when we were younger. None of us thought we'd live long with the way we grew up, but we clung to life like fucking leeches, desperate to crawl out of the pit of hell we'd been born into. It was mostly down to Quinn that we were here now.

Quinn fought our battles.

Quinn protected us when everything got tough.

And Quinn accepted us no matter who we were.

So regardless of what had happened this evening, I wasn't about to put it all on him. He'd earnt our loyalty. He'd earnt the right to call on us to help him now. To repay him for everything he'd done for us. That's why we'd gone along with this evening. That's why we'd even gone along with taking the girl clinging to us in the first place.

"What does your father have on Gregor Bykov, Ash?" I asked because it suddenly occurred to me Gregor had acquiesced to Russo's demand he put his gun down without a single complaint.

I felt her pull away rather than saw it. Xav released me next and I sat back, staring at the blonde girl who had answers we wouldn't find elsewhere.

"I honestly don't know. As far as I'm aware Papa considers the Bykovs and Villettis his rivals."

Xav frowned.

"Are you sure?"

She nodded. I saw no dishonesty in her expression but Ash had every reason to lie to us.

"I might be his heir, but Papa doesn't tell me everything. He doesn't think I need to know right now. He's far too secure in his position, although now, I think perhaps he feels the need to exert his power. He can't afford to show weakness, especially not after you took me from him. He doesn't know it was you four... does he?"

I looked at Xav who shrugged. We weren't supposed to talk to Ash about this, but after tonight, I didn't care any longer. To me, it seemed Ash wasn't completely loyal to her father.

"Your father thinks *Il Diavolo* has you, but he doesn't know that's Quinn. Very few people do."

Quinn hadn't hidden who he was from her so this bit of knowledge didn't matter. Ash knew enough about us now that if she did go back to her father, she could use it against us. Something inside me told me she wouldn't. For some unfathomable reason, I felt as though I could trust her because Ash had been through hell just as we all had. You could tell from looking deep into a person's eyes. They couldn't hide that darkness. Ash's eyes betrayed her inner turmoil and I would bet my life it stemmed from her father and his treatment.

"Quinn has a lot to answer for," she muttered, her fists clenched by her sides.

I looked at Xav again. He was eyeing Ash with concern painting his features. There was something else there too. Longing laced with affection. It made my heart lurch in my chest. Xav had never looked at me like that. Never with such intensity in his gaze. It's as if Ash was the very person he'd been searching for his entire life. It made me edge further away from them when Ash looked at him and her eyes softened, betraying her own feelings towards Xav. He reached up and stroked her cheek with such reverence, it made me queasy. And she didn't push him away. She leant into his touch as if she was starved of it.

"Feel free to give him hell, angel."

She gave him a tight smile, but it did nothing to stop the pulsating lust between the two of them.

What the actual fuck is happening here?

CHAPTER FORTY ONE

Quinn

Getting the measure of a man like Frank Russo was nigh on impossible when he gave very little away. I needed to prove to myself he was weak because I'd taken his daughter, but Russo seemed as unruffled as ever. Tonight had only shown me one thing. Ash was right. Her father didn't care about her. He cared about power and his own reputation remaining intact. Although likely he wouldn't show how her disappearance had affected him to those he considered his enemies.

And he'd proved his power base was far more secure than I anticipated. If he had that much influence over someone as formidable as Gregor Bykov, I had my fucking work cut out taking him down. Stealing Ash from him wasn't enough. Had I misjudged everything? I was sure Ash was his most prized possession. Everything pointed to that. He'd made sure his daughter was watched at all times. It was nigh on impossible to take her without him knowing. Our careful planning and help was the only reason we'd got close enough to do so.

The last half an hour had left me feeling vulnerable in a way I hated. I hadn't been able to protect Eric and that fucking had me on edge. As much as Xav's behaviour when he'd stormed in here had been fucking dangerous, he'd only been looking out for his best friend. I couldn't exactly begrudge him that even though I wished he'd see what was right in front of him. He and Eric needed their heads bashing together.

The tournament had continued without further interruptions. It seemed after Gregor's outburst, no one wanted to rock the boat any further much to my irritation. This was meant to force Russo into showing his weaknesses. My efforts had failed spectacularly and backfired on me instead.

Gregor was right about one thing. I had been throwing every hand until I'd depleted my chips and folded out of the tournament. I wasn't playing to win. This had never been about that. The only three players left were Moran, Russo and Villetti. Bykov was a sore loser. He'd practically stormed out the moment he realised he'd lost it all. No one commented on his abrupt departure. He'd cool off in time, but I was sure this wouldn't be the end of our troubles with the man. Tonight we'd made brand new enemies. Of that, I was sure.

I felt Rory next to me and looked up. He'd made his silent approach from his station by the door without anyone else noticing. He leant down close to my ear.

"We have a problem," he whispered.

"What's wrong?" I asked, my voice just as low.

"I should've said you have a problem… with a girl."

I stiffened. My little girl. I'd put her to the back of my mind during this shit, but I'd known her seeing her ex-boyfriend and her parents wouldn't sit well with her.

"She's angry."

"It's more than that, Quinn. You're going to have to answer her questions if you don't want her to hate you."

"She's going to hate me regardless of what I say."

The sad truth of it all was I couldn't stop her from hating me. Or at the very least, feeling like she'd been lied to. Deceived. I kept the truth of why I took her a secret and forced my friends to as well. When she realised, when she understood, there'd be nothing but hate left. She'd hate me far more than the small part of me which still hated her for what she'd done.

"You should've told her the truth from the start."

I shifted in my seat, aware that perhaps he was right, but there was no point in trying to fix the past. I couldn't change it.

"Now isn't the time, Rory."

"It never is."

There wasn't anything left to say. This evening was always going to force many secrets out into the open.

"Get Eric and Xav to take her home. I'll deal with it when this is over."

I glanced at him. His expression was grim but he nodded and slunk back into the shadows by the door again.

I sat back and ran a hand through my hair, watching the proceedings with tension flooding my veins. Rory's tone told me I would be in for an earful later. Perhaps it was for the best she found out. Dragging it out wasn't helping anyone. I needed answers to the questions plaguing me about why she'd allowed it all to happen. She could've stopped it if she'd been brave enough. Then again, Ash had shown me she was brave when she stood up to me. She'd proved she had a backbone and wouldn't allow me to get away with shit if she wasn't on board with it.

My eyes fell on her father. I couldn't blame Ash for being afraid of him. If I was a lesser man, I'd have cowered in the face of Frank Russo. But I wasn't about to let the cunt scare me into submission. He couldn't be allowed to win the war brewing. It simmered under the surface of all the players this evening. They all knew Frank had lost his daughter. They all knew that showed a huge chink in his armour no matter how much Russo had tried to show it hadn't affected him. It was fucking clear it had. Just by the way his wife, Isabella's expression was that of abject misery when she thought no one was looking. The tension lining Russo's brow when he looked at her. Things were not all fun and games in the Russo household.

Isabella's eyes met mine for the briefest of moments and she gave me a subtle nod. I smirked but didn't acknowledge her otherwise.

Tearing my gaze away from the Russos, I wondered who would win this tournament now. The longer it went on, the longer it delayed the inevitable confrontation between Ash and me. I wasn't sure if I was wishing for it to come sooner or not.

Was I really prepared for the ensuing fallout? Or was I just kidding myself into thinking everything would eventually work out in the end?

CHAPTER FORTY TWO

Ash

I sat in Quinn's chair in his office after Xav and Eric took me back to the house. There was a weird atmosphere between the three of us. I think it started when I hugged both of them at the same time. Xav hadn't seemed to mind, in fact, he'd encouraged it, but Eric, I was sure he felt off about the whole thing. It was only after Xav had stroked my face I realised just how much. Eric looked like he'd been burnt and I couldn't understand it. He'd shut down his emotions pretty much immediately after that, his face turning expressionless. Then he'd walked away to the monitors leaving Xav and me alone. I didn't know what to make of it all.

It didn't matter right now. I couldn't deal with that mess. Besides, I was far more focused on what I was going to say to Quinn when he got back. I had so many questions. So many answers I needed to demand from him. The whole thing made my skin prickle.

Tonight had been like a punch to the gut. Seeing Nate and knowing he'd colluded with Quinn made me ill. Made me feel as though our entire relationship had been a lie. Maybe everything I thought I knew had been one too. How could I believe anything anyone said any longer?

Seeing my parents was worse. My mother looked tense and Papa? He looked ready to take no prisoners. Most people wouldn't recognise the subtleties of my father's expressions and moods but I did. I'd had to learn so I could survive in the Russo household. Didn't mean I always got it right and certainly didn't mean I got out unscathed, but things could've been far worse for me.

I wasn't sure why Xav and Eric trusted me to be left alone in Quinn's office, but I hadn't touched anything. It wasn't really my place. I could've searched it high and low. Except I didn't feel the urge to. And if Quinn came back and found me, that wouldn't help my cause. He'd be instantly suspicious. So instead, I sat there pretty much twiddling my thumbs, waiting for the one man with all the answers.

How much time passed, I had no idea, but when the door was flung open and Quinn walked in, my whole body tensed. His eyes fell on me straight away. They were dark and full of unrepressed rage. Whatever was meant to happen this evening clearly hadn't judging by the way his jaw ticked and one of his hands clenched into a fist.

"What are you doing in here alone?" he all but barked at me.

"Waiting for you."

He raised a hand and curled a finger.

"Come here."

312

I didn't want to obey him but my body had other ideas. I was up and out of my chair within moments, my feet carrying me over to him. Barely having a chance to register what was happening, I was unceremoniously pressed against him with his hands in my hair and his mouth covering mine. He took what he wanted from me without compunction. And for some stupid reason, I just let him. This might very well be the last time I got to kiss this man. My body craved him in ways I hadn't ever expected. Quinn was my drug of choice and I'd allowed myself to get addicted way too quickly.

"Little girl," he murmured against my mouth. "I don't want to talk."

He might not want to, but I sure as hell did. So why didn't I stop him when he backed me towards the desk and pinned me against it. Why didn't I prevent him from tugging up my dress and finding out I had no underwear on? Why did his resulting groan which reverberated across my skin set my body on fire? Why did I still grow wet under his touch?

"Quinn," I whimpered, desperate for more.

His fingers parted me, stroking across my wet and pulsating pussy like he owned it. I should be angry at him. I should push him away, but I didn't have it in me. It's as if his touch stole my ability to think clearly.

"You're angry," he whispered against my neck as he placed kisses down the column of my throat. "And yet you crave it all the same. Crave me."

I needed to get my head back on straight, fight through this haze of lust surrounding us, consuming us from the inside out.

"I need you to stop."

He went completely still at my words.

"Are you sure, little girl?"

"No… Yes… I don't fucking know. You scramble my brain so much sometimes. I hate it. I feel so weak when I'm around you like I'm no longer in control of my own actions because all I want is to feel you against me. You drive me fucking crazy and I'm pissed as hell at you right now, but it doesn't change how much I want you."

I hadn't meant to confess such things to him, but I couldn't take it back now.

"We need to talk, Quinn."

I felt him withdraw in that moment, not physically, but emotionally. Like all of his shutters had come crashing down and I was left outside in the cold. A shiver ran down my spine and dread settled in my stomach. Nothing about what came next would be pleasant. I could feel it.

He pulled back, his dark eyes betraying his frustration with me. Betraying something much darker. Something I'd not felt from him before.

Hate.

Sure, he'd been scathing about my father and how much he hated him, but that had never been directed specifically at me.

Feeling vulnerable and exposed, I tugged my dress back down, covering my intimate parts. There was no fucking way I was letting him touch me further when he was looking at me like that.

He released me completely and paced away, his fists clenching at his sides.

"Talk then."

314

I swallowed as I straightened. It was now or never.

"Was my entire relationship with Nate even real?"

His back stiffened.

"If you're asking if I told him to pursue you, the answer is no."

"Then why did he?"

My heart had already been in pieces before Quinn took me since Nate had wrecked me by proving he didn't care. He used me in the worst way possible. But then again, Quinn was using me too. Using me against my own family.

"His only brief was to get close to your father by whatever means necessary. He chose to involve you. I didn't ask questions and he volunteered no answers. I needed information and I didn't care how he obtained it."

I trembled, gripping the desk behind me as my knees threatened to buckle. Quinn sounded so matter of fact as if causing me pain meant nothing to him.

"Nate is your double agent."

"He needed money, I gave him a way to obtain it. It was win-win for both of us. The more I learnt about your father, the more I had to use against him. And in turn, I learnt about you too, but not as much as you might think. Nate didn't like to discuss you. Contrary to what you might think, I do believe he genuinely came to care for you."

I took a shuddering breath.

"Then why did he break my heart?"

Quinn's body tensed at my words and his knuckles went white as he clenched his fist harder.

"I have a feeling your father told him to end it the moment Nate obtained entry into Russo's inner circle. When you told me your father would choose your husband, I guessed the reasoning behind the demise of your relationship, although, I don't know for certain obviously."

My world felt as though it was beginning to crumble around me. So many lies from the people I thought I could trust. So much deception. My father was the worst culprit of all.

"Did you really love him, Ash?"

I blinked. I hadn't expected that question and, in all honesty, I wasn't quite sure I had an answer. When I looked inside myself, I no longer knew what was real or not.

"I thought I did, but what do I fucking well even know any longer? My life has been built on lie after lie fed to me by my father and everyone else around me. I can't trust anyone's words. Not even yours."

He turned, unclenching his fists as his dark eyes fell on me.

"Everything I'm telling you now is the truth whether you want to believe it or not."

I took a step towards him.

"Then tell me why you took me. Tell me why you went to all this trouble. What did Papa do to you that made you hate him so much?"

His eyes flashed with pain for a moment before it morphed into anger.

"What did he do? What didn't he fucking do?"

"That doesn't bloody well answer my question."

He strode towards me, gripping my chin and tipping my face up towards his.

"You've heard of the name Marotta, have you not?"

My blood turned to ice in my veins. Memories assaulted me one after the other, ripping me to shreds as I stared up into the eyes of the man I was beginning to care far too much for.

"Yes," I whispered, not having it in me to lie to him at all.

"Then you know what you did, Ash. You know what your father did."

I shook my head, not understanding what he meant by that. Not understanding how it related to Quinn. It didn't make any sense. None at all. Yes, I knew a Marotta. That name only brought up my very worst memories. The ones filled with blood. The blood on my hands I couldn't wash off. The day my father had turned me from a girl into a monster. That day was awful on every level. I couldn't get away from it. I couldn't hide. It haunted my waking hours and when I slept.

How did Quinn know about what happened with Casey Marotta?

"What does that have to do with you?"

"Look closely, Ash, then you might understand."

I stared at him. Taking in every one of Quinn's features just as I had done many times during the two weeks I'd been with him. It took me a while to see it. To really look at what had been staring me in the face all this time.

"You have the same eyes as him," I whispered.

Why did Quinn have Casey's eyes? They looked nothing alike otherwise. Casey's hair had been light brown and his build stockier. He didn't share Quinn's high cheekbones. Nothing about Casey was attractive whereas everything about Quinn was.

"I do."

"But how?"

His grip on my chin tightened.

"Casey was my older brother."

It was as if everything was in free fall and the life had been sucked out of me. My eyes were on Quinn's but I wasn't really seeing him. I was remembering that night six months ago. That horrific night I'd told no one about.

"But you don't have the same surname."

It was a stupid thing to say but it was the only thing I could think of with the images assaulting me at every turn.

"I changed mine when I turned eighteen so I no longer had to associate myself with our fucking parents."

"Why?" I whispered, completely confused by this entire situation.

Nothing he'd said made sense but I knew he was telling me the truth. I could feel it and see it in his eyes.

"You grew up in luxury," he practically spat. "I grew up in hell. They didn't give a shit about me or Casey. All they did is chase their next high and beat the shit out of my brother for just being alive. They never cared enough about me to try it. I was just another mistake they didn't want to deal with. They up and fucking left us to burn when I was fourteen. Then Casey ran too, joined up with your father's fucking family and I never saw him again. They all left me in the dirt."

His eyes were wild and his chest heaved with each breath. His voice got raspy and low, dripping with agony and disdain.

"The only reason I survived is because of those three out there. I kept them fucking safe from all the shit we'd been dealt with. I made sure we rose from the fucking ashes. Me."

He dropped his hand from my chin as if it burnt him.

"I did that. I made it possible. You'll never fucking understand any of it because you've never had to beg, cheat, lie and fucking steal just to stay alive."

His words struck me. Each and every one like a blow to my chest. I ached for him. My heart broke for him. For the suffering he'd gone through. I wanted to hold him. To take away his pain. Damn it, I cared. I cared too much.

"You and your fucking father took away the only blood family I had left. I hate him for it and I used to hate you too. I hated both of you so fucking much. You want to know why I enlisted Nate's help two years ago? It was to get Casey out of that life. To find a way to break your father's hold on him. I was so fucking close and then the two of you killed him. You fucking murdered my brother." He dragged his hands through his hair as if he was trying to tug it out by the roots. "The worst part of all is I don't even fucking hate you any longer, Ash. You fucking messed with my head. I can't think straight or see straight when I'm near you. You're like toxins coating my veins. My need to have you, be inside you consumes me from the inside out. I want to hate you for it but I can't. I fucking can't and it kills me."

I took a step back, needing space between us. His words all but destroyed me. He hated how he felt about me. That cut so deep. I might hate how he controlled me, but he took me in the first place. I was fucking entitled to hate it since I was the captive and he was the captor. But maybe it was just as bad for him as it was for me. Maybe this whole thing was fucked well beyond repair.

Quinn didn't understand what happened with Casey. He didn't know why my father had taken his brother's life. He didn't know what Casey had done. What he'd tried to do. That he'd turned into a monster capable of the unspeakable.

"He wasn't a good person, Quinn," I whispered.

"He didn't deserve what you did to him."

I agreed with Quinn but I hadn't done it. I'd tried to stop my father. I didn't want any of what happened.

"I know he didn't. I tried to save him. I tried so hard to save him. There was so much blood." I stared down at my hands, reliving that night all over again when blood coated my fingers after I'd tried to put pressure on his wounds. "I tried, Quinn, but it was too late. There was nothing I could do."

Tears welled in my eyes. The whole thing broke me inside.

"Why did he do it? Why did he take Casey's life?"

I swallowed. My knees almost buckled. I didn't want to tell Quinn about this. I never wanted anyone to know. Those damn tears fell down my cheeks. I held back from moaning with pain. I dug my nails into my palms, trying to steel myself against the avalanche of turmoil threatening to consume me whole.

"Casey tried to rape me," I choked out, the words making my tongue stick to the roof of my mouth. "He wanted to hurt my father for promoting someone else over him. He was psychotic, Quinn. He didn't care about the people he hurt. He only cared about himself. He tried to rape me even though he knew I was with Nate. He tried and he failed."

My nails dug harder into my palms.

"And when Papa found out because he bragged about it to someone else, he took Casey's life."

CHAPTER FORTY THREE

Quinn

sh's words struck me hard. It couldn't be true. It couldn't possibly be true. Casey wasn't that sort of person, was he?

Why else would she say it? Ash isn't the girl who cries wolf.

How could my own brother try to take what wasn't his? Take her. *My* little girl. Though she wasn't mine six months ago when he was butchered and his body never found. I only knew he was dead because Nate told me, but even he didn't know why, which meant Ash hadn't told him the truth.

"Why didn't you tell Nate?"

She stared at me, tears streaming down her cheeks. Ash didn't fake her own pain. She didn't have to. It was clear as day, written all over her body.

"He would've ended up dead if I told anyone. I didn't want that. I stopped him from doing anything by kneeing him in the balls and running. I ran until my lungs burnt and my legs felt like jelly. He didn't come after me."

"He ended up fucking dead anyway."

A fresh set of tears ran down her face.

"That wasn't my fault! He bragged about it. Told someone close to my father he'd got inside the boss's daughter's tight cunt behind her boyfriend's back. It got back to Papa. I begged him not to do anything. I told him it wasn't true and he believed me, but no one disrespects Frank Russo personally. You must know this about my father. He made me watch whilst he beat Casey with brass knuckles then he took a knife to him. One of his men held me back as I screamed at him to stop."

She choked on her own words as if it physically pained her to say them.

"He told me this was how I would be expected to deal with it all going forward. That I was weak for allowing a man to disrespect our family. He broke me when he murdered your brother in front of me. He made me into a monster, Quinn. He made me an accomplice. I can never wash the stain of that night from my hands. The blood haunts me."

She took another step back, her hand coming up to her chest as she sucked in oxygen.

"Do you think I wanted any of this to happen? I didn't want Casey to die no matter what he'd done. I never wanted any of this. I never wanted this life. I'm not my father. I'm nothing like him."

She stumbled backwards into the desk and slid down it, her legs no longer able to hold her up. Ash buried her face in her knees and sobbed. The sight of her like this shattered me, but I was stuck watching her, unable to move.

"Little girl," I choked out on a whisper. "Little girl, please don't cry."

Helpless. I felt utterly helpless. I believed every single word of what she'd said and yet I still couldn't go to her. It was as if chains bound my chest and held me back. I struggled to even breathe. The pain of knowing my own brother tried to hurt *my* little girl tore through me. Of knowing despite her trying to protect him even after what he'd tried to do ended with him dead anyway shredded every single last piece of my blackened heart.

"I'm sorry," she sobbed. "I'm so, so sorry."

I wanted to hold her close and tell her everything would be okay, but that would be another lie. Ash had been lied to enough to last a lifetime. So I stood there staring down at her instead. Watching her body shake with her wracking sobs. Watching her fall apart before my very eyes. The girl who'd wreaked havoc through my household the moment she stepped foot in it. And yet despite everything she'd done and been involved in, I still couldn't hate her. I couldn't do anything but want her so desperately, it really did consume me whole.

She raised her head off her legs and blinked as she took me in. Her tear-streaked face destroyed the part of me still standing. How was it possible to feel so much for someone you barely knew? I'd never cared before. Not like this. Not with such visceral intensity.

I didn't want to talk about Casey any longer. What I needed was for Ash to be on my side. If she regretted that day, then maybe she could give up what she knew. Maybe she could help me.

"I need you to tell me his weaknesses, Ash. That's why I took you. So I could use you to get to him, but it's not enough. I need more."

She stared at me for the longest time without making a sound.

"I can't do this anymore," she whispered. "I want to go home."

"You can't."

She knew I wouldn't let her go. Especially not now.

"You want things I can't give you, Quinn. I can't tell you how to destroy my father. I can't give you his secrets. No matter what he's done, he's still my father. I still love him."

It wasn't like it hadn't occurred to me Ash would be loyal to her family, but she knew what type of a monster her father was. It'd been my intention to break her so she'd spill her secrets. That was until she'd arrived and all those plans went to hell in a fucking handcart. Now I just wanted her to help me because it was the right thing to do. I wanted her to feel the things I felt.

I wanted her mine. All mine.

"You'd protect the man who made you feel like you're a monster?"

"He's still my family."

"Do you even care about what he's done?"

Her eyes widened.

"You make it sound like I agree with everything he's done."

"Do you?"

"Of course not!"

The urge to reach out for her was overwhelming me, but my body remained frozen to the spot.

"Do you care about me?"

Why the fuck did you just ask that?

More tears flowed down her face, making everything infinitely worse.

"More than you realise, but that doesn't matter. You want me to help you destroy my father. You're asking me to choose between you and him. I'm telling you right now, I won't choose. I refuse to take part in this war between you and him. I'm sorry he took away the last of your family, but that doesn't mean I can help you."

Hearing her say it was like a thousand knives digging their way into my skin. Why did I care about this fucking girl so much? Why had I thrown all of my carefully laid plans away just so I could have her when it was clear she would never give me what I needed?

Because she's so much more than you ever realised. Because she's everything.

And I was the stupid fool who'd allowed myself to get caught up in all these ridiculous feelings and emotions. I'd allowed myself to get wrapped up in her.

"Let me go, Quinn. Please. Just let me go. I'm useless to you now, aren't I?"

I shook my head. She was never going to be useless to me. Not whilst she had such a tight grip on me.

"Never."

Despite everything, I couldn't do it. I couldn't let her go back to her father and tell him who I was. And I couldn't allow her to go because I still wanted her.

"You're still mine, little girl."

She shook her head.

"I don't belong to you."

Breaking free of my invisible bonds, I strode towards her and tugged her up by her arm. She stared up at me, her blue eyes betraying all of her wildly conflicting emotions.

"You will always belong to me. No matter what happens, you will always be mine."

She reached up, her fingers brushing across my face and causing me to shudder under her touch.

"You can't possess me," she whispered. "If you want me so much, you have to let me in. You have to let me have you too, but I know you won't do that. That's exactly why this will never work. I need more than you can give me. I need so much more."

I didn't understand what she was getting at. If she wanted me, she could have me. Hell, I think on some fucking level she already did. Didn't she see that?

"Are you saying I'm not enough for you?"

"No... I'm saying what you're willing to give isn't enough."

She dropped her hand and bowed her head.

"Until you can give me everything, then this conversation... this thing... it's over."

I didn't know what the fuck to make of anything she'd said. And I didn't stop her as she left the room even though it killed me. She'd walked away. Walked away from all the shit between us. Was I asking too much of her? Had I pushed her too hard?

God, you sound like such a fucking pussy.

Yet in that moment, I didn't give a fuck.

It didn't matter how long she'd been in my life. I knew what I wanted was her. All of her. I thought I had her. Turns out I never had her at all.

And that thought brought me to my knees. I stared down at my hands wondering how the fuck I was going to fix this. Because if what Ash had said was true. If we were over, whatever the fuck we were in the first place, then things were far worse than I ever anticipated.

How can I give you everything, Ash, when I don't even know what everything is?

CHAPTER FORTY FOUR

Ash

didn't know what the hell I was doing. What happened with Quinn broke me further, as if I wasn't fucking well broken enough. Having to tell him about Casey. Having him ask me to betray my father. And then telling him I was done. All of it was devastating.

I wandered through the ground floor listlessly, semi-surprised I hadn't run into anyone else, but then again, it was late.

I didn't want us to be done. That said a lot about how fucked up things had become that I couldn't even imagine my life without him in it. Who the fuck felt that about someone they'd known such a short period of time? He'd given me so much but it was all physical. I needed emotions. I needed feelings. I needed something real.

He might have revealed why he really took me. Why he hated my father so much. And that he'd had a fucked up childhood. But what did I really know about Quinn other than that? It didn't feel as though he'd ever really open up to me. He was so closed off. All of his emotions locked up tight.

Pacing the house wouldn't do me any good. I was already overwrought from everything which happened this evening. And I really didn't want to be alone. There was only one person who'd told me I could go to them no matter what. After all this shit, I needed a hug. I just needed something to ground me. My emotions were all over the place and I felt as though I was falling apart at the seams.

I trudged upstairs and walked along the landing until I stopped outside his door. Raising my hand, I knocked twice. A few moments later, the door was pulled open and Xav looked me over before he frowned.

"What's wrong?"

"I had a fight with Quinn."

He stepped back, letting me enter. I walked in and he shut the door behind me. I stood in the middle of the room, not really seeing anything around me, but also unable to turn and look at Xav either.

"I take it you didn't get the answers you were looking for."

"I did… I understand why you all took me now. That's not why we fought."

I felt him lay a hand on my shoulder.

"What happened, angel?"

I almost broke down again at the concern in his voice. I sniffled instead, feeling stupid. He moved away for a moment before coming back and circling me. He held out a bunch of tissues. I took them and dabbed my face.

"It's such a mess," I mumbled. "All of it."

He took me by the arm and led me over to his bed, forcing me to sit on the end of it. Sitting next to me, he put an arm around my shoulder and gave me a squeeze.

"You've had a pretty shitty evening."

"You can say that again."

I looked over at him. He was half smiling and I couldn't help but want to smile back. Xav had stripped off his suit jacket and tie. His collar was hanging open and his sleeves had been rolled up exposing his tattoos. No matter how much emotional bullshit I'd been through, I was still very much affected by his closeness and the way he smelt. It was a woodsy masculine kind of smell. In so many ways it comforted me.

"So Quinn told you the truth, huh?"

"That he's Casey's brother... yeah... the thing is, I never wanted Casey to die. That was my father's doing. And he didn't find out from me what Casey did."

Xav didn't seem shocked at the mention of Quinn's brother so I assumed all of them knew.

"What did he do?"

"He tried to force himself on me, but he never got very far... then he bragged about having fucked me. It got back to my father and he killed Casey for the disrespect he'd shown. I tried to stop it from happening. Tried to save him. It was too late though. I'm not my father. I would never take another person's life."

Xav's expression darkened and his eyes narrowed.

"That's fucked up."

I nodded. It was fucked up just like everything else in my life.

"Things are very cut and dry in Papa's world. I don't agree with his methods. It's been a sticking point between us for as long as I can remember."

I sighed, looking down at my hands.

"Quinn asked me to tell him my father's weaknesses, but I can't. He doesn't understand how I can protect my father, but he's my family. I love him. So I can't let Quinn destroy him even though I hate everything he represents. Everything he does. He's not a good man, Xav, but he's my father."

His arm around me tightened.

"I know, angel. Quinn has nothing but hate for his own parents so he doesn't get it. But me? I've lived through shit with mine and yet I still can't get away from my own conflicting feelings towards my father. So trust me, I understand your dilemma."

I didn't ask him to elaborate knowing that if he wanted to tell me what happened, he would. But his voice rang with his sincerity. Xav did understand why I couldn't just forgo my loyalty to my father. Doing so would put a huge target on my back as well as all of theirs. I cared about these four men enough that I didn't want my father to hurt them.

"That's not everything… I told Quinn I was done with whatever the fuck is going on between me and him. I didn't want to, but he'll never let me in. God, it hurts… why does it fucking hurt so much? I barely even know anything about him or any of you. Why do I care?"

Xav tugged me closer and wrapped his other arm around me. I buried my face in his shoulder, breathing him in to keep myself from crying all over again.

"You know what makes you so beautiful?" he asked quietly.

"No."

"Your ability to see past all the bullshit walls people put up and truly look at them for who they are. That's why you care, angel, because you see what's inside."

No one had ever given me such a compliment before. I suppose I did try to look past people's outward appearances and focus on who they really were. First impressions could lie, but what was in your heart? That was real and true.

"Quinn's been all kinds of messed up since you got here. The way you've stood up for yourself in the face of his shit makes you special. He sees that. He's just too fucking stubborn to allow you past his barriers. You've seen and dealt with him at his worst. If you can handle that, then you're good. Give him time, angel."

Xav made sense and yet I still felt hopeless about the situation between me and Quinn. I could tell myself it was ridiculous because I'd known him two weeks and that was too short a time to become attached. It would be a lie. I was attached all right. Attached to all of them in a way I'd never expected. So even though I'd asked Quinn to let me go, I didn't really want to leave. I wanted to stay right here with them because even though I wouldn't betray my father, these men would protect me from Papa and his plans for me.

I shifted and peered up at Xav. He looked sympathetic but there was something else simmering in his blue eyes. Something I knew very well he felt for me. It's just it seemed hopeless before, but now... now everything was so up in the air. And I was so fucking lost.

"He told me I'd always be his."

He rolled his eyes.

"Quinn and his possessive bullshit."

I tried to smile but I couldn't.

"I don't want to be just his," I whispered.

Some part of me deep down recognised the truth of Quinn's words. That a part of me did belong to him. It just wasn't all of me like he assumed. No, parts of me belonged to his friends and I was beginning to see I'd never get away from that. I'd never truly understand what it meant until I allowed myself to feel these things.

Tonight had been an emotional minefield, but I'd never been so sure about anything in my life. I needed to feel what it would be like to be consumed by them all. And I knew very well the man in front of me would be on board with it even if the others would not.

"No?"

I shook my head and raised it higher so we were eye to eye.

"I don't want to deny what I want any longer."

I could see the comprehension in his blue eyes, but he still asked me the question anyway.

"What are you saying, Ash?"

I swallowed hard and leant closer until my mouth was a hair's breadth away from his.

"I'm saying I don't care what anyone else thinks, says or does. You said you'd share me. You said you'd be okay with it… I can't hide from how I feel. I can't run from it. I want you…" My hand rose and I cupped the back of his neck. "And I know you want me too."

To be continued in

DeFied

ACKNOWELDGEMENTS

Thank you so much for taking the time to read this book. I really appreciate all of my readers and hope this book gave you as much joy reading it as I did writing it.

HUGE thank you goes to my bestie, critique partner, fellow dolphin hater and romance enthusiast, Sab. Without you, this series would not exist. I know you were like Sarah, why are you writing a reverse harem at first, but I proved just how much these five belong together. You get me through the tough times when I feel like throwing my laptop at the wall. You listen to my frustrations and you keep me on the straight and narrow. Every time you come back to me after I send you chapters telling me how much you love the characters and their stories, it keeps me going. I love you so much, bruv. You're one of the very best people in my life and I appreciate you more than words can say.

Elle - sharing our writing journeys together over this past year has been amazing. Finding someone so like me, who has the same process, same taste in books and the same pet hates is crazy, but also pretty damn cool. And as always, keep up with those #oliviapopegoals!

Matt – our daily talks get me through the day. Your encouragement is a little unorthodox at times, but it works. I always love reward day when I finish a book and your specially curated hot guy and girl pictures. Plus, your reviews are pretty awesome and insightful.

All my readers – you're the reason I do this. Yes, I love to write, but without you, I wouldn't be where I am today, so thank you. I really hope you're enjoying this new series!

Mum – thank you for all your proofreading and support!

Husband – you're my number one forever. I love you. Never stop being weird because that's partly why I married you.

ABOUT THE AUTHOR

Sarah writes dark, contemporary, erotic and paranormal romances. They adore all forms of steamy romance and can always be found with a book or ten on their Kindle. They love anti-heroes, alpha males and flawed characters with a little bit of darkness lurking within. Their writing buddies nicknamed Sarah: 'The Queen of Steam' for their pulse racing sex scenes which will leave you a little hot under the collar.

Born and raised in Sussex, UK near the Ashdown Forest, they grew up climbing trees and building Lego towns with their younger brother. Sarah fell in love with novels as teenager reading their aunt's historical regency romances. They have always loved the supernatural and exploring the darker side of romance and fantasy novels.

Sarah currently resides in the Scottish Highlands with their husband. Music is one of their biggest inspirations and they always have something on in the background whilst writing. They are an avid gamer and are often found hogging their husband's Xbox.

Made in the USA
Middletown, DE
19 May 2024

54546646R00205